Elvis Takes a Back Seat

Elvis Takes a Back Seat

Leanna Ellis

Nashville, Tennessee

Printed in the United States of America

978-0-8054-4696-8

Published by B&H Publishing Group,
Nashville, Tennessee

Dewey Decimal Classification: F
Subject Heading: CHRISTIAN LIFE—
FICTION \ SINGLE WOMEN—FICTION \
ADVENTURE STORIES

Publisher's Note: This novel is a work of fiction. Names, character places, and incidents are either products of the author's imagination or used fictitiously. All characters are fictional, and any similarity to people leaving or dead is purely coincidental.

1 2 3 4 5 6 7 8   11 10 09 08

A.S.

Chapter One

I Forgot to Remember to Forget

I used to dream.

But now it's as if the TV in my mind has been turned off and a blank screen waits for me when I fall asleep at night. At least I'm not having nightmares. But I'm afraid the bulb has simply burned out.

Maybe I've simply forgotten how to dream. I've tried warm milk, sleeping pills, and staying in bed for what seemed like days (maybe it was). I've tried power naps, suffered restless legs, counted sheep, frogs, backwards. I've slept on the floor, in a chair, crossways in bed. Nothing works.

My dreams used to be miniature Broadway productions. Once I dreamed about a Laundromat with industrial-sized washers and dryers. Clothes spun around, *th-thunking* against the dryer walls, reminding me of a kettle drum pounding in a royal cadence. My father, his head as bald as

Yul Brynner's, his cheekbones bold against taut skin, strolled toward me whistling "Shall We Dance?" Then he asked about Mother. She went to be with him five years ago.

Mother visited me occasionally, still wearing the auburn wig she bought during chemo. She bustled into my subconscious, her voice chirping "Pick a Little, Talk a Little" right out of *The Music Man*. She would remind me to fix dinner, sweep the floor, go to church. Duty was Mother's idol.

Old boyfriends made brief guest appearances, congregating on the beach, kicking up sand, and tanning their torsos, belting out "There Is Nothing Like a Dame."

But Stu has never rock-and-rolled his way into my dreams. If he did, I'm sure he'd be dressed like Elvis, hips swiveling, blond hair dyed black bobbing in rhythm, lip trying to curl. Maybe it's better not to think of him that way.

Stu had been my dream. His absence is the source of my emptiness, the reason my dreams have evaporated like dew on a hot, dry June day (which in Texas is hotter and drier than normal). Even when I had dreamed, I always turned toward Stu, reaching for him in the night. Now his side of the bed is empty. His glasses lay on the side table, beside the alarm clock, the lenses dusty from neglect.

As is the case most nights, I roll out of bed, not bothering to check the clock. I blink against the darkness. It's so early it's late. Before the paper boy has delivered the paper that I probably won't read. Before the neighbor's teenage son drives home after a late night with college friends and rolls a tire onto the curb. Before I've managed to get enough sleep.

I pad my way to the den and bang my toe into a box.

A curse word pops out of my mouth and makes the house sound more empty. The silence aches in my bones.

Leaning my elbow against a wall, I rub my bruised toe. I'd forgotten about the boxes scattered throughout the house. With the help of my Aunt Rae and Ben, Stu's best friend and my boss, I hauled down from the attic garbage bags of clothes and boxes of mementoes and forgotten items wrapped in newsprint and memories. Most everything is stuffed in the garage now, waiting to be sold tomorrow . . . this morning.

It's too quiet. There are no car sounds, no dogs barking. I power up the stereo—Stu preferred a turntable—flip the record player on, and an album drops down and begins to spin. Elvis's voice floats out of the speakers, crackly and supple, wrapping around me, tightening into a fist, squeezing my heart.

I curl up on the sofa and bury myself under a knitted blanket that used to hold Stu's scent, but over the last year and a half even that has faded. I miss the smell of Paul Sebastian cologne. I suppose I could buy a bottle or find Stu's under his sink, but it wouldn't be the same.

I poke my fingers and toes through the thick, soft yarn latticework. I vaguely remember, as a kid going to Sunday school, a story about somebody dreaming of angels climbing a ladder to and from heaven. I imagined the ladder being gold and glittering in the moonlight. I wonder if I could climb that ladder now or if Stu could descend.

Finally night gives way to the new day, but my mood remains dark and restless. My future is the same. There are no angels pointing me in the right direction. God is a black hole, engulfing my hopes and dreams.

♪♩♪♩.♩♪♩

"HERE GOES EVERYTHING," I mumble and push the button. A whirring noise starts. In its cantankerous manner that reflects my own attitude, the garage door shifts against its will, lurches, and swings upward.

"What's this?" Aunt Rae pats an unmarked box, large enough to hold a small refrigerator. The oscillating fan we set up to combat the Dallas heat stirs her long gray hair. "A hidden treasure?"

"Might be that old lamp Stu's first boss gave us for a wedding present. Pretty hideous." I straighten a poster-board sign that reads "$1 each." Stu's business ties remind me of dinners and dances, parties and pain.

Rae separates the arthritic box tabs, sending dust particles in every direction. The dust sticks to my sweaty legs. I dig beneath the crumpled packing paper until I reach gleaming black pottery. Recognition slams into me, and a prickling heat crawls up the back of my neck. My stomach turns lumpy and sticky with irritation, like my mother's fig preserves that Daddy pretended to like but that I scraped off into the trash. The heat of the day presses in on me, intensifies like a solar flare. At the same time, sounds and awareness of others recede into the distance like a fog curling back toward the bay.

I shake off my crazy reaction. It's nothing. I won't let it be anything. I slap the tabs down, push the box toward the corner. Cardboard scrapes concrete. "It's nothing."

"Oh, come on." Rae puts a hand on my arm. "This lamp I gotta see."

"Leave it alone," I snap. In my head I hear my mother's

shocked gasp. "Claudia," she'd say, "if you can't say something nice . . ."

I should go through these things alone although I haven't bothered. My weakness angers me more than my aunt's interference. "I'm sorry, Rae."

She waves off my apology and dips her arms into the mounds of paper. Heaving, she lifts the object from inside the box and staggers backward. "What *is* this?" She grunts and struggles under the bulk.

The box catches on a chiseled nose. I step forward and tug the box loose. My stomach folds in on itself like cardboard crumpling. I kick the box out of the way (a little harder than necessary) and wince at my already-sore toe.

I embrace the hard edges of the base. Propping one knee beneath the bust, I brace an arm under the ceramic chin and a hand on the smooth, round head. "Aunt Rae," I say, embarrassed as I maneuver the bulky pottery around to face her, "meet—"

"Bless my blue suede shoes!" My aunt's mouth goes slack. "Stu—"

"No," I give the bust a quick glance, "Elvis."

It isn't a sculpture of any report. Cheap and tacky, the Elvis bust ranks right up there with black-velvet wall hangings from Tijuana. Since the first time I saw him more than twenty years ago, I've wanted to get rid of Elvis. The heat of my anger burns hot until it slowly begins to evaporate, forming at first a barrier in my thoughts like a steamed-up mirror.

I remember Stu's college apartment where the bust held a place of honor on a stool in the corner of the den. Stu's giant stereo speakers were laid on their sides next to Elvis as if bowing to his sovereignty.

"What he said then," Rae whispers, "it was true."

Confused, I start to question her, but a flurry of expressions flicker across her face. She reaches out to touch the bust, then pulls back. Her many silver rings flash in the early morning sunlight, sending a kaleidoscope of colors bouncing around the garage, as uncatchable as her look. "You can't sell this, Claudia."

"You're right." I laugh off her theatrics. "No one in their right mind would buy it."

"No, no." She waves her hand, her bangles and charms clinking together. "It's too . . ." She pauses, stumped as I was when I first met "Elvis" more than twenty years ago.

"Too much?" I supply. The bust weighs more than I remember and starts to slip out of my hands. I shove it onto the closest card table, pushing aside my mother's linens. From chest to pompadour, Elvis is a good three feet tall, a garish glorification of an American icon.

Rae touches one of the silver studs on Elvis's upright collar. In a low tone, she starts singing "All Shook Up." In all her years away from Texas, she never lost her accent. Her twang gives the words of the song an extra lilt. Her voice is husky, warm and engaging. Her hips rock agilely, making her long, flowing skirt sway. Two customers enter the garage and watch my sixty-year-old aunt. But she doesn't seem to notice or care that she has an audience.

I can't help but think how different she is from my mother, her sister, who, if I gyrated like that, would have said, "Be still." But Stu . . . he loved loud music, unreserved affection, and all things Elvis. He would have loved Rae's rendition. My eyes burn.

"Stu would have had a conniption fit." I try a laugh that snags on my jagged grief. "If only he'd known you shared the same taste in music."

She halts her dance, her long skirt swishing around her ankles and clunky sandals. "We had many discussions of Elvis, Stuart and I."

My smile falters. "No wonder he liked you so much."

I remember how fond he was of Rae, while I remained lukewarm, uncertain, and wary. Maybe I'd inherited my mother's attitude toward her baby sister. Aunt Rae was absent most of my life, sending us brief and rare postcards. Mother always said Rae was "different." When I questioned her, Mother remained vague.

"Rae chose a more bohemian lifestyle," Mother once said.

At twelve, I'd never heard that word before. "What's that?"

"Different."

So I never got further in those conversations.

After Mother's death, Rae moved back to Dallas. Occasionally, I felt obligated to invite her over. Stu thought she was hilarious, like a novelty white elephant gift. But I silently agreed with Mother's assessment.

Then Stu started chemo, and Rae volunteered to sit with him when I ran occasional errands. My irritation and indifference toward Rae turned to belligerent gratitude. Slowly she inched her way into my life until now she is as much a part of my world as this Elvis bust. I never wondered what she and Stu had talked about till now. I feel an odd pinch of jealousy that they bonded over Elvis, something I never cared about or wanted.

I never understood Stu's Elvis mania. Sure, the man had a good voice. But Stu's obsession was more than that. Frankly it got on my nerves. It became an odd quirk which his good friends and I laughed and teased him about. Sometimes I think he bought bizarre Elvis items just to exaggerate his reputation as an aficionado.

"Elvis was Stu's before we married," I explain to Rae. "He wouldn't part with it. And I wouldn't let him put it on the coffee table. So Elvis took up residence in the attic."

Rae nods, still focusing on Elvis. Paint on one wide sideburn has been chipped. The pouty top lip curls in the King's trademark expression.

Suddenly a car door slams. Other neighborhood sounds intrude. Children squeal as they ride bikes along the sidewalk. I feel exposed, as if I've strung up my utilitarian panties and B-cup bras across the front of my house for all to see and touch and wonder about. Maybe I'm more like my mother than I thought, more comfortable keeping my hopes, dreams, and secrets to myself.

"How much?" a man asks, his T-shirt too short to cover his round, hairy stomach.

I stare at the cardboard record covers the man holds. A dusty picture of Elvis stares up at the ceiling. Memories compress upon me. "I better keep those."

"Which ones?"

"All of them."

"But Claudia," Rae interrupts. "You wanted to say good-bye to all of this and begin a new life."

No. Others wanted that. I'm not sure what I want. Weeks ago Rae told me (*pushed* would be more accurate),

"Claudia, you must get on with your life." Then one day last week Ben said, "It's time, Claudia."

I've known Ben as long as I've known Stu. They were college roommates. Now he's the founder and executive director of the nonprofit where I work. If he's right, if it's time, then why does this feel like a betrayal?

I can't meet Rae's questioning glance. "I changed my mind."

The man scowls, drops the albums in Stu's office chair, and stalks out of the garage, mumbling about a crazy woman.

"Am I crazy?" I ask Rae.

"No more than me." She hums "All Shook Up," which is how I feel.

I bend down to pick up the crinkled papers of Elvis's shroud and toss the packing paper into the empty box. A folded card flutters away from me. Reaching for it, I scrape my nails against the concrete floor. Then I recognize Stu's scribbled writing. Carefully, I pick up the card, rub my thumb over Stu's awkward and labored script. Why was a note hidden inside Elvis's cardboard coffin? I slide it into my back pocket.

"I think I'll get a soda." But I hesitate when two new customers wander into the garage. "Want one, Rae?"

She waves me off, telling me she can handle the few customers milling about my garage. "Looking for something in particular?"

A woman with dark hair and a skimpy T-shirt that reads "J. Lo's Twin!" glances around the garage. "Kid toys?"

"Depends on the age of the child." Rae steps toward Stu's assortment of basketballs, footballs, and tennis rackets.

I block out the rest of the conversation as I step inside my house. A blast of cold air stirs the damp, sweaty ends of my hair. I close the door behind me. Stu would want me to get rid of all this stuff. When he carried box after box of my mother's things to our attic after her death, he said, "It's stuff, not your mother."

I push away the memory and head for the refrigerator. The door makes a sucking noise as I open it. Along the bottom shelf a puddle of orange juice has congealed. The health department would be appalled at the expiration dates on a few containers that remind me of all that is so easy to toss away and all that I long to hold onto.

I pull out a soda and close the door. Leaning back against it, I clutch the cold can in my hand. Exhaustion weights my limbs. Tapping the top of the can three times, I yank the tab and take a long pull of Diet Coke. The cold liquid bubbles down my throat, evaporates the emotional congestion.

Mother remained stoic after my father's death. I was in high school; my mother in her early forties. It suddenly occurs to me she must have been widowed about the same age I was. How did she manage without my dad? She seemed so strong, so brave. I'm not like her at all.

I pull the note from my back pocket. Stu probably wanted to make sure I didn't get rid of Elvis. Maybe he wanted me to donate Elvis to some pop culture museum. Or maybe he wanted me to put Elvis on the coffee table so I wouldn't forget. How can I? Yet how can I ever say no to Stu?

I unfold the note. A trembling starts deep within me. There are only a few lines.

Deer Claudia,

I'm waiting for the end. Can't stop thinking. Elvis is in the basement. And he belongs in Memphis. He haunts me.

I draw a shaky breath. Stu was a magna cum laude graduate, yet the cancer stole his intellect, his dignity, and finally his life.

I reread the first paragraph, remember how the tumor affected his speech. I translate "basement" to mean "attic" since we never had the former.

A memory lurks of Stu sipping Sprite through a straw. "You know, he was forty-two."

In the background Elvis sang about being lonesome. His heartbreaking vocals made me believe he'd experienced that very emotion.

"When Elvis recorded this song?"

"When he died." A sharp hook of comprehension snagged the edge of my stomach. Stu was the same age.

I slam the mental drawer on that memory. He knew. But I hadn't been ready to face the truth. I'm still not.

Stu always felt a connection to Elvis. In college he told me as an adolescent he'd felt awkward and geeky. "I was a loner," he told me. "But I didn't want to be. I learned how to be cool through Elvis."

I focus on Stu's note again. Was he thinking about Elvis at the end of his own life? Or was he thinking of me? I force myself to read the rest.

I regress it now.

Regret? I wonder. Regret what?

I figure once I've left . . .

Like it was his choice.

. . . you'll say bye to Elvis.

But can I?

Will you refund it for me?

Return?

It belongs at Faithland. It was his fault. He was so real.

Who was real? Who was at fault? And for what? Maybe Stu had been hallucinating. Faithland? Did he mean Graceland?

Rae must go too. She can help.

I miss you. Miss your laugh. It's been gone a while now.

I miss the you and me.

This dizeez has changed both of us, hasn't it?

Hold me, like you used to do, in your dreams.

I don't want to leave.

Always yours,

Stu

I fold the note over, rub my thumbnail across the crease. My eyes are dry, my heart cracked like the ground during a summer drought.

Chapter Two

I Want You, I Need You, I Love You

A knock at the back door jars me out of my stupor. I should have relieved Rae before now. How long have I been inside? I stuff Stu's note in my back pocket just as the door opens. Ben steps inside my house carrying one of Stu's golf clubs.

I salute him with my Diet Coke. "Need a drink?"

He walks into my kitchen, his face shadowed beneath the A&M baseball cap he wears. "You don't have anything strong enough."

"Bad day?"

"I'm okay." He rubs his hand over his face as if trying to ease the tension, erase the worry lining the corners of his eyes. "How's the garage sale going?"

I rub my thumb around the edge of the soda can. "What did Rae tell you?"

He balances the golf club between his hands like he's about to mimic Gene Kelly's soft-shoe routine. "Why?"

I shrug. "Let's just say sales isn't my forte."

"I want Stu's clubs." He lays the one club—a driver, I think—on the counter.

"You can have them."

"See, you made a sale." He grins, planes of his face creasing like a paper fan.

"No, they're yours. I should have asked if you wanted them. I wasn't thinking."

"Stu would make me pay."

"Yeah," I laugh, "he would. I'll give you a good deal on a bunch of record albums."

"Are they warped?"

"Not the way you mean. But some of Stu's collection was a bit twisted."

A wry smile tugs one corner of his mouth. He readjusts his baseball cap, lifting it off his head and settling it back a notch. "So what's going on with the garage sale? From what Rae said, you sound like my daughter. One minute Ivy says this, the next minute the opposite." He studies me like a pimple might pop out on my forehead. "Are you a teenager?"

"You better stay back then," I warn, my tone light and airy. "I've got the hormones for some scary behavior."

His laughter is a short burst, then silence expands between us. I sip my Diet Coke, which foams up like the tension building inside me. "Are you having trouble with Ivy?"

"Depends on the moment." He grins, but there's tension around the edges. "She's normal. I think. But I don't have a lot to compare her to. It's times like this when I miss Gwen."

I don't know how to respond. I don't know how to help. I know the damage Gwen caused, the anger and betrayal. Ben rarely mentions his ex-wife anymore; but when he does, it feels like a shovel jabbing at a pile of hurt, anger, and betrayal.

"There's no guarantee if Gwen had stayed that she and Ivy would be close." Case in point: my relationship with my mother. "There's no such thing as a perfect teenager. Or the perfect parent." Or a perfect life. Over the past few years I've discovered uncertainty is the one certainty.

"That's true." He leans against the kitchen counter, one shoulder tilted downward. "Thing is, I've been meaning to talk to her about her mother. Explain some things she should know and understand. But it's never a good time. She's always angry or upset. Usually at me. And this would make it worse."

Despair washes over me. There's so much hurt in the world, in this very room. Sometimes I feel as if I'm drowning in it. "Do you ever wonder why this has happened? Gwen . . . and Stu? Why she abandoned your family? Why Stu had to die? I mean, what's the point?"

"Are you asking why God allowed it?" His brown eyes narrow on me.

I shrug, shift from one foot to the other. Maybe that's what I've been asking but secretly was afraid a lightning bolt would hit me if I dared. "Maybe I am."

"I'll tell you, Claudia, I haven't a clue." His answer stuns me. Then he laughs, a caustic sound. "I've wrestled with that question a lot. Sometimes I think it's my fault about Gwen. The consequences of sin and all that."

"Your fault?"

"Sure. Did I miss the warning signs? Looking back, there were things about Gwen that I should have noticed, should have worried about. Before and after we married. But I ignored them."

"It's not your fault that Gwen walked out."

"Maybe. Maybe not. But maybe I could have spared all of us this pain if I'd paid attention to the signs. Then again, I wouldn't have Ivy."

"So what's the reason for Stu suffering, dying so young?"

He leans back against the counter and crosses his arms over his chest. "I don't have an answer. I don't have answers for all *my* questions. I trust there's a reason."

"Trust," I scoff. "Like trusting Santa's going to come down the chimney?"

"God isn't a myth. Or some jolly elf that brings presents."

Maybe that's why I'm disappointed. Maybe I expected more. But then what or who is this God who's supposed to be running things?

The back door opens and bangs against the wall. Rae rushes into the kitchen, her face reddened, her fists tight.

"What's wrong?" I ask, rushing forward.

"I caught someone stealing!"

Ben grabs the golf club like a baseball bat.

Rae slaps a baby rattle on the counter. "Can you believe that?"

"Someone stole a baby rattle?" Ben asks. "Where'd—"

"Where's the money box, Rae?" I ask, thinking of the Monkees lunch box I'm using for a bank.

"I gave it to Ivy to watch." She shifts her gaze to Ben, then back to me. "Was that okay?"

"I'm sure it'll be fine." I ignore Ben's frown. "Ivy's trustworthy."

Even if Santa isn't.

"I was telling Claudia," he says, "I've been having trouble with Ivy."

"Stealing?" Rae asks.

"No."

"Drugs then?"

"Nothing like that. Angst. Mood swings. Boys. They're here one minute, gone the next. Which I prefer."

"Love isn't easy on a young heart," Rae says. "Claudia, you should spend time with the girl."

"That would be great." Ben's eyes fill with hope.

"Uh . . ." I stall, feeling a band tighten around my chest like the tiny yellow ribbon tied around the rattle's handle. "I'm not the motherly type."

"You have a woman's heart," Rae says, as if that's the only requirement.

Remembering Ivy's birth, her childhood years when Stu and I babysat often, I ache for the girl who knows even less of her mother than I do about mine. At least my mother was able to make bologna sandwiches for me to put in my Monkees lunch box.

"She needs a woman's influence." Ben watches me.

"Of course," I say. "I'll help Ivy anyway I can. You know that." I place a hand on his arm, then pull back. "But you need to find a time to talk to her about her mother.

Everyone needs to know as much as they can about their own mother."

"Knowledge like that," Rae says, a flutter of emotions flying over her features like a butterfly's course, "is overrated. I better get back to the garage sale. Check on that money box."

♪ ♩ ♪ ♩. ♩ ♪ ♩

"THAT IS THE ugliest thing I've ever seen!"

I don't have to see the Elvis bust to know that's what Ivy is talking about. Still, her blatant honesty rankles me. I don't know why I feel defensive about Elvis. Maybe I'm protecting Stu even now as I step back into the heat of the garage.

Rae surges past me and grabs the lunch box, which rattles with change, from Ivy. "I'll take care of that now."

Ivy glares at Rae, her chin jutted forward.

I'm surprised by Ivy's appearance. I haven't seen Ben's daughter in a few months or since she dyed her blond hair black. She now wears heavy eyeliner, making her look older and wearier than her fifteen years.

"Sorry, Claudia." Carrying the golf club, Ben steps down onto the concrete floor. He shrugs as if saying, "What can you do with a teen?" I wonder what I can do with an aunt who lacks diplomacy.

Ben's tried his best to be father and mother to Ivy. He even started Abandoned Families, a nonprofit organization, to help others who've experienced devastating losses the way he had. But obviously Ivy needs a little feminine advice.

"It's okay." I offer a smile to Ivy like a pact not

blaming her for the sentiments we both share. "Elvis *is* rather nauseating."

She gives me a sideways glance but no smile when I walk up beside her and put a casual arm around her shoulders.

"It's good to see you, Ivy. Like the color." I flip one of her locks off her shoulder. "Very chic."

"Dad hates it."

"I never said that." Ben drops the club into the golf bag and heaves it onto his shoulder.

"Whatever."

A group begins to form around us, everyone staring at Stu's pride and joy. It almost looks like those gathered are worshipping a shrine of the late King.

"It's amazing," an older man says.

"Unbelievable," someone else adds.

"Very true in its likeness, don't you think?" Rae joins in.

Irritated once again at the King for his intrusion into my life, I cross my arms over my chest. Slowly customers saunter away to look at the rest of my junk for sale.

"Brings back memories." Ben clunks the golf bag on the floor at his feet and drapes an arm around my shoulders.

Uncomfortable walking down memory lane with anyone else, I move out from under his arm. "Too many."

Ivy steps sideways, then back the other direction. "I swear his eyes are following me."

"Ivy thinks every hot guy is watching her." Ben winks.

His daughter rolls her gaze heavenward in that forever-old teenage prayer of disdain.

"I think he's creepy, too," I say for Ivy's benefit.

"Stuart loved this," Rae says. She makes a statement, not a question, making me wonder all over again what she and Stu discussed about Elvis. She places a handful of change into the Monkees lunch box, pressing her palm against Davy Jones's smiling face as she closes the lid. Seeing her next to Ben, I realize how tall and elegant she looks, if a bit gypsy-esque with her free-flowing clothes and assorted rings and charm bracelet.

"Who does Elvis belong to?" I ask Ben.

"What'd you do?" Ivy looks at her dad with a mixture of teen rebellion and cool admiration. "Steal it?"

He lifts his baseball cap and settles it further back on his head. "Not me." A gleam of mischief sparks in his brown eyes. "I wouldn't have done such a thing."

"But Stu would have," I say.

Ben shrugs, not confirming my suspicions but not denying them either. "That's not what he told me."

Didn't I have confirmation in my back pocket? Elvis belonged in Memphis, according to Stu. Obviously to someone else. What else could that mean?

"I'd forgotten all about the King." Ben peers closer at the bust. His athletic build is apparent in his running shorts and tank. Stu and Ben were about the same height, but Stu was slender as a two-by-four while Ben is broad and husky—not overweight, just ex-college-football-player big. "Where's he been hiding all these years?"

"The attic."

"Elvis has left the attic," Ben's voice rumbles through the garage.

"Dad!" Ivy huffs a sigh and rolls her eyes.

Customers glance up from jumbles of linens and sports

equipment. Ivy edges away from us, meandering through the garage. She walks along the far table, her nose crinkled at the collection of my mother's knickknacks that are as far from a teen's tastes as garden teas are from MTV.

Ben shrugs. "I've always wanted to say something like that."

"That guy," a customer nods toward Ben, "has left his brain."

Ben and I share a laugh. For a moment, it's like we're back in college, joking around. But one important element is missing—Stu. In moments like this my laughter freezes in my chest, hard and heavy.

A crash makes me turn. Ivy curses, rubs her knee, then kicks the crib she knocked to the floor. "Why would anybody put a stupid crib here?"

"Ivy," Ben says with a warning note.

"Why do you have this?" Ivy asks, her face red with embarrassment and the flush of anger, as if the crib jumped out like a rabid dog and bit her. "It's not like you have a kid."

"That's enough, Ivy." Ben steps toward his daughter.

My pulse thrums in my ears. I stare at the piece of furniture made to hold a baby and wonder what I was made for.

"So . . . what?" Ivy crosses her arms over her chest. "Did you lose it or something?"

"Claudia," Ben says, "I'm—"

I put a hand on his arm to let him know it's okay, I'm okay. But I'm not sure I am. I feel the repercussions of Ivy's jab echoing through my body. At that moment all sympathy for the little girl whose mother left her drains out of me.

A hardness tightens within me. A nasty part of myself wants to lash out at her.

"Actually," I say, looking straight at her, "I did."

She stares back for a moment, then shrugs and mumbles, "Probably for the best."

Heat surges to my face, makes my eyes fill. I blink. I know she's right. I'm not the motherly type. But the pain lingers and picks at an old, forgotten wound.

Chapter Three

Love Me

"Claudia," Ben starts.

I know what he's about to say so I look toward Elvis, as if he holds the answers to my questions. "So where did Stu get him?"

He studies me for a moment. "You want a matching set? Like bookends?"

"How much?" A man with an Elvis-sized pouch steps toward the King.

I catch myself blocking the man's way. I tried to get rid of the bust a few times in the past but Stu always said, "Love me, love Elvis." I touch Elvis's shoulder protectively. "He's not for sale."

"What do you want?" the man persists. "Fifty?"

"No." I cross my arms over my stomach.

"All right, a hundred."

"No, really. I don't want to sell it."

"One-fifty then."

Rae waves her hand at him, as if shooing a bothersome fly. "She said no!"

The man points a stubby finger at her. "Who are you?"

She takes a step forward, flings her long, steel-gray hair over one shoulder, and glares right back. "I'm—"

"It's okay." I step between them. "Look, I'm sorry, Elvis isn't for sale."

"Are you sure?" Ben asks, his brow furrowing.

The man grunts. "Why not?"

A ready answer eludes me. "He's just not."

His mouth twists, then he turns and stalks out of the garage.

Ben rocks back on his heels and cocks an eyebrow at me. I ignore him. I don't want to defend my actions. I don't want to try to explain myself. I'm not sure I can.

"I'm glad you didn't sell Elvis, Claudia," Rae pats my arm. "It's worth—"

"Oh, I'm going to get rid of him," I say, feeling suddenly rebellious, more like Ivy than I care to admit.

"I doubt it's worth much," Ben says. "Stu probably bought it at some Elvis gift shop."

I shake my head. "If he had, then it wouldn't have bothered him at the end of his life."

"It did?" Both of his eyebrows go up this time.

"Do you remember when Stu showed up with Elvis?"

"Sure, it was the trip we took to Memphis in '87. Beat the Memphis State Tigers in a nonconference game early our senior year." If I ask, I'm sure he can tell me the last play of the game. "Stu took pictures as always." He'd been one of the school photographers for the *Cavalier Daily*. "We toured Graceland, ate barbecue. After the game Stu disappeared for a few hours. He showed back up with his friend here." Ben gestures toward Elvis. "We questioned Stu, but he gave no answers."

I notice Ivy inching closer, pretending not to listen, but her gaze shifts from the upside-down CDs she's holding to her father.

"A few weeks later Stu told me a different tale."

"What?"

Ben's chest expands with a deep breath. He moves a little closer and speaks in a low voice. "He picked up a hitch-hiker outside of Memphis."

"A hitchhiker?"

"Looked like Elvis," he says. "That's what made Stu stop. An impersonator, he decided, when the guy climbed into his car. And about fifty or so. Had stark white hair. He told Stu he needed a lift."

"Do you think that's what really happened?" I ask.

Ben shrugs. "I don't know. Stu seemed pretty shaken by the experience. Talked about it being a ghost or something."

"A ghost? Stu said that?" I stare at Ben, trying to decide if he's pulling my leg, the way Stu might.

Ben snaps his fingers. "Years later he gave me an Alan Jackson CD. I didn't like country music. But he said, 'Listen to track 4.' So I did. It was that song 'Midnight in Memphis' . . . or 'Mayberry' . . ."

"Montgomery," Rae corrects.

Ben jerks as if he's been electrocuted. "That's it. And it was about—"

"The ghost of Hank Williams," Rae says. "Stuart saw him."

"Who?" I ask, confused. "Hank Williams? Or Alan Jackson?"

"Elvis," she says without a trace of humor.

"I doubt it." Ben rubs his jaw. "When did Elvis die?"

"Seventy-seven." Rae's knowledge of country music and Elvis trivia surprises me. I wonder what else she knows. Maybe Elvis's current address? She's the type I imagine who would believe he's still alive.

Ben shifts from foot to foot. "The whole meet-and-greet with Elvis made Stu think some weird things."

"Great," I say. "So I should look in the cemetery for the owner of the bust?"

"Elvis was buried at Graceland," Rae says.

"Even better." I grimace. "I think I'd rather call Ghostbusters."

"What are you talking about?" Ben asks.

I pull the note out of my back pocket. "See if you can solve the mystery."

Ben reads the letter silently, pushing his arm out straight in front of him. I've teased him about needing granny glasses. He rubs the back of his neck as Rae leans close to see the note. She makes a tiny gasp. Her face suddenly pales. Ben gives me a questioning look.

"Stu was having trouble writing," I explain. "Could he have been delusional?"

"I doubt it." He studies the note again. "He must have meant Graceland."

"That's what I thought. But how would he have known it belonged there if he got it from some old Elvis wannabe?"

"Elvis told him," Rae says.

"Elvis was dead," I remind my aunt.

"He told him," she emphasizes.

Skeptical of my aunt's sanity, I ask Ben, "So what do I do? Ignore this request? Go up to Graceland's gate and say, 'My late husband stole this and wanted me to bring it back?'"

"He didn't steal it," Rae says.

"We don't really know that." Anger simmers inside me. Stu told Ben and Rae about Elvis. But not me. Why? Then I turn on my aunt. "Why would Stu want you to go with me anyway?"

"Because . . ." She stares down at her feet for a moment and draws a slow breath. "Because I knew him."

"Him? Of course you knew Stu."

She remains silent, her lips squeezed together.

"Elvis?" Ben asks.

She gives a hesitant nod. Ben and I glance at each other.

In some ways, if I know little about Rae's life, it's my own fault. After all, I rarely ask about her life, and when I do she dodges the questions like a politician, like my mother. I've seen my baby pictures with occasional appearances by her, a doting aunt. Then nothing for too many years. Maybe I've simply accepted the blank pages of Rae's past like lost pictures never to be recovered. But could it be true that she knew the King of Rock 'n' Roll?

"You actually knew Elvis?" Ben lowers his voice to a whisper.

She shrugs as if her claim means nothing. "I've known many people in my lifetime."

"Then you have to go with Claudia to Memphis," Ben says.

"Whoa!" I put a hand out. "I never said I was going to Memphis." Everyone in the garage—neighbors, customers, Aunt Rae, and Ben, even Ivy—stare at me.

Rae puts an arm around me as if siding with me. "You're right. It's too much. It wouldn't be good."

Ben frowns.

I look at Stu's note, my husband's last request. Frustration rises in me, but I press it down.

"This is Stu's last request," Ben voices my own rebellious thoughts.

"A fool's journey," Rae says. "How can you leave work? Everything? Just like that? What was Stuart thinking? He wasn't. He was delusional. Forget Elvis. Sell him."

Hadn't she told me to keep the bust? What made her suddenly change her mind? Is there something she's hiding? Frankly, I'm tired of secrets. "But you said—"

"I'm her boss," Ben says. "She can have the time off." He looks at me then, his gaze dark. "You need to do this."

"What if it's one of Stu's pranks?"

Ben has no answer.

"I'll go," Ivy says, suddenly standing beside us.

"What?" I ask.

"To Memphis?" Ben stares at his daughter.

Uncertainty grips my stomach. Elvis is bad enough, but I'm not sure about being responsible for a teenager. Especially one who has the ability to cut me to the core. "No, I'm not going. This is pure insanity."

"But it's Stu's last request," Ben says.

"That we know of. What if I find another crazy request in a potted plant next week?"

"Have you found any other notes in almost two years?" Ben challenges.

I look away, then admit, "No."

"You have to do this," he says, his voice low.

My heart hammers. I want to smash Elvis with one of Stu's golf clubs. "No, I don't."

"YOU'RE NOT SELLING this dress, are you?" Rae slides a green silk dress off the unstable metal rack, holds it up to her, and smiles through the hanger.

"Apparently not." I hit the button on the wall and the garage door slides down, creaking in protest, closing the sale for the day. "You're welcome to it."

"It's your color," she says.

"Stu hated that dress on me."

"And we know what good taste he had." Ben grins.

I have to admit, Stu never acquired better taste. He always used to say, "I married you. That's as good as it gets." My insides warm like chocolate squares in a hot pan and melt into a dark puddle, shapeless and bitter.

Ben leans an elbow on Elvis's head. "Maybe Stu was jealous."

Laughter bursts out of me. "You're saying Stu wanted to wear my dress?"

"Of looks you'd get from other guys."

"No way." Yet I feel the truth of his words in the sudden tautness of my stomach.

"You should keep this," Rae says, handing me the dress. "You might go to a party."

"Not likely. It doesn't fit anyway." I wonder if my memories have downsized from reality as well as my weight over the past year. "Where's Ivy?"

"She went inside to borrow your bathroom."

"Is she sick?" Rae asks. "She looked pale."

"That's her look," Ben says. "The latest rage in teen fashion."

"Do you think she's upset that we're not going to Memphis?" I ask.

He shrugs. "The question is, are you? I think you should go."

"I think you're crazy." I swat his elbow off Elvis's head. "So why do you think Ivy wanted to go to Memphis with me?"

"Maybe she wants to spend time with you. She used to, you know."

I nod. Guilt swells inside me. Maybe that's the reason for her cruel remark. Maybe I've let her down with my absence. "I know. I'm sorry. I'll take her to dinner." I've been introspective—okay, a hermit—the past year, even longer as Stu's illness kept me busy and distracted for a long while, too. It's just another way of saying I've been selfish, not reaching out to help anyone else. "I promise."

"She'd like that."

Doubting that, I rub my hand over the contours of Elvis's head, feeling the smooth pottery beneath my fingers, the slight grooves and creases. "So if I did go . . . and I'm not saying I am, would you let Ivy go with me?"

"Would you want her to?" Ben asks.

Lifting a shoulder, I sigh. "As long as it's okay with you."

"She can be difficult."

"Because you're her dad. Isn't that how it is with teenagers? They're difficult with their parents but not so much with others." I'm not sure I'm buying that line myself.

"Maybe." Ben's desperation shows in his eagerness to believe. "So are you thinking of going?"

I notice Rae is watching me too. Her expression tightens with worry. "No." I laugh to relieve the tension. "Then I'd be crazy."

I pick up a bag of knitting yarn someone left tipped on its side. I remove a lace doily from the top. My fingers poke through the empty spaces. Mother kept her feelings tightly woven, hidden from view. I've tried to do the same, but my feelings seem more like twisted and tangled yarn unraveling at the ends.

I lift another sack of yarn and begin sorting it by color, plopping a mauve ball into the sack with a pink mountain growing within. Mother belonged to a group called the Knitwits. They make baby blankets and lap blankets, donating them to hospitals, charities, and old folks' homes. Maybe they could use all this yarn. I don't know why I've kept it so long. But then, I do: Letting go is painful. Memories might replace the need for all this stuff. Maybe I'm simply searching for more.

"Why have I lost everyone?" Hearing my own voice, I realize I spoke out loud.

"At least you had them once," Rae says.

"So I should be grateful?"

Rae shrugs. "It's better than not ever."

"Then I wouldn't know what I've lost." It would be easier. Wouldn't it?

Rae's green gaze is steady, somber. "You're going to Memphis, aren't you?"

"You are?" Ivy asks, coming out of the house.

I shrug. "I don't know." But I do. *Love me, love Elvis.* The words play over and over in my head like a scratched record. Stu's voice vibrates in my head, resonates in my heart.

I never felt like I had a choice in the matter. Stu filled the holes in my life. My response to Stu was automatic and overwhelming. Even now in death he calls and I answer.

"Maybe," I say.

"I'm sorry I said what I did earlier." Rae places her hand on my arm. "Maybe you should go. Maybe Stuart was right. Maybe it's time. If so, then I'll help you find where Elvis belongs."

"You'd do that? For me?"

"Of course."

"What about me?" Ivy asks. "Can I go?"

"Why?" Ben questions.

"Because." She huffs out a breath. Her defensiveness returns. "Oh, forget it. What do I care?"

I shift my gaze toward Ben, unsure if I'm pleading for Ivy or not.

"I didn't say you couldn't go," Ben says to his daughter. "Maybe you should. If it's all right with Claudia."

"Is it?" Ivy looks to me. Something in her eyes looks desperate, like she needs this trip, maybe more than I do. Maybe she needs time away from her overwhelmed father. Most definitely he needs a break from her.

"Sure." What else can I say?

"Then there will be three of us," Rae says, looping an arm through mine.

An odd feeling swells inside me. I nod my appreciation. But I'm not sure if I'm relieved or more apprehensive. I pat Elvis on his pompadour.

"Make that four."

Chapter Four

Moody Blue

"He won't fit," I say one week later.

Having caught up with work and Ivy's school letting out for summer, we're ready to take Elvis home. Wherever that may be.

Stu's hunk-of-burnin'-love red vintage Cadillac sits in front of the house, the trunk gaping like an open mouth, the bust sitting in it like a bug that can't be choked down. Exasperated, I push the trunk lid down. It knocks against the base of the bust.

"I don't remember Elvis being so big." Rae stands beside the rear bumper. She's wearing a sparkly top that matches a pair of black capri pants and the same clunky, comfortable-looking sandals that she wore to the garage sale.

"Maybe he swelled up in the heat."

Rae laughs. "Maybe our heads did, thinking we could do this."

Okay, I don't need an excuse to back out. I have a bad

case of what Stu would have called the moody blues, after Elvis's album.

"Tell me about Elvis," I say.

Rae remains silent for a moment, looks up at the sky. It's been light for an hour, the gray of dawn cracking apart into a pale blue. "He was larger than life."

And so is the bust. With a grunt I shift its position again. "Heavy, too."

"He did have a weight problem."

Laughter sticks in my bad attitude. I try laying Elvis on his side, but the base is too wide and knocks against the trunk lid when I attempt to close it again.

"But," she says, "that was after I knew him."

I glance at my aunt, still not quite able to believe she knew the King. "What was it like to know Elvis?"

"Oh, he was like anybody else." She rolls her wrist and the charms on her bracelet make little chiming sounds. "And yet . . ."

I roll the King onto his back, but still the base proves too broad. I feel a sudden kinship with Elvis, sympathizing with how he was pushed around by the Colonel, yanked around by his own desires. I've been pushed into a corner by my own grief and Stu's letter. Rae even pushed me into the garage sale.

"Mother never mentioned you knew Elvis."

"Beverly thought my life—my 'antics' as she called it—was unimportant." A slight breeze ruffles the bright yellow scarf encircling her head, the tail ends trailing out into her long, peppery hair. "But she liked Elvis once upon a time."

"Mother?" She preferred Frank Sinatra and Bing Crosby. Didn't she? I lean against the side of the car, but knowing

Stu would have objected, I straighten. The trunk stands wide open, and Elvis stares up at the brightening sky.

"Didn't she ever tell you when we saw him?"

"Elvis? My mother saw Elvis?"

"We were young. Foolish. Elvis came through Dallas on a train. Father—your grandfather, that is—didn't care for Elvis. Didn't like his moves." She performs a quick pelvis thrust for emphasis, making me laugh. "If Father had ever met Elvis, I believe he would have changed his mind. Elvis was really a nice young man. Very courteous. Very mannerly. But back then Beverly and I probably liked him because Father did not."

"A rebel," I say, intrigued. An only child myself, I always did as I was told.

She winks. "I was just thirteen and your mother was eighteen, I think. But what trouble we could get into! We snuck out of the house to run along the train tracks and wave to Elvis." She sighs as if she were once again a young girl. "He was very handsome."

I smile, having had my share of crushes. Davy Jones was probably first, then David Cassidy came along and stole my heart. I almost laugh out loud remembering John Travolta from his *Welcome Back, Kotter* days. But I never met one of my objects of infatuation. I'm not the type to scream or faint or go into hysterics. I'm more the type to stand back, stare or gawk, but not say a word. I remember David Cassidy giving a concert in Dallas, but Mother wouldn't let me go. I sulked for a whole week. I wasn't as brave as Rae.

"Elvis was on the train tracks?" I ask.

"On a train. Traveling through Dallas on his way to the army or Germany." She shrugs. "What did it matter where he was going? He was here! There was a crowd. Screaming girls. Such fun. Such foolishness."

"But why didn't Mother ever tell me that story?"

A shadow of an emotion crosses her face, but not one I fully recognize. "Maybe Elvis never came up in conversation."

I can't remember. If Elvis ever did come up, as in "Turn down that music!" or "*Blue Hawaii*'s on TV," the conversation didn't progress to anything else. That is, nothing personal and exciting. It was probably as dull as watching an Elvis impersonator instead of the real deal. So why did Mother keep it a secret? Wouldn't it have been a fun story? So many conversations I feel as if I've missed out on with my mother. Maybe I simply failed to ask enough questions.

"Maybe she didn't want you sneaking out the way she did." Rae crosses her arms over her chest. "Beverly took her job as mom very seriously."

A frown pinches my brows together. "She always wanted to set a good example."

"So," I give up trying to make Elvis fit inside the trunk, "what was it like when you met Elvis?"

"Like you'd imagine."

I can imagine a lot. But before I can ask more specific questions, a heavy bass booms out a familiar beat. Ben pulls up in his Jeep and parks along the curb. Spilling out of the speakers are the rocking sounds of "Bossa Nova Baby." My own smile catches me off guard as I remember how Stu's friends ribbed him about always playing Elvis music.

When he cuts the engine and the beat dies, I call out, "Feeling retro?"

"He won't stop playing that music!" Ivy slaps down the visor and looks in the mirror as she brushes her windblown hair.

Grinning, Ben hauls Ivy's suitcase out of the back of the Jeep along with a cooler full of iced soda cans. "Seeing Elvis the other day brought back memories. Where is he?"

I point at the open trunk.

He carries the suitcase around to the back of the Cadillac then drops it on the pavement with a *thunk*. "That's not going to work."

"You're quicker than us." I prop a hand on my hip. "Any suggestions?"

We all stare at Elvis lying in the trunk as if he were a dead body we've suddenly discovered.

"Did you get the belts checked?" Sunlight picks up strands of gray sneaking into Ben's brown hair. "Oil changed?"

"As ordered, Captain." During the last week, I decided Stu's vintage 1959 Cadillac would be better to take than my car, only because my Z-4 won't hold three women, luggage, plus an Elvis-sized bust. "Are you ready, Ivy?"

She saunters up to us in that slow teen way of showing she isn't a slave to anyone else's time frame. Wearing a T-shirt, shorts, and flip-flops, she slings a purple backpack over her shoulder. "Not really."

Neither am I. "What's wrong?"

"Don't ask." Ben mimic's his daughter's rolling of the eyes.

I wonder if he had time to talk to Ivy about her mother.

"I like your flip-flops, Ivy." Around the edges of her toes are sparkly silver stars.

"I've gotta pee."

"The front door is unlocked." I gesture toward my house.

Carrying her backpack over her shoulder, she goes inside.

"Sorry," Ben says.

"For what?"

"She's a teenager."

"She's fine. Don't worry."

"This trip will be good for her," Rae predicts. She puts a hand on my shoulder. "Claudia will be good for her."

I don't know why she thinks that. But if this weekend gives Ben a break, then it'll be worth it.

"I think she had a fight with her boyfriend." He props a foot on the back bumper. "But I'm not sure. She won't talk about it."

"Oh, the joys of love," Rae says.

"Yeah," Ben huffs.

"Don't worry. Really, she'll be fine." I'm not sure my words are comforting. They're not to me. Simply because I don't believe them myself. "So, thoughts on what to do with Elvis? Ship him FedEx?"

Ben looks down at the bust and laughs. "We could tie down the trunk with a rope. It would only be open a few inches."

The front door shuts and we look up as Ivy joins us again.

I wonder if I have rope in the garage. "Let me check—"

"Elvis could sit in the back seat," Rae interrupts.

"That'll look stupid." Ivy cuts her eyes toward the bust as if it's a nerd at school who's been annoying her.

"Might prevent anyone breaking into the trunk when we make stops along the way," I add. I'd hate to lose my change of clothes.

"You think someone would steal Elvis?" Ben asks.

"No." I laugh. Who would want this ugly bust? I should have taken the hundred dollars I'd been offered. I wouldn't complain if someone did steal it. Maybe I should advertise with a sign in the back window: *Elvis. Please take.*

Ben clears his throat. "Claudia, you will be careful."

"Dad," Ivy says, "don't worry so much."

"It's my job."

I remember the way my father worried about me, asked what time I'd be home, insisted on meeting boys I went out with, and generally aggravating me with too many questions. Then he was gone, victim of a massive heart attack. His overprotectiveness suddenly became endearing.

The way Stu would walk me to the dorm at night was one of the first things I liked about him. "I'll be fine," I always said. "Yeah, I know," he'd answer, then keep me company in the dark. His presence made me feel secure, *loved,* before he ever used the word.

Dragging myself back to the present, I ask, "What if Elvis shifts and slides in the back seat?"

"What's to stop him from doing the same in the trunk?" Rae asks.

"Good point. Might rub his nose off," I say, not really caring and yet not wanting him damaged.

"The luggage would wedge him in somewhat." Ben lifts

his baseball cap and swipes his forearm over his brow. "But a seat belt would keep him safe in the back seat."

I start to laugh, then Rae and Ben join in. Only Ivy stands solemn and funereal, as if she's a weary adult tired of our childish antics.

I stare at Elvis. "If Stu wanted to play one last trick on me . . ."

"This would be a doozy," Rae agreed.

With Ben's help I move Elvis to the back seat. It's possible to lift him by myself, but he's bulky and awkward to maneuver. I grab the retrofit seat belt and lean into the car to strap Elvis into place. Kissing distance from the King, I feel a connection with him. He's trapped and so am I. And I'm not sure where either of us is going.

Chapter Five

Burning Love

This is a mistake.

Five miles outside of Dallas, I regret the trip already. The wind whips at my hair, which lashes my cheeks. The Cadillac drives like an unwieldy ship. I clutch the thin, slick wheel, which seems too wide and moves too easily. When I push sixty miles an hour, the car starts to shake. It also shakes while idling at a light. Before we pulled onto the highway, Rae felt the jiggling at the last red light and said, "Shaken, please, not stirred." One of my flaws is that once on a path I keep going, chugging along until I see it through. No matter what the shaking or stirring.

"Bullheaded," my mother used to say, shaking her head.

"Tenacious," Stu once told me.

"A fool," I mumble to myself.

"What's that?" Rae asks, sitting beside me in the Cadillac.

"Want some music?"

"Sure." Her sunglasses are dark and impenetrable, her hair a shimmery wave of gray. She stuffed most of it down the back of her shirt, but strands float out like long, luxurious strings.

I punch the 10-disc CD player that Stu had specially installed after he'd restored the vintage Cadillac. He said it only played Elvis music. Although Ivy might protest, she probably wouldn't like any contemporary music I'd choose. Besides, she's got an iPod plugged into her ear. I've caught snippets of electric guitar and drums leaking from the earphones. My father would have said, "You're gonna ruin your ears." But I am not her parent and will offer no alienating advice of that sort.

Elvis's voice finally bursts out of the speakers with confidence and assurance as he sings about partying in the county jail. The tension in the Cadillac is anything but jovial; it feels more like a prison to me.

Ivy was the one who requested the top to the car be left down. Since she was irritable, I had hoped it would cheer her, maybe even make me look cool in her eyes so we could bond on this trip. But that doesn't seem to have worked. And now the wind is chapping my lips.

I glance in the rearview mirror at the large Elvis bust strapped into its own seat. I imagine it getting splattered with bugs. Sunlight glints off Elvis's painted pompadour. His lip curls at passing cars. I notice other drivers rubbernecking as they pass on either side of our slow-moving parade float.

"Turn it up," Rae directs, reaching for the volume herself. Her hand taps out the rhythm on the seat between us.

Her face splits into a wide grin, revealing a lifetime of finely etched lines in her skin.

"Hey!" Ivy yells from the back seat. Up until that moment she'd been silent. "That's getting on my nerves."

Frowning, I readjust the speakers, turning off the ones in the rear of the car. I remember an icy blast of February frost the last time Stu rode in the Cadillac. He wanted the top down, to feel the wind against his face. While he napped, I struggled for an hour to get the top fastened in place. Sweating, disheveled, I'd tapped on the horn and he'd poured himself into the passenger seat, content for once to let me drive. "Burning Love" blared from the speakers. The bitter wind whipped at my hair and clothes, reflected my thoughts. But Stu's grin warmed me inside and out and temporarily brightened the gray hue that had started to seep into his skin.

Sudden tears threaten like the storm clouds popping up on the horizon. The love we shared still burns inside me. It's why I couldn't say no to Stu about a drive in February or, now, this bizarre trip to Memphis.

We drive over the long bridge that stretches across Lake Ray Hubbard. Bass boats, speeders, and sailboats glide over the smooth water. It's a beautiful day for being out in the sunshine. Once again I resent having to take this trip. Not that I'd be out on the water today. I'd probably be working or piddling around the house.

Movement in the rearview mirror shifts my attention from the road. Ivy leans against the door and props her bare feet on Elvis's shoulder. Irritation twists inside me like a cap on a prescription bottle. I put my arm over the seat and wave my hand toward her feet. "Do you mind?"

Her eyes are closed, and she's absorbed in her own music, her own life, her own problems. I wonder why she wanted to come on this trip. To get away from her dad? To escape her own life? To irritate me?

"Hey!" I arch my back, straining over the seat to get her attention while still trying to maneuver the car, which drives more like a barge through a cramped harbor. I flap my hand until my fingertips brush Ivy's long brown leg.

"What?"

"Do you mind?" I meet her startled gaze in the rear-view mirror.

She lifts an earphone. "What?"

"Your feet! Do you mind not putting them on the King?" Stu would have been horrified.

She looks at her feet, pops her big toe, then slowly pulls them away from Elvis's shoulder. "Whatever."

"Thanks." But I know she's already tuned me out.

A blast of a car horn jerks my attention back to the road where I drifted out of my lane and into the next. I wrench the steering wheel to the right and try to breathe. I remember how my mother rode with me as I practiced driving before I turned sixteen. Most of the time she clutched the side door and shrieked whenever she thought I was slow on braking. But her sister doesn't seem to have a care in the world right now. Rae leans back, her head tilted to absorb the sun's rays, caught up in the moment. I wish I could be so carefree.

BY THE TIME we reach Greenville, we've stopped once and are behind schedule. Ivy needs bathroom breaks more often than a toddler. Other drivers keep checking out Elvis in the back seat, doing double takes, then honking. Some wave and point like they're trying to make sure I know Elvis is hiding in my back seat. Like I don't know this. More truckers have blasted their horns at us until my nerves are frayed.

"Do you think you're going to be able to do this?" Rae asks.

"Do what?"

"Say good-bye to Stuart."

"You mean to Elvis." I shrug. "I've already . . ." My throat tightens. I've already done the impossible. Haven't I?

"You had a happy marriage. For a long while."

"Yes." Feeling the sticky barbs of truth, I turn the questions back on Rae. "Were you ever married?"

"No, no."

"Why not?"

"It's not as if I never had offers. Handsome men. Wealthy, affluent. Oh, the men I've known." She sighs. "But I never loved one enough to sacrifice my freedom. I like adventure."

"Mother always said I should meet a man at church."

"Is that where you met Stu?" she asks.

"No. We met while I was on a date."

"With another man?"

"Ben." I glance back at Ivy, not sure I want her to know this about her father. "It was a setup. A mutual friend at the church we both attended hooked us up. And while we were at dinner, we ran into Stu. He was on a date with someone else."

"Fruit basket turnover," Rae laughs. "I always thought men at church were boring."

"Ben wasn't boring. I don't really remember what

happened. But we never went out again. And soon Stu started calling. I guess I figured Ben wasn't interested."

I think back on the twenty years I was married to Stu. It took me along paths I would never have ventured on my own. "Don't you think marriage can be an adventure?"

"Maybe." Rae readjusts her sunglasses. "With the right someone. But I know how painful loving can be."

I nod, knowing the pain, the sacrifices mingled with the joy.

"After . . ." Her voice drifts, her gaze seems to be looking more in the distance than the smattering of car dealerships we are passing. "Well, I never allowed myself to love deeply again. The pain," she waves her hand, "was too much."

"I know. I don't think I'll ever marry again either. It's too hard to let go." I think back to my mother, who never spoke of lost loves or the pain of losing my father. "Who was it that broke your heart?"

"I did." She taps her chest. "And my heart never recovered."

"How is that possible?" I ask.

"Hey!" Ivy interrupts. "It's raining."

At that moment a raindrop plops against my scalp, then another fat one hits my arm. Up ahead, dark clouds bump together. We seem to be reaching the edge of a storm. "We need to pull over and put the top up."

"Don't worry, I won't melt," Rae says.

"Yeah, but Elvis might." I'm not sure what he's made of, or what I'm made of either, but I can imagine Elvis's pompadour dripping down his face, like the tonic Michael Jackson used to put on his hair, and a puddle of plaster forming in the back seat.

♪♩♪♩.♩♪♩

"GRAB THAT AND pull," I shout. The wind has picked up. Eighteen-wheelers rumble past and shake the car.

Rae tries to help but doesn't know what to do. I end up racing from one side of the car to the other. Rain begins to fall, first in random drops, then more steadily, as if the clouds have figured out what to do.

By the time I've wrestled the top into place, I'm sopping wet with sweat and rain. I brush damp strands of hair out of my face and fall into the driver's seat, slamming the door closed. Bubbling with laughter, Rae climbs in beside me on the front bench seat. Behind us, not a care in the world, Ivy sends a text message through her cell phone, probably to her friends that she is with two lunatic adults.

I stare out the windshield at the rain sluicing down it. Only a few feet away from the car is a purple ostrich. I blink, lean forward. That's when I see a whole row of statues—a giraffe, buffalo, lion, and a giant marlin. Maybe Elvis belongs with these guys. I could dump him on the side of the road and turn for home. But as soon as the thought enters my mind, I bat it down. I think of Stu's note and know I'm bound for Graceland.

"Does it hurt badly?" Rae asks.

I glance at my thumb, which I smashed while putting the top up. The side of it is red, and I feel it pulse with anger. "It's okay."

We sit on the side of the road for a moment longer as I catch my breath. Rain splatters on the windshield and plunks on the canvas top. It reminds me of another rainy day, cold and bitter. Stu lay in his hospice bed, staring up at the pockmarked ceiling, watching the slow spin of the fan. It was toward the end. Every breath had become precious. "How much will you miss me?"

His voice floats back to me across the space of time—that look, the electricity he elicited in my body crackled like the lightning flashes up ahead—and I clench the steering wheel.

"Are you okay?" Rae asks, and I realize she's watching me closely.

I shake loose the memories, pull my seat belt across my body. "I guess we better move on now. We won't get to Memphis sitting on the side of the road."

Ivy makes no comment, not verbally anyway; she's focused on her cell phone. But Rae touches my arm, her warmth startling to the coolness of my skin, as if to say, *You're not alone.* But I feel alone. So very alone in all of this.

♪♩♪♩.♩♪♩

"HEY," IVY CALLS over the roar of the engine, the buffeting of the wind against the canvas top, and Elvis singing "Love Me Tender." "I gotta pee."

"Again?" I glance over my shoulder, then back toward the highway. "Okay. There's a town coming up."

"Is this Arkansas?" Rae asks, seeming to wake up. Her head has been nodding sleepily for the last twenty minutes.

The rain stops as we pull into a gas station that looks newly constructed. The pavement is wet, and everything seems to glitter with remnants of the rain. I see a sign for restrooms and a refrigerated compartment of Coca-Colas and Budweisers.

"I might fill up the gas tank while we're—"

Ivy slams the door and heads toward the building without a word or a glance back.

"—stopped," I finish, then sigh. Teenagers. I'm beginning to be glad I never had children. I pity Ben, who has to deal with his daughter on a daily basis. No wonder he needs a break. I do, too.

After choosing the grade of gasoline—the top grade, Stu always advised me—I open the car door and lean in. "Rae, would you like something to drink or snack on?"

"Good idea. I'll come in with you."

Together we walk into the gas station. Immediately the scent of incense tickles my senses and makes me sneeze.

"It is not what he said," the woman sitting behind the counter says into the phone attached to her ear. She has a thick Middle Eastern accent. Sufi music weeps out of the speakers. Nothing in this place makes me think of Arkansas.

"Peanuts or crackers?" Rae asks, perusing the shelves for snack foods.

I'm not hungry, but my stomach feels empty. Or maybe it's just me. "I'm thinking an apple turnover."

"Ooh, I haven't had one of those in years. Beverly used to love those."

"Mother?" I ask, remembering how she wouldn't let me have those fat-laden empty calories.

"Oh, yes. She would walk me over to the Gulf station, only a couple of blocks from our house, and we'd buy two—a lemon one for me and an apple for her."

"You'd pass on the pickled eggs and pigs' feet?" I joke,

passing a five-gallon jar of each, which is the first clear indication of the state we're in.

Rae laughs. "Maybe on the way home."

We each select a turnover and grab an extra for Ivy. The paper crinkles beneath my fingers. After we pay and walk back toward the car, I ask, "Was my mother a good big sister?"

"Of course. Sometimes she would take me with her, include me in her trouble so we could share the blame. Then other times she'd shun me."

"Wait a minute . . . Mother, *my* mother, in trouble?"

"Oh, the trouble she could find! When she started dating your daddy, she missed her curfew a few times." Rae grins at my surprised expression. "Don't be so shocked. Where do you think I learned to rebel?"

"This just doesn't sound like Mother."

"I remember her buying Coca-Cola bottles, then taking them home, dumping out part, and filling it up with rum that she snuck out of Father's closet."

"Grandpa had rum?"

"Oh, sure," Rae says. "But he wasn't a big drinker. Someone at the office would give him a bottle for Christmas, and Momma would make him put it in the closet. He had a whole collection. Every now and then, he'd pull some out and add it to the eggnog at Christmas. But most of the time, Beverly was sneaking a snortful."

"Mother?" Rae's memories of my mother and mine don't coincide. "She was always so prim and proper."

"Not always. But eventually that is the path she chose. Maybe I shouldn't tell you these things."

"No, that's okay." I want to know more. I unlock the trunk of the Cadillac. The lid pops open.

"Beverly may not have wanted you to know about the wildness of her youth."

"Probably not." I unlatch the cooler. "But it makes her seem more real, less perfect."

Rae shrugs and takes out a can, brushes off the ice, and hands me one. "A Coca-Cola in memory then?"

"Thanks. Do you think Ivy will want one?"

"Young girls drink Diet nowadays." She pulls out a diet soda from the icy slush. "Always worried about being skinny."

I tap the top of my can three times. With a glance at my watch, I sigh. "What's keeping her? Do you think she's sick?" I can imagine Stu's horror at the thought of someone puking in his beloved Cadillac. "You know, carsick?"

"Or maybe it's something else." Rae's mouth thins.

"Like what?"

"Could be anything." She purses her lips together as if contemplating myriad reasons that I don't want to imagine.

"But you think . . ."

"Smoking, maybe." She taps a finger against her mouth.

"Cigarettes?"

"Or . . ." Rae pauses, "weed. Isn't that what kids call pot nowadays?"

"Marijuana?" I stare at my aunt. What did she know of drugs? I sense somehow she does. Maybe because Mother told me Rae lived a bohemian life, I conjure up wild parties in my own mind.

I remember walking through a shopping mall with my mother. A group of teenagers grabbed our attention with their boisterous laughter. They leaned against a metal railing near the food court, laughing and cutting up. Mother sniffed derisively, "Drugs." But I'm not sure Mother would have known a weed if she'd met one or even knew that young kids were often more likely to try crack than marijuana. But then I never would have guessed she'd ever tasted hard liquor.

The question running around my mind now is, does Ivy know anything about drugs? I think of her suitcase in my trunk. Could I—should I—search it? After all, I'm responsible for Ivy. Would that be responsible or just nosy?

I wish I could call this trip off, turn around, and go home. I pray it's short. Which is saying something. I can't remember the last time I prayed. Probably when Stu was sick . . . but those prayers went unanswered. Praying feels more like making a wish on the first star of the evening or a hay bale. But I figure I need all the help I can get. Once we find Elvis's owner—and I don't bother thinking we won't—then I can turn my questions, doubts, and concerns over to Ivy's father, where those things belong.

Chapter Six

Suspicious Minds

I lean close to Ivy as we pile back into the Cadillac and sniff her. She jerks around and glares at me. "What are you doing?"

"Nothing." My face feels like I just pressed a curling iron to it. "The pine trees must be getting to me. I feel like I'm going to sneeze."

I didn't smell smoke on Ivy. Only citrus hair products. So much for theories of smoking and drugs.

An hour later we stop—again!—at Cracker Barrel in Arkadelphia. As Ivy zips past the souvenirs to the restroom, I wonder again what's going on.

"In the restroom again," Rae whispers, as if I hadn't noticed. I pick up different lotions and lip balms while we wait for a table.

We amble around looking at frog T-shirts and quilts before my name is called. With Ivy still in the restroom, Rae and I settle at a table. I stare at the menu and try to decide between fried catfish and salad. Nothing actually sounds good. Nothing has since Stu. But I've learned to eat a few bites anyway, swallowing automatically.

I glance out the window next to our table, past the rocking chairs lined up along the porch to the parking lot. Along the side of the restaurant sits the Cadillac, its top securely in place and Elvis still strapped in the back seat.

Feeling Rae staring at me, I shift my thoughts back to her speculations. "Ivy might have a weak bladder. Or an infection."

"I don't think so."

"Maybe the hilly roads made her feel ill. When I was a kid, I got carsick."

"It's not that hilly and the road is straight."

"Well, I can't follow her into the restroom every time she says she has to pee."

"I didn't say you should." Rae sips her water, then wipes the condensation off the glass with a paper napkin.

"I'm not the parental type," I say, wondering why I'm searching for excuses.

"You have a woman's heart. It's enough."

I wish she wouldn't say that. What does a woman's heart have to do with it? Obviously mine isn't masculine. But as a kid I felt closer to my father than my mother, so does gender really matter?

"Let's just eat and get back on the road." I glance at my watch again, a present from Stu. "Leather," he'd said, handing me a gift-wrapped box, "is for the third anniversary. So says Hallmark."

"Did you give me a belt?"

"A whip," he'd joked.

The watch helped keep me on track, so I wasn't as late as was my tendency. Almost twenty years married to Stu and now I laugh at how I like to stay on schedule, rarely running late. But today, because of Ivy, we're more than an hour behind the schedule I'd planned.

"How far are we from Memphis?" Rae asks, cutting off my memory.

"Only a few more hours, depending on"—I feel Elvis staring at me from the parking lot, like Stu used to wait for me, already in the car, motor going, clock ticking—"how many more stops." To divert Rae from her concerns for Ivy, I say, "How long has it been since you've been to Memphis?"

"A few years. Twenty." She pauses as if she's just now added up the years and realized how long it's actually been. "Forty maybe."

A family with four young children is shown to a nearby table. The disheveled mother jiggles a baby against her shoulder. The father takes another off toward the restroom. The wait staff brings booster seats and high chairs.

"Think Memphis has changed?"

Rae twists the straw sticking out of her water glass. "That's the one certainty in life—change."

"Are you excited about going back now?"

She takes a long sip of water. "Not really. I don't like to visit old haunts."

Walking down memory lane for me these days often includes puddles of tears. But I don't sense heartache in Rae. She seems strong, as if she can simply block out memories she doesn't care to reexamine. Hoping to fill up the emptiness between us, I ask, "Why'd you leave?"

"It was time. Time for new adventures."

I wonder how she knew it was time. Or was it simply an offhand comment in retrospect? In the past year I've tried on new lifestyles in my mind, imagining myself becoming a hermit in the mountains with the solitude of earth and sky for company, or traveling abroad and letting the crowds of tourists press memories out of my mind. But I'm frozen with uncertainty.

Rae once told me, "God will reveal his plan. In his time."

But frankly, I've heard nothing. I doubt my ability to hear God's voice. And if Stu's dying was God's plan, then I'm not sure I want what he has planned for me. So the question for me is, what do I want?

Others pushed me into a garage sale. Stu pushed me into this trip. I don't know which direction I'd push me.

"I came here . . ." Rae waves her hand, her charm bracelet jangling, as if to erase that remark. "I came to Dallas for a while and stayed with your mother."

"When I was a baby," I said, remembering the pictures in my mother's photo albums. "Then you went to the west coast?"

She hesitates as if uncertain of her response, then nods. "I worked my way there by way of Chicago, New York, Santa Fe, and L.A. Then I eventually landed in Oregon. I came back to Dallas once more. You were a girl, maybe three or so. Do you remember?"

"Vaguely."

"No, you were four."

I remember lying in my bed, my pink-checked pajamas tickling my chin. Aunt Rae came in to say good night and good-bye. She'd be leaving early the next morning. I clutched the little doll she'd given me, which I'd named Emily.

She told me a bedtime story of a little girl who went to Topsy-Turvyville. "Everything is upside down and backwards. Cars go backwards. Elevators go sideways, too. Houses have their chimneys on the ground, their front doors way up high. People even eat upside down."

"I bet that's messy," I remember saying as I giggled.

"Sometimes," she chuckled. "But the people who live there are used to it, so they take special care not to dribble food or let it plop on the floor. Anything is possible in Topsy-Turvyville."

"Anything?"

"Anything. So when you get lonely or sad or miss me, as I will be missing you, think of Topsy-Turvyville. Okay? And remember it is the place where things are not what they seem."

I'd forgotten that time, repressed it or locked it away somewhere safe—until now. I feel like I'm living in Topsy-Turvyville. My life has been turned upside down and backwards. But unlike Rae's imagining, this place is messy, unkempt, and overwhelming. I want to go back to the way things were, to my normal life, to my hopes and dreams, to the time when I felt safe and secure—with Stu.

Silence settles between Rae and me, but around us continues the noise of other conversations, plates clattering, a baby fussing. The children at the table near us drop crayons on the floor and whine for their food. Once more I shift my gaze out the window. Even from here I can see the dark outline of Elvis's head safely tucked inside the back seat.

"Did you miss your friends from Memphis? Your family, when you moved around so much?"

"I made new ones."

New family? But I don't voice my question. She makes starting over sound easy, but to me it seems as difficult as telling a lame man how to stand and walk. How can I ever make a new life for myself? Everything reminds me of Stu.

Seeing Ivy emerge from the bathroom, I give her a wave. She drifts toward the table and slides into the chair beside me. She looks thin and pale; her shoulders slump with what seems like unhappiness. Still, she's a beautiful young woman. Her short shorts and tight-fitting T-shirt grab the attention of several men sitting nearby.

"Are you okay?" I ask.

She sniffs and looks around. "What is that smell?"

"Lunch grease," Rae says. "I'm having chicken-fried steak."

I hand the menu to Ivy. "I think I'll have the vegetable plate. What are you going to have? That is, if the waitress ever returns."

"We're in no hurry, Claudia," Rae says. "No rush."

There's no deadline. No one waiting for us . . . or Elvis. But I want to get this trip over with as soon as possible. I don't want to linger and stroll through Memphis or down Memory Lane. This isn't a vacation.

My gaze veers toward Elvis. An older couple walks past the Cadillac. First the man turns and looks back, probably noting the make and model. He touches the woman's arm, then points at Elvis. Together they bend over, peering into the back seat. Eventually they enter the restaurant, their heads bent together as they share a laugh. It's tiny moments, snippets of others' lives, that make me miss Stu the most.

Ivy clicks her short nails against the wooden table. "Do they have soup here?"

"We'll ask the waitress." The conversation dies as we wait for the gal who brought us water when we first sat down. She gave us a toothy grin and said she'd be back "quick as a bunny." But we are still waiting.

Looking at Ivy, her thin arms, heavy makeup, and shocking black hair that contrasts with her pale skin, I remember Ben wanting me to impart some motherly wisdom to his daughter, but I am at a loss for words. I figure if I can get us talking at all, it might put us on the right course. But I don't know what teenagers talk about. Boys? Movies? The latest music? I feel way behind the times. "I thought it might be fun to stay at the Heartbreak Hotel in Memphis."

Ivy shrugs.

"Have you been there, Rae?"

"No."

"I called and got reservations last week." No one seems interested. "I thought we could immerse ourselves in all things Elvis."

Ivy looks around at the other tables, her gaze settling on the family next to us. The children wiggle and squirm. The baby starts to cry.

Finally the waitress returns and takes our orders. When she moves on to the next table, I continue, "Heartbreak Hotel is named for one of Elvis's songs. It's very famous." That garners no response either. "I thought it might be kind of retro"—I feel desperate trying to sound hip enough to interest Ivy—"to go to Graceland. Have you been there, Rae?"

She unwraps her utensils and lays her curled-up napkin in her lap. "A long time ago."

"What about you, Ivy? Have you been to Graceland?"

"What is it?" Her lip curls as if the word is distasteful.

"It's Elvis's home. Elvis Presley. It's a mansion really. Still decorated the same way it was when he died. I've heard there's purple shag carpet and a Jungle Room."

"Whatever."

I swallow a heavy sigh. "Rae, was that where you met Elvis? Or later?"

"I *knew* Elvis."

"Oh. Well . . . okay." I cut my gaze toward Ivy, but she isn't paying attention. "Tell us about him. What was he like? Was he as generous as everyone says?"

Rae narrows her eyes and yells, "Stop!"

Her shout startles me and everyone around us. Suddenly the restaurant is silent except for Rae as she yells and waves her arms. She bounds out of her chair, knocking it over. It clatters against the brick floor. Without a backward glance, she runs toward the nearest exit, which sets off an alarm.

"I wouldn't talk about Elvis anymore," Ivy says.

"Get up!" Through the big window, I see two middle-aged women bent next to the Cadillac. "They're stealing Elvis!"

Chapter Seven

Jailhouse Rock

Pushing out into the muggy heat of the day, I race down the porch, past wooden rocking chairs with price tags, and stumble to a halt in front of the Cadillac. Rae's screaming at the two women. Through the windshield, Elvis stares at me unblinking as if he can't figure out what all the fuss is about. The two women Rae's cornered shift nervously, cut their eyes toward each other as if they've awakened a lunatic. I gulp air and try to figure out a way to interrupt Rae.

"What is going on?" I finally yell.

Rae keeps yammering away, her words running fast and furious, bumping into each other.

One woman stands beside the Cadillac, backing toward the parking lot, her face as red as a summer tomato. "Nothing! Everything's okay." She points at Rae. "Except she's a nutcase."

The other woman—her accomplice, I surmise—can't stop making a high-pitched yodeling sound, some kind of a bizarre laugh.

I put my arm on Rae's arm. "Okay, Rae. It's okay now."

"It's not okay." Her eyes are wild.

"Take it easy, Rae. It's o—" I stop myself from saying "okay." I don't want to agitate her any more. "It's going to be all right." Then I remember how she reacted to the woman who tried to steal a baby rattle from my garage sale. "Are you all right?"

She blinks at me, her lips pressing tightly together. "They stole Elvis."

But there he is still sitting in the back seat of the Cadillac.

"We weren't going to steal it," the woman who looks as if she swallowed a can of V-8 juice says.

The laughing hyena sputters and coughs. "We wanted to see it. Up close and personal, you might say. We wouldn't do nothin' illegal."

I narrow my gaze, squinting at her, noticing the bent-out-of-shape hanger in her hand. "You can't see Elvis through the window?"

"Not clearly, no."

A man who looks like he eats down-home cookin' every day of the week walks up, spits tobacco out the side of his mouth into the bushes. "There a problem, ladies?"

Rae launches into another tirade.

He stares at her as if her head had suddenly become dislodged, rubs his thumb against the edge of his cowboy hat. "Say that again, ma'am? Slower maybe."

"Rae," I interrupt, "it's okay."

The door to the restaurant opens behind me, and Ivy steps outside. "What's going on?" She holds her cell phone. "Need me to call 911?"

I stare at the two women, not quite believing them, yet not believing anyone would want to steal Elvis either. "No," I finally say. "It's okay. They were just going to have a look at the King. Who can blame them for that, right?"

The cackling woman says, "He isn't your regular tourist hereabouts."

The red-faced woman readjusts a bra strap and backs away. "Y'all have a nice day."

"Where you takin' him?" her accomplice asks.

"Mem—"

I cough, stopping Ivy from revealing our destination. "Back to Texas."

Rae shifts her gaze toward me, concern deepening her green eyes.

The woman looks through the window at Elvis, then says, "Guess that's as good a place as any. You know, Elvis spent a good amount of time in Texas."

"Uh-huh." She'll never know how much time this Elvis has spent there.

After the two women disappear, I meet Rae's gaze. "Don't worry, I'm not taking him home. I was just throwing them off the scent." When she nods her understanding, I add, "Thanks for noticing that they were—"

"They were trying to steal Elvis!"

"They won't be back," the man says.

"Yes, well, it's over," I say. "Maybe Elvis is considered haute decor here in Arkansas."

"You'd be surprised." The man grins, revealing tobacco-stained teeth.

"No harm done anyway." I run my finger along the car door, check to make sure the door is locked still.

The small crowd that gathered when the commotion started begins to disperse. Folks entering or leaving the restaurant give us long, curious glances.

"Uh," Ivy grunts, jerking her head toward the restaurant, "lunch is served."

Through the window, I can see our waitress setting plates and platters on our table.

"You ladies staying or heading out?" the man asks, opening the restaurant door wide.

"Staying." But I can't leave Elvis. What if someone else decides to take a closer look at the King?

Rae touches my shoulder. "You go on in and eat. I'll guard Elvis."

"No, no. You should eat. It's okay. I'll stay out here. My car, my Elvis, my problem."

"Who's gonna steal him now?" Ivy asks.

Everyone suddenly appears suspicious to me. I know Stu didn't ask me to bring Elvis to Memphis only to have him stolen. With a heavy sigh, I say, "Okay, there's only one thing to do. Hold the door, please."

I unlock the car door, unbuckle Elvis, and lift him out of the car. I wobble, then gain my footing and waddle toward the trucker. Rae shuts the car door behind me and grabs hold of Elvis's shoulders.

"What are you doing?" Ivy asks.

Already huffing with the exertion of carrying the King,

who feels as if he's gained weight on the drive, I say, "Elvis is hungry."

"He's talking to you?" Ivy asks.

I grin and thank the man, who tips his hat as we pass (whether it's to us or saluting Elvis, I'm not sure). A minute later we place the bust on the chair next to me. Ivy shifts to the other side of the table, sitting next to Rae.

The waitress does a double take as she passes, then comes back grinning. She plunks a ketchup bottle on the table. "Coffee, sugar?"

"He's cutting back on caffeine," I say.

"'Bout time he started to eat healthy." She props her fist on an ample hip. "Heard tell Elvis come through these parts years ago."

Ivy blows out a puffy breath that lifts her bangs, then she slumps down in her seat across from the King.

"Really?" I unscrew the lid and pour ketchup on the side of my plate. "Did you meet him?"

"Oh, heavens, no. But I sure do wish somebody like Tim McGraw would come through now. I'd give his wife, Faith, a run for her money. Guess I shouldn't say that, being a good Christian woman. But he sure is somethin'." She laughs. "You girls need anything else, just let me know."

A husky man stops at our table, rolls a toothpick to the side of his mouth. "Where'd you get him?"

"A souvenir," I say.

"My wife sure would like one of those."

"Who wouldn't?" I swirl a fat French fry through the ketchup.

"You're not eating," Rae says to Ivy.

The girl pushes her salad around in the bowl but hasn't eaten anything. "I think I lost my appetite."

"You know what Elvis would say?" I ask, putting my arm around my stiff and unresponsive dinner companion.

"What's that?" Rae asks, her eyebrow lifting with amusement—or was it a challenge? Frankly, I had no idea what Elvis would say; I simply want to lighten the mood, add a little laughter. "Well, uh, he'd say . . ." I try a stumbling, bumbling impersonation of the King. After all, I'd heard Stu do it a thousand times. "Try the pie. Two helpings is better than one. Thank you. Thank you very much."

Rae laughs first. Relief washes over me.

Then she orders a piece of pecan pie. When it arrives, she places it in front of Elvis. With a shrug, she says, "It was one of his favorites."

♪ ♩ ♪ ♩. ♩ ♪ ♩

"TENNESSEE," I READ the highway sign before the bridge as our headlights pave the way. "Welcome to Memphis, ladies."

"Over the river and through the woods to Elvis's house we go." Rae sits straighter and peers through the windshield.

We can't see much but concrete and steel.

"Could you reach in the glove compartment and get the map?" I ask Rae. Before we left Dallas, I printed off a map and directions leading to the hotel.

She pushes the button, but the door doesn't budge. "It's now," she sings out in her best imitation of Elvis, "or never."

"You have to push really hard," I say.

She does and the compartment door clunks open. Pulling out the map, she reads the directions.

"Stay south on 55," Rae directs.

I avoid a big semi that doesn't seem to see me.

"Not much has changed," she says, more to herself than me. "And yet I don't recognize any of it."

I glance in my rearview. Ivy uses her backpack as a pillow propped against Elvis' side. Her eyes are closed. We've been driving since Little Rock, almost two hours of straight, flat highway and no restroom stops. I'm glad for the darkness that has fallen as I feel less conspicuous with Elvis riding in the back seat.

The electronic beeping of a rock beat interrupts Elvis's rockabilly rendition of "Little Sister" playing on the stereo. "I think that's yours, Ivy."

She wakes quickly, which makes me wonder if she was only playing possum. "Yeah," she says brusquely into her cell phone. "I don't know." She leans her arm on the front seat. "Where are we?"

"Memphis. Is it your dad?"

"You wanna talk to him?" She shoves the phone toward me. Placing my left hand on the steering wheel, I hold the phone with my right. "Ben?"

"What happened to Ivy?" he asks, his voice sounding amazingly clear.

"She handed me the phone. How are you?"

"I'm fine. Where are you now?"

"Memphis. But we haven't reached the hotel yet. I can call you with our room number when we get settled. I reserved us a suite, so we'll be together." A room together seemed the safest solution with a minor. But a suite will give us more room and some privacy.

"Sounds good," he says. "How's she doing?"

"Okay." I shift my gaze to Rae, remembering her concerns. I wonder if she'd tell Ben. But now isn't the time. No need to worry Ivy's dad when I have no facts, no way of knowing anything delinquent about his daughter yet. "We're all kind of tired from being in the car all day."

"What took you so long? You didn't have car trouble, did you?"

"Oh, no. We, uh . . ." I glance at Ivy in the rearview mirror as she digs through her backpack. "We just made more stops than we anticipated."

"She's not being a pain, is she?"

Red brake lights flash in front of me, and I touch my foot to the brakes. After a moment the long line of cars moving along the highway slowly picks up its pace again.

"No, not at all." Ivy is respectful. Just quiet. Yet I also know, or suspect, something is wrong. But I can't say so in front of Ivy, or even over the phone.

"You'd tell me, right?"

"Of course." When I have something to tell. Until then . . .

"Take the next exit," Rae says.

"We're almost there," I tell Ben on the phone.

"Okay, call me later."

"You should have come with us," I say.

"Nah. Somebody has to hold down the fort."

"Okay, Dad," I tease with a wry smile, as I know he's going to worry about all of us until we arrive safely home. "I'll keep you posted."

"Here," Rae says, pointing to Elvis Presley Boulevard. "This is it."

"Okay." I fumble with the steering wheel and the phone, letting it drop into my lap and yell, "Bye!" as I signal and take the exit. "Imagine having your own street named after you." In the rearview mirror, I catch Ivy's eyes rolling upward. I consider keeping a count of that particular expression. I bet we can break one hundred before the end of the trip. "I wonder what it must have been like for Elvis."

"Confining," Rae says, folding the map.

"Let's get checked in, then we'll find some dinner." I turn right on Lonely Street and then veer left into the Heartbreak Hotel parking lot.

♪♩♪♩.♩♪♩

"SEE SEE RIDER" blares out of the hotel's sound system and can be heard throughout the parking lot as we unload our suitcases. Temporarily, we leave Elvis in the back seat.

In the lobby a small old-style television shows Elvis boxing in *Kid Galahad*. The hotel boasts Elvis movies twenty-four hours a day. Already I'm getting weary of the King.

The Heartbreak Hotel is as worn and weary looking as I am after a long day of travel. We pass the cherry-red couch and purple chairs to check in at the desk. Then we head up to our rooms and settle in.

The suite is large and roomy, and we each go to our separate rooms to unpack. I lay on the bed for a minute, stretch my back, and wish I were home. A rumbling in my stomach gets me back on my feet.

I knock on Ivy's door.

"Yeah?"

"It's me." I open the door a crack. "Are you ready?"

She sits up on the bed, her suitcase open, her backpack slung over the chair in the corner.

"Are you hungry?" After checking into the hotel and unloading our luggage, we all took a few minutes to freshen up for dinner.

"Not really."

"But we haven't eaten since our late lunch. Come on."

"I'm tired." She has dark circles under her eyes. Or is it remnants of mascara?

"We could order room service—"

"Go to dinner. I'll be fine here."

"We might need your help." I try to figure out a way to get Ivy to come with us without demanding it and alienating her in the process.

"With what?"

"Elvis."

"Whaddya mean?"

"We've got to get Elvis into the room. And we don't exactly want to make a big deal of carrying him through the lobby."

"Embarrassing, huh?"

"And heavy." I lower my voice. "It might be too heavy for Rae. You know?"

She puffs out a hefty breath. "Okay." She scoots to the edge of the bed. "I'll come."

"Good. You never know. You might be an Elvis fan by the time this is all over."

She sticks her toes into her flip-flops. "Not likely."

Chapter Eight

(Now and Then There's) A Fool Such as I

"We're not taking him to dinner with us, are we?" Ivy asks, standing outside the Cadillac.

Elvis lies in the back seat hidden beneath a beige hotel towel. We brought several out to the car as the towels are small. I covered him so no passersby would decide to make off with him.

"No, of course not." I remember the ruckus he caused in Arkansas. "But we shouldn't leave him in the car either."

Rae nods. "We'll take him into the hotel for safekeeping."

"I don't think I can carry him that far alone." I glance

across the parking lot at the five-story hotel and think of the walk to the elevator, then to the suite. "It's a long way."

"Not to worry." Rae touches my elbow. "I'll help."

Ivy laughs. Both Rae and I stare at her, surprised since she's been somber all the way to Tennessee. "I can't wait to see you two carrying this thing through the lobby."

I smile, but it feels strained. I was hoping Ivy would help carry him, not Rae. "I don't want to advertise that we have him. Most people who stay at the Heartbreak Hotel are Elvis fans. Someone might get the idea to steal him."

"Can't imagine that happening," Rae says with a grin.

"We'll have to sneak him in through a side door."

The clerk at check-in didn't encourage us to use any door but the front one. But a side one is available.

"Is there one of those carts for luggage?" Ivy asks.

"Not that I've seen." I want to ask someone to turn off the Elvis music that carries through the parking lot like the odor from a fast-food restaurant. "I didn't even see a bellboy."

"We'll have to carry Elvis," Rae says. "Ivy, you run ahead of us to the side door. We'll go in there."

"Maybe you should hold the door, Rae," I suggest.

"Are you saying I'm too old?"

"Of course not, but—"

"Ivy doesn't look strong enough to pick up a toothpick. I'll help carry the King. Besides, I knew him personally."

"Okay." Not wanting to hurt her feelings or risk an argument, I open the car door and lug the Elvis bust out of the back. The towel slips to the concrete, and Ivy picks it up and holds it until Rae and I balance Elvis horizontally between us. Then Ivy lays the towel over his face, shrouding him like a corpse. I start to laugh, then Rae joins in, followed by Ivy. We look as if we're pallbearers for one of the munchkins from the land of Oz.

The bust starts to tip over, and I almost lose my grip on Elvis's ear. We sober immediately.

"No more laughing," Rae says, taking on a stern expression, "or I won't be able to hold onto him."

I nod, fighting a sudden need to giggle. Together we begin the slow, shuffling walk across the parking lot. I walk backward and Rae cautions me, "Slowly, slowly. One more. Careful of the speed bump."

Ivy walks far ahead of us, turning to look back occasionally to see if we need help, but I can tell she doesn't want to be seen with us. Not sure I blame her.

"Wait!" I yell as the towel starts to slip off, revealing half of Elvis' face. I edge closer to Rae, pushing his pompadour into my stomach, propping it with one hand beneath, and pull the towel over his face again with my other hand. Rae grimaces under the weight.

When we reach the corner of the building, we wait for a car to pass, then another. I'm thankful for the cloak of semi-darkness. Then we toddle along again and begin the slow trek toward the side door. A motorcycle zips behind me, roaring as it goes. I gasp. Rae yells, "Hey, buddy! Slow down."

"Careful," I say. "Don't drop him."

Ivy jogs ahead of us to the side door. By the time we inch our way up onto the sidewalk, she comes back. "It's locked. We need our room key to get in."

We stop. Elvis nudges my hip. My arms start aching. I know Rae has to be tired too. "Should we set it down here?"

"No, no." Her breath comes in little huffs.

"Ivy, grab the car keys out of my pocket. The room key is in my purse in the Cadillac." My words come out gruff. My fingers have gone numb. Standing still takes effort as Ivy fishes in my pocket and removes the keys.

"I'll be right back."

We wait at the side entrance, losing patience and strength with each passing minute.

"Could she be lost?" Rae asks.

I shrug, then regret it as the towel slips off the bust and falls in a heap on the concrete. "She might have needed to pee again."

Rae chuckles.

"Let's set it down for a minute. Give our arms a rest."

The base clunks against the concrete.

"Whoa!" Rae loses her balance on the wheelchair access ramp and tips over backwards, landing on her rump.

The bust teeters on a corner of its base. I reach for it, but it flops forward. The King nosedives into my aunt's lap. With my arms outstretched, I freeze, unable to move, to believe my eyes. "Oh, Rae! Are you okay?"

She tilts her head back, fluffs her long hair Mae West style. "I could use a cigarette."

Chuckling, I lean forward and pull the King off my aunt.

"He always was a bad boy," she says.

I feel my face reddening and am grateful for the darkness. I give him a playful slap on the hard cheek. "Behave yourself."

"He never could keep his hands off me." Rae demurely rearranges her skirt to cover her long legs.

Shaking my head, I say, "Need a hand up?"

"I think I'll rest here for a minute. But I'm okay."

I push Elvis out of the way of the door and cover him with two towels, just in case anyone walks by. But if someone does, they'll think it's E.T. in his Halloween costume. Then I plop down on the sidewalk beside Rae. "You don't really smoke, do you?"

"Not anymore."

"Well, I'm glad you quit. It isn't good for you."

"I have so much to live for."

Her statement surprises me. I give her a sharp glance. What I thought was sarcasm seems genuine and somehow pricks my soul. I remember what she told me about my mother drinking, and I wonder if she smoked, too. Never before this weekend would I have considered that a possibility. "Did my mother smoke?"

"Beverly? She gave me my first cigarette. Then she quit cold turkey and turned into a Goody Two-shoes."

"But you weren't?"

"Not at all. I wasn't a bad kid, but I wasn't a follower. My mother used to say I marched to the beat of my own drummer. I guess she was right."

Knowing what little I know about Rae, I can see that. She exudes confidence, as if she doesn't care what anyone else thinks or says. I lean more toward the opposite, having always been concerned with what Stu thought or, before that, my mother. Ivy, however, acts more like Rae. But I wonder if it's all a pretense to cover up a deeper pain.

"How did you get to be that way? I mean, it's so hard for me not to think about others. What they think or would say. I still worry about what Stu would say. Ridiculous, huh?"

Rae shrugs. "I'm not sure. Maybe I was always that way. Maybe I was rebellious." She winks. "Or maybe I just saw how it never really mattered. You can't please everyone all the time. It's impossible. Your mother tried to please our parents. But in the end she still disappointed them. They *expected* me to disappoint them, so when I did, it wasn't a major catastrophe."

"Were their standards so high?" I ask.

"I don't know about that. Maybe just different. They were worried about what neighbors would say, about what people at church would say." Rae laughs. "I always said if they were talking behind our backs, then that wasn't right. My folks frowned at that, but they didn't have an answer for it either."

"I think I tried to please Mother. Being an only child, I was a pleaser. But I wasn't always sure I did."

"Oh, you did. Beverly was very proud of you, Claudia."

I shrug, feeling uncomfortable. "She never said that. She wasn't very demonstrative with her feelings."

"That was just her way. She was a lot like our mother, your grandmother. Maybe it was a sign of the times."

"I wish I knew more about Mother. She never liked to talk about herself. Or her past."

"Oh?" Rae looks away from me, stares off as if she's looking into a mirror reflecting days gone by.

"After Stu and I became engaged, I asked Mother how Daddy had proposed to her. Know what she said?"

Rae gives a tiny, almost indiscernible shake of her head.

"She couldn't remember." Incredulous still, I laugh. "How can someone not remember how their husband proposed?"

Rae lifts one narrow shoulder in a shrug.

Worried I've upset her, I lean forward. "Are you okay? Does it upset you to talk about my mother?"

She gives me a reassuring smile, but there's something in her eyes that I can't quite read. Is it pain? Regret? "I never knew what your relationship was like with Beverly. I wasn't around you two much. Except when you were little."

I look at my aunt, sitting cross-legged on the ground in a filmy skirt. My mother would have been mortified if Elvis had fallen face first into her lap, but Rae thought it was funny. "Maybe you're right. Maybe you were different from others. Ahead of your time." I try to peer across the parking lot but can't see the Cadillac or Ivy. "What's taking Ivy so long?"

Then I hear footsteps, the snapping of flip-flops against heels, and Ivy walks up. She slides the plastic key into the slot and pulls the door open.

"Okay. Here we go." Rae pushes herself up to stand, brushes off her skirt, and flexes her fingers. "Hold the door now." She bends, and we again perch Elvis horizontally between us. He stares up at the stars. "The towel?" She glances at Ivy, who looks suddenly pale.

Then Ivy lunges forward, pushes past me. I stumble, joggle Elvis. The door knocks against my shoulder and a sharp pain shoots through my arm, making my fingers tingle. I brace the door with my foot. Elvis's head tips toward the concrete. Rae and I bobble Elvis but manage to right him. We look at each other for a moment, breathing a sigh of relief, knowing how close we came to destroying this stupid, cheap bust. Once again I wonder if Stu is getting a good laugh out of all of this.

Caught in the doorway, I hang onto Elvis. From the

corner of my eye, I see Ivy bending over the bushes. I don't know what to do. I wish someone would stop and help us, but then pray no one sees us.

"Do you need help, Ivy?" Rae asks, looking over at the girl.

Ivy gags, but it seems to be a dry heave.

"Are you okay?" I start to put Elvis down, but how? I'm trapped. "Ivy?" She turns finally, her face pale, eyes wide. She presses a hand to her mouth.

"Do you need a towel?" I ask, seeing it on the concrete at the tip of my shoe.

Ivy picks it up, dabs her mouth, then lays it atop Elvis, carefully straightening the folds and edges.

"Now what?" Rae asks. "It's getting heavy."

"I can't put it down." The weight of the door pushes against me. Elvis's head presses into my stomach.

"I'm okay." Ivy steps behind me and pulls the door open wide. "Go on."

"I'm glad we aren't attracting any attention," Rae says.

We shuffle through the stairwell, then into a narrow hallway. The walls are painted yellow, but there are no decorations. Nothing but door after door of rooms. At the end of the hallway, I notice a sign with the silhouette of a woman.

"There's a restroom."

But Ivy heads straight for the elevator, which has a sign pasted over the buttons. "Out of order."

"Great," I mutter. "There's another elevator down the hall."

This time we have to pass the Jungle Room bar and the entrance to the lobby. No one seems to notice us as we scurry along like mice carrying a block of cheese the size of

Wisconsin. When we reach the other elevator, I lean against the wall, my arms aching. "Ivy, are you sick? Do you think I should take you to a doctor?"

"I'm fine. Just carsick."

I hesitate to mention the obvious, then say, "We're not in a car."

"I'm not over the drive yet."

"It could take a few more hours," Rae says as if she's had experience with this sort of thing. "You'll feel better when you get something in your stomach."

Ivy doesn't look too sure about the idea.

"Should we call your dad?" I ask.

"I'm fine. Really." Her voice takes on that huffy quality of irritation, and I drop the subject.

I glance up at the lights above the elevator. How much longer? The hallway is deserted except for a framed poster of Elvis and a vending machine selling water and Cokes.

Ivy lifts the corner of the towel covering Elvis's face. "That's creepy."

"Why do you think I banished Elvis to the attic?"

Finally the elevator arrives. It's empty. We board it, inching forward, careful not to scrape Elvis against the doors. A minute later we carry him down the hallway to our suite.

"Where?" Rae asks.

"Over there." We shuffle our way to the sitting room and set him on a corner table.

Ivy flips the towel over his head, covering at least his face. "He was staring at us."

"Laughing at us is more like it." I feel laughter bubble up inside me.

"WHEN IN MEMPHIS, eat like the natives," I say, pulling into Corky's, one of the best barbecue joints in town according to *Southern Living.* Weaving the unwieldy Cadillac through the narrow parking lot is an exercise in holding my breath. It's usually my personal rule not to eat at places with big pigs on the side of the building, but it's also my rule not to chase impossible dreams. This trip is an exception to all.

The air inside the restaurant smells tangy, mingled with the succulent scent of roasted pork. If I was looking for a quiet dining experience, this isn't it. But at least the music piped through the restaurant isn't Elvis. After a short wait we're seated in a booth.

"Sweet tea?" the waitress asks.

"It's been years," Rae says, "but I believe I'll indulge in the house wine of the South."

"You must not have been in the South much, sugar," the waitress remarks. "Or else you have great self-control."

"I've never been accused of that."

"Tell us about Oregon," I say, when the waitress has taken our orders.

"Where do I begin?" she asks wrinkling her forehead.

I'm relieved to find a topic she's willing to discuss. "Why did you choose to live there?"

"It seemed as far away from Dallas and Memphis as the moon. It's also where I found myself . . . and God."

"What do you mean?" Ivy asks.

"More like God found me. Because I don't think I was looking. But he got my attention."

"How?" I ask.

"I quit looking inward and looked for help. And I found it."

"God helped you?" Ivy asks.

"He always does."

"What did you need help from? Were you trying to escape? Trying to avoid seeing someone?" I ask, wondering if that someone was Elvis.

"Someone? You mean Elvis? No, it was over. I was over Elvis. But other things are not so easily forgotten. I needed to get away. It was too confining in Dallas."

Or was our family, my mother and grandparents, too reserved for her? "What did you do?"

"Do?"

"For a living."

"A little bit of everything. I waitressed in a little café for a while. Modeled in New York."

"You modeled in New York?" Ivy leans forward.

"Sure. I did a couple of runways, but I wasn't much good. I didn't want to show off the clothes. I preferred grabbing everyone's attention myself. Designers don't like that. I did a couple of magazines. But mostly I modeled for art students."

Ivy leans back, shading her eyes with her eyelashes, wary and watchful.

"Somewhere there's a picture of me in the buff on some stranger's mantle." Rae starts to laugh.

Ivy's eyes widen. "Really?"

Rae arches her back, pushing her small breasts forward. "Well, I wasn't Brigitte Bardot in my day, but I certainly wasn't a dachshund either. I had plenty of men interested back then. And I made a good living in the different art schools. Of course, I liked to think of myself as an artist then. But I had no talent. And certainly no determination. Just a willing spirit."

"A free spirit," I say.

She nods.

"And what did my mother think of all your adventures?" I ask, remembering Mother's dislike of Holly Golightly in *Breakfast at Tiffany's*.

"Oh, Beverly didn't ask anymore what I was up to. We had very little contact back then. She never wrote."

"We never got letters from you either," I defend my mother. "Just an occasional postcard."

She shrugs as if indifferent. "It was for the best. Beverly didn't want to hear from me. She was busy with her own life. She had no need of me, no desire to remember . . ."

"Remember what?" I ask, leaning forward, resting my elbows on the table.

"Her dreams. She had them with you."

I lean back into the booth. "Mother always said she wanted to be a wife and mother."

"That's true." Rae's mouth flattens into a thin line. "Our food should be coming soon."

"Was my mother really satisfied with that?" I ask, needing to know more. I thought I'd known Mother, but maybe I hadn't. Maybe no one had. It didn't seem like she let anyone into her thoughts or her heart. Maybe Rae hadn't really known her either. After all, they hadn't spoken for many years before Mother died.

"I don't know." Rae lifts a narrow shoulder, then fingers the base of her iced-tea glass. "Dreams come true are rarely as satisfying as we imagine."

Wondering if she's thinking of my mother or her own lost or forgotten dreams, I place my hand on hers. I wonder if it's painful for her to be back in Memphis. Memories, I know full well, can soothe like a violin sonata or jolt like a discordant note on a steel guitar.

Rae places her other hand on top of mine and her warmth surrounds me. I feel a sudden closeness to her, the same feeling I remember when she visited when I was a child. A tingling delight and solid connection took hold. If nothing else, my aunt and I share a love for my mother.

"I miss her . . ." My voice breaks.

"I know," Rae says, her eyes fill with tears. "I do, too."

"My mother left when I was three," Ivy says suddenly. Beneath the layers of makeup, there is a dusting of freckles across her nose. She looks so young and vulnerable. Twisting her fork over and over, she stares at the candle in the middle of the table.

I don't know what to say. But I know loneliness, the kind that weights the heart until it cracks and break. I understand the need to reach out to my mother, to feel her arms come around me and hold me as she whispers that everything will be all right. "I know."

"B-but why?" she asks, her tone flat. Then she looks right at me, searching for answers when there are none. "You knew her, right?"

I never understood why Gwen walked out on Ben and their young daughter. "I don't know what happened."

I wonder what Ben told his daughter, if they discussed her mother's disappearance since the garage sale. Or if it's been too painful, too difficult a subject to broach when their father-daughter relationship seems at a standoff. "What did your father tell you?"

"Not much."

"She didn't leave a note." I remember Ben coming over, carrying a sleeping Ivy against his shoulder, pain as deep as any I've ever seen darkened his eyes. Now Ivy squints at me, anger burning in her gaze. "No reasons. No excuses. Not that anything Gwen could say would explain it away." The hurt had been dealt with a harsh blow, the emptiness, all these years later, still resonates. "I always thought your mother was overwhelmed . . . that she felt inadequate—"

I stop. I don't want Ivy to think she's the reason her mother left and blame herself. Suddenly I understand the briar patch Ben has tried to pick his way through, knowing if he said the wrong thing, it would be Ivy who would be hurt. Tread carefully, I tell myself. "It didn't have anything to do with you though. You know that, don't you, Ivy?"

She looks away. My heart aches for her, for Ben, for elusive answers, haunting questions.

Rae's somber gaze shifts between us, watching, listening, waiting.

"How could she leave like that?" Ivy asks. "Maybe she hated being a mom so much. Maybe she knew she'd make us all miserable. Maybe we made her miserable."

Rae makes a disgruntled noise of disbelief.

As a baby Ivy had an easy, full-bodied smile, wiggling her body, kicking her legs, waving her arms with joy. Now she's somber, so sad. Her eyes tilt downward at the corners, as if weighted with misery. "I remember when she was pregnant with you."

"Was she happy?" Ivy asks.

"Yes. For a while. Now that I think back, she wasn't typically a happy person. She was always fussing, worrying about something. But I remember her rubbing her tummy affectionately." She always said everything was all right, but her eyes told a different story.

"So why'd she leave?" Ivy asks.

"I don't know." I feel unprepared and wish Ben were here to field these questions. But maybe Ben doesn't have any answers either. No amount of explanation, I've learned, can cover the heartache. I remember the doctor painstakingly explaining the way cancer can spread and grow. But knowing, understanding the physical, biological reasons didn't answer the deeper struggle of why.

"Sometimes," Rae chimes in, "we don't know what is in another's heart. It's a mystery. A mother's heart . . . is as deep as an ocean. You must know that whatever took your mother away, you are in her heart. Wherever she is, whatever happened. A mother never forgets her child."

Her words strike a chord in me that resonates outward, like sound carrying across water. I can never forget my baby either, the hopes, dreams, promise of a new life. What do you do with those dreams?

"How do you know?" Ivy asks pointedly.

"Because I have been a mother."

Rae's admission stuns me. "You have? You are?"

"Yes."

Mother never mentioned Rae having a baby. Did

Mother not know? Had the child died, I wonder? What happened? "When?"

The waitress picks that moment to serve our meal. By the time we finish passing barbecue sauce and having our tea glasses refilled, Rae has deftly changed the subject. She chatters about the pictures of famous people on the wall and the different barbecue sauces. I try to think of a tactful way to ask about Rae's child. "So where is this cousin of mine?" I want to ask. "Is your child in Oregon still?"

I don't realize I have spoken out loud until everything at the table stops. Ivy stares at me with the same blank, frozen look of the Elvis bust. Rae looks at me, then methodically places her forkful of pulled pork back on the plate and readjusts her napkin in her lap.

"I'm sorry," I say. "It's none of my business. But I was just surprised to know you had a child." *Had* a child implies she lost the child, and I instantly feel a connection with her. I want to reach out to her, tell her I know the pain as I've felt it myself every day since I lost my baby in a late-term miscarriage. But as quick as the connection between us formed, fragile and slender, it snaps in two.

"You're correct," Rae says. But I'm not sure if she means it's none of my business or that the information is accurate.

"Did it die?" Ivy asks, and I'm suddenly grateful for a young, assertive teen who doesn't feel the constraints of propriety.

"No." Rae sighs, then gives me a secretive smile. "I think I would rather talk about Elvis."

I laugh and apologize again. "We don't have to discuss this. I shouldn't have brought it up."

"My own pain shouldn't be yours. I'm the one who should apologize. For many years I've tried to outrun my past. It's proving difficult." She looks around the restaurant. "I never thought I would return to Memphis, either. But you can't outrun who you are, your problems, or mistakes." Her gaze settles on Ivy, then switches to me. "Or hide from them. True?"

I feel the barb of her remark like a splinter embedded under my skin. Does she think I've been hiding from my grief? Anger rushes through me. I live it every day, in every moment, in every way. It flows into me with each breath and out again as I exhale. It is a part of me that I can't escape.

Slowly, with her steady gaze, unwavering and soft as a baby's blanket upon me, I begin to see what she means. I've been hiding myself in the grief, in long, dreamless sleep, in extended hours at work.

Ivy belches, a loud eruption that makes heads turn at a nearby table. Her face turns bright pink with embarrassment. She places her hand on her flat stomach.

"Are you okay?" I ask.

She nods, then races from the table to the ladies' room. Rae and I glance at each other. I start to rise from my seat and go after her, but Rae places a hand on my arm.

"Wait. She'll share when she's ready."

"Share? But what if she needs help? What if she's still experiencing motion sickness."

"She'll let us know."

I waver between acting like the girl's mother and trying to give her space and a bit of her dignity back. I figure if she's throwing up in the bathroom, she's probably old enough not to need me to hold her hair for her. Thank God for that, as I have a weak stomach. But of course, if she needed me to, I would. I have done similar things for my mother and Stu.

"So," I say, trying to fill the awkward silence between us. I can't ask Rae about her child, and I don't want to analyze my propensity for hiding. I tap my fingers on the table. "You said you would rather talk about Elvis . . ."

Rae smiles, her eyes twinkling, and laughs. "What do you want to know?"

"How can we figure out where Elvis, the bust, came from?"

"We'll start at the most obvious place and work our way down."

Elvis's voice sings in my head, *Way on down* . . . "How way on down do you think we could go?"

"I'm afraid far," she says.

"So where's the most obvious? Graceland?"

"Of course."

Chapter Nine

Too Much

I wish I could shake off the melancholy that wraps around me like tentacles. But tonight with so much talk, with so much heartache lingering like an ink stain, I feel trapped, unable to breathe.

Ivy emerges from the ladies' room looking pale and unsteady. Worried, I suggest, "Why don't we go back to the hotel?"

Rae reaches for her purse.

"But what about your dinner?" Ivy asks.

"We're finished." I leave cash on the table for a tip. Rae offered to help pay, but I refused. This trip is Stu's fault. It's only fair I pick up the tab.

Accompanied by the sound of laughter and clinking dishes, we escort Ivy to the car.

"Maybe we should call your dad." Concern creases my brow.

While I unlock the Cadillac, I glance over at Ivy.

Something's going on. She's pencil thin, her arms and legs bony. But so much anger and pain churn in those eyes. I recognize the look now: It's the same look I saw in her mother's face so long ago. A chill sweeps over me.

"Do you think we should go to the emergency room?" I ask. "Get you checked out, make sure you're okay?"

"No! I just don't do well in the back seat. And the drive got to me. Again."

"The dinner was spicy," Rae says, then scolds, "You should have told us. I would have switched seats with you." She climbs into the back seat.

I flip on the headlights, glance again at Ivy, who has closed her eyes. In the rearview mirror I see Rae staring out the side window, lost in her own thoughts and memories. Memories, I know, can be probing, penetrating, making me cringe as if I were being grilled under an interrogator's lamp. Or they can be fuzzy, like a distant glow, warm and enticing and just out of reach.

"That was here," Rae whispers, more to herself than to Ivy or me as we pass an old diner that looks straight out of the 1950s. The Cadillac rocks slightly, acknowledging every bump and ripple in the road. Rae *tsks*. "So much has changed, yet . . ."

The blinker ticks. The Cadillac jiggles like a nervous mother joggling a baby as we wait for the left-turn signal. When the green arrow blinks, I accelerate through the light.

Rae suddenly sits forward and places a hand on Ivy's shoulder. "Are you doing okay?"

The girl nods.

"Are you going to be sick?" Rae asks.

Immediately I brake, a bit too hard, and Rae falls forward against the front bench seat. "Sorry." Anxious, I glance from the road to Ivy, making the steering wheel bobble and the car weave, pitching Rae right, then left in the back seat. "Should I pull over? You can't—"

"I'm okay," Ivy says through clenched teeth. I'm not sure if she's holding back vomit or irritated at our hovering concern. Cautiously, I maneuver the Cadillac over to the right lane.

"Don't worry," Rae says, handing a Styrofoam container to Ivy.

"What's this?" Ivy opens it.

"I swiped it from the waitress on the way out of the restaurant. Just being cautious. You looked a bit green."

Ivy tosses the container to the floorboard.

"How much did Stu pay for this car?" Rae asks.

"Too much," I answer, remembering my shock over the sticker price. But I hadn't said anything. "He bought it after . . ." My voice drifts. "Stu was obsessed with everything Elvis."

"Why?" Ivy asks, wrinkling her nose as if she couldn't understand it any more than if Stu had collected skunk tails. "All of this is so cheesy."

"He was the King." I shrug one shoulder. "Many people loved Elvis. Still do. Right, Rae?" But my aunt doesn't answer. "He was the epitome of cool. At least to Stu."

"I think it was more than that," Rae finally says. "Sounds like Stu was running from something. Or avoiding something . . . to spend so much money on an old car."

"I guess we're all running and hiding, aren't we?" I manage, feeling my throat tighten. I'm caught between irritation at Stu for spending so much on this car and questioning what I always believed about my husband. Have I had it wrong all these years? Why *did* Stu love Elvis so?

"I ran away from my problems," Rae says, "when I was young. Not as young as you, Ivy. First I left my folks to get away, to escape what felt like a suffocating life of boredom." She laughs. "Then I ended up running back to that security. Life can be crazy sometimes. Or maybe it's us . . . our actions that are crazy." She sighs, looking back out the side window. "Anyway, I couldn't stay any longer and I left . . . went even farther away. But you can't outrun the pain, the past, or your problems. It never works. Never."

The hotel looms large ahead. Cars line the streets. Elvis's voice floats from the speakers. It's not the words or the tune that stirs me, just his voice. The deep, melodic voice.

"For thirty years I ran. I stayed away. Even after . . ." Rae shakes her head as if cutting herself off. "I was off on my own. But then I finally had to stop. I couldn't run anymore."

I pull up to the front of the hotel. It's a covered area where benches line one side for folks waiting for free shuttles to various tourist spots. Overhead Elvis sings about a tiger. With the car idling, I look at Rae over the seat separating us. "What changed?"

"Everything. And yet nothing at all."

"What were you running from?" I ask.

"Oh, I could give you a litany of things, but mostly I was running from myself. Fear. Fear dictated my life. And that's no way to live."

"I can't imagine you afraid of anything."

"We all have feelings below the surface, undetectable to others. Most of the time."

"Was my mother ever afraid?" I ask.

"Aren't we all afraid of something?" Rae returns. "But Beverly never ran. She was braver. She had more faith."

"So are you better now?" Ivy asks, half turning in her seat to look at Rae. "Now that you're facing up to things?"

"In some ways, yes. It's hard to face up to my own weaknesses and inadequacies. My mistakes. My sins. But everything is magnified again here. In Memphis."

"Like your getting pregnant?" Ivy asks.

"No," Rae says quickly, almost sharply. "That wasn't a mistake. Ever. I cannot say bringing a baby into the world is ever a mistake. It's after—" She stops herself. "I've said too much. Enough."

"So it's possible," Ivy asks, "for someone to change what they've done? Fix their mistakes?"

"You cannot change what's done. You can make the best of what is." Rae places a hand on Ivy's shoulder. "That's what I'm trying to do. Maybe that's all I've ever done."

I wonder what mistakes Rae means. And Ivy . . . what could she have done? She's so young, and yet there's a weariness in her eyes that many forty-year-olds don't have.

"You want us to get out here?" Rae asks.

"I'll park and meet you in the suite."

"Good idea." Rae gives me a secretive wink as if to say she'll take good care of Ivy.

GUILT FALLS ON me hard. It's the same guilt I felt every time I had to leave Stu's side for even a short time. I feel as if

I should accompany them to the suite. What if Ivy gets sick on the way upstairs?

I watch them walk into the hotel. They are such different women, yet similar in a way I cannot pinpoint. Maybe it's the squareness of their shoulders, their long strides. Ivy has an independent streak that I'm not sure I ever possessed. Even though at the end of Stu's life he depended on me, I believe that during twenty years of marriage I leaned more on him. Not financially, as I always worked, but emotionally. I needed him. Maybe more than he needed me.

Weaving the Cadillac through the parking lot across the street from the hotel, I search for an empty space. I wonder why Rae continues to bring up her story of running away, of not escaping the past. Is she anxious to get out of Memphis? My heart pounds in empathy. Going through Stu's belongings, as well as my mother's, before the garage sale, I felt an urgent need to run.

Or maybe Rae was simply rambling on for Ivy's sake. But why? I sense something is going on with the girl. Is it simply her mother, the confusion of her loss? Did she come all the way to Memphis with us just to get away from her dad for a while? There has to be something else. Or maybe I'm just so uneasy around teenagers that I assume the worst.

I remember flying to New York on business a few years back. It had been an unusually turbulent flight that had me reaching for the barf bag in the pocket of the seat ahead of me. Luckily I hadn't needed to use it. But I had felt off kilter the rest of the day. If I stood too quickly, I felt dizzy, my stomach unsettled. I was cautious what I ate at a business meeting that night. Maybe that's all it is with Ivy—car sickness and spicy food.

As I walk through the parking lot toward the hotel, I notice the night sky has begun to grow gray with clouds. A heaviness settles in my chest as I enter the hotel. Yet my pace takes on the tempo of the ever-present Elvis music rocking and rolling through the small lobby. I purposefully slow my stride and take the elevator up to our rooms.

Thankful for the relative quiet of the suite, I check on Ivy, getting her a cold cloth for her head and a drink of water. "If you need anything in the night, just let me know."

I watch her lying on the bed, looking so thin and frail, and wonder if I should let Ben know that his daughter is sick. "Do you want me to call your dad? Have him come get you? You could have the stomach flu or something."

"Don't tell Dad. He'll just worry."

That's true. Knowing Ben needs a break—he's carried the burden of parenthood alone for so long—I decide to wait. Surely I can manage as a stand-in guardian for a long weekend.

"You think Rae really ran away?" Ivy asks in a hoarse whisper.

"So she says. I know Rae was around when I was little, and then she wasn't. My mother would never talk about Rae. She always changed the subject when I brought it up. I figured they'd had a fight or something. Maybe it was hurt and resentment that kept Mother silent."

"Dad acts the same way when I mention my mom," Ivy says.

"I'm sure it's just hard for him. I know he wants to talk to you. Maybe he just doesn't know how. Maybe he can't find the right words."

"Well, I can't answer my own questions!"

"I know. Just give him a break. Okay? It was rough on him. It can't be easy to relive the pain of that time. Keep trying. When you get home, try again. Ask him the questions you asked me. He may not know the answers. It might be really hard for him . . . and you, too. But afterward, I think you'll both be glad you talked."

"It just makes Dad mad."

I sigh and sit on the edge of the bed. "He's not mad at you. When it happened, when your mother left . . . he took it really hard. He blamed himself. And he was angry at your mom. You can't blame him for that. I'm sure your questions just stir up old hurts. Just know it's not you. Whatever happened between your parents was about them, not you."

I finger the corner of the pillow. Cautiously I venture deeper into dark emotions that I'm not sure I can fully understand. "Ivy, I know it's hard not having a mother. I was lucky and had mine until I was thirty-five. And still it seems too early to have lost her." I realize it's the lost memories of her stories, things she held back from me, that make her absence so sharp. Maybe it's the same way with Ivy. She has no memory of her mother, nothing to hold onto. "So, if you need anything . . . a substitute . . ." My throat tightens. "I'm not your mom. I won't pretend to be. And I've never been a mom." My throat feels full, stretched, as if I've swallowed a ball of my mother's yarn. "But if you need somebody to listen, someone to talk to, I'm here. Okay?"

She closes her eyes.

I wait for an answer but don't really expect one. Turning off the light, I close her door most of the way, leaving it open a wedge so she can make her way to the bathroom if she needs to. There is a sharp pain in my heart, and I press my hand against my chest as if I might find Mother's knitting needles sticking out of me. Slowly the pain eases.

♪♩♪♩.♩♪♩

I FIND RAE in the sitting room, already in a green silk robe, her long, silvery hair loose and flowing about her shoulders. The television is on, the sound muted. But Elvis sits in a Hawaiian jail singing "Beach Boy Blues." In the corner, quiet yet noticeable, is our own Elvis shrouded only partially by a hotel towel, yet the profile is obviously that of the King.

"How is she?"

"I guess okay. I wish I knew what was wrong. Can," I whisper and move closer to Rae so my voice doesn't travel down the hall to Ivy, "can drugs make you sick to your stomach?"

"Of course." She sets a brochure about Sun Records on the coffee table.

"Why did you say all that tonight about running away from your problems?"

Rae lifts her chin. "She has problems. She wants to hide from them. But it's impossible. I learned that the hard way. I was hoping she might share with us."

I nod. "I hope she will. Maybe tomorrow. Her mother ran away from her problems, from her responsibilities. It's been really hard on Ivy. Ben, too."

"I can imagine. A young girl needs a mother."

"I'm not a mom. But," I shrug, feeling uncomfortable with my latest role, "I hope I helped." I look back at Ivy's partially closed door.

"Don't worry. She'll talk when she's ready. She wants a mother. And she'll find that in you."

Her statement shocks me as if she's thrown a dart into my heart. "In me?"

"You don't have to be afraid, Claudia. You're a natural. You have the gift of caring for wounded creatures."

"I don't know anything about being a mother." The empty space fills with a hard, weighty substance. Could it be fear? I don't have answers for Ivy. I don't have any solutions. Aren't parents supposed to have all the answers? Mine certainly seemed to. Mother never hesitated in scolding, in pointing out right and wrong, in speaking her mind. And yet I sense there is more to parenting, maybe something I missed out on.

On the television Elvis chases after an angry teen, then turns her over his knee and spanks her.

"You know more than you think," Rae says. "Caring for a creature in need is the best way to feel alive." She stifles a yawn as she unfolds from the couch and stands. "I'm going to turn in, too. It's been a long day. Who knows what tomorrow will bring?"

Graceland, I think, my gaze shifting toward Elvis.

"Good night." She turns to go.

"Aunt Rae?"

She looks back at me. Something flickers in her eyes, and I wonder if my calling her "aunt" is a good thing or troubling to her. "I'm sorry, I didn't realize coming to Memphis would be so hard for you."

She gives a little lift of her shoulder. "If everything were easy, what would be the price of love?"

I nod, not entirely sure I catch her meaning. "You know, I've seen pictures of when you would visit us, when I was little. I, well . . . I wish you had kept in touch with us."

"There is a time for every season."

I nod, supposing the old adage is true. "Why did you leave? I always assumed you had a fight with my mother."

"With Beverly? Not at all. Your mother, she saved me in many ways. She managed to do what I could not."

"What was that?"

"The right thing. As she always did." She rocks her hips to a mysterious rhythm. Slowly she starts singing the words to Elvis's "Love Me." The words speak of fools and the loss of love. Her voice sounds deep and seductive, mimicking Elvis's rendition of the slow ballad. With a jaunty smile and a flippant wave, she sings her way to her bedroom and closes the door.

But I know she is no fool. No fool at all.

I turn off the television and the main lights in the sitting area. The neon lights from a fast-food restaurant, souvenir shops, and car lots draw me to the window. With the air conditioner blowing on me, I stare out at the black sky. A haze of clouds drifts in over the city, and the neon lights take on an eerie cast. "Love Me" circles around my mind, and I can hear Elvis's mournful tone.

Stu and I slow danced to that song once upon a time. I can almost feel his breath against my neck, the heat of his body pressed tight to mine. Closing my eyes, I feel my own heart pounding and imagine Stu's own thumping against me. Slowly the beats merge into one. I wanted to stay like that forever, with Stu's arms securely around me, swaying to Elvis's slow tempo and tempting voice. It was just us, and I'd felt contentment, security, peace.

Our dance came to a stumbling halt when Stu joined in to sing with Elvis. His voice made me laugh. Actually, I think I snorted. At first he acted offended, but then Stu picked up where he'd left off, exaggerating his inability to impersonate the King with a reedy thin voice and hips that didn't swivel with the same oomph.

My heart feels a sudden pinch, as if I've been running on a treadmill, my side aching with fatigue. My breath comes sharp and fast. I brace my hands against the window, feel the coolness of the glass against my palms. The words of the song swirl through my mind, lonely and blue.

I know loneliness well. It's been my cold companion during the last year. But now Rae's words filter down into my heart, and I recognize the truth of them. I've tried to outrun the pain of losing Stu, the loss of all our dreams. But I can't. Everywhere I turn, I end up back at the same place: Without Stu. Without hope. Or direction. Ashamed, I realize I no longer have him to lead me in this lifelong dance we began together. Perhaps this is not something a woman of this century should feel. But Stu's lead gave me a sense of security I had never known before.

I press my forehead to the glass. My eyes swell like the dark clouds outside. I can almost hear Stu's rumbling laugh tumble through my thoughts. Is he laughing now? Laughing at my inability to dispose of Elvis? Laughing at some stupid joke he's pulled, getting me to escort Elvis to Memphis?

I jerk around and glare at the table, at the shrouded Elvis. He's silhouetted in mystery and darkness, but the outline is clear under the thin towel, the shape unmistakable. For so long Elvis was my nemesis. I tried to get rid of him, tried to banish him from our lives. But finally I gave in, more ignoring his presence, the music, its effect on Stu. Now I cling to him, fearing that if I let go I will lose Stu. Forever.

I remember when the hospice nurse came to our house and declared Stu dead. She covered him with a sheet until the hearse from the funeral home could arrive. I stared at the sheet a long time. Just above the top, I could see Stu's bald head. I wanted to jerk the sheet off him and yell, "He can't breathe under there!" But I was unable to move.

Now I yank the towel off Elvis's head, throw it as far as I can. It lands on the floor in a shapeless lump, just as I feel I am without Stu.

"Why?" I whisper to Elvis as if he were Stu. "Why did you bring me here?" Was it a practical joke? I remember when we first started dating, he'd call me on the phone and start playing "You Don't Have to Say You Love Me" or "Hound Dog." When I called his name into the phone, I would hear him laughing in the background, but later he'd deny calling. He was notorious for short-sheeting beds and putting Saran Wrap over toilet seats. I wonder if the note Stu left along with the Elvis bust was some elaborate prank? What if some impersonator had played a joke on Stu? Or had he bought the bust from some cheesy tourist shop? What if he'd stolen it? Had he felt guilty at the end of his life? The questions churn inside me, give me something to focus on other than grief.

"Don't be cruel," I whisper. "Please, for God's sake, don't be cruel."

I draw a ragged breath and know I must find the answers to all my questions, even though I want to toss Elvis right off the balcony. It's time to say good-bye once and for all. But I'm not sure I'm strong enough.

Scooping up the towel off the floor, I wrap it around my arm, twisting as the past seems to tighten its hold on me. It was a typical day, the day it happened. Blue sky. Eighty degrees. Nothing interesting even in the news. No war mentioned on the front pages. No major disasters. Yet my life changed that day. Irrevocably.

Of course, in what had become our very small world, no day was typical anymore. A hospital bed had been brought to our home. Hospice came three times a week. Bottles and pills and such covered the bedside table. I'd tried to make the room happy and bright. I'd placed a vase of mixed flowers I'd picked up at the grocery store in front of the bed where Stu could see them. But he hadn't opened his eyes in two and a half days.

Elvis music drifted from a CD player atop the dresser. At first I'd played the usual top-ten hits, but I noticed Stu's breathing became agitated during "Hard Headed Woman." I switched to Elvis's gospel songs and hymns. That silken voice crooned "I Believe," "Take My Hand, Precious Lord," and "You'll Never Walk Alone." The songs seemed to soothe Stu, but I became more anxious, watching for each breath, each twitch, knowing I would be walking alone from then on.

Stu and I attended a large church, so large that we often got lost in the crowd. But as Stu liked to say, "No one knows when we sleep in on Sunday morning." And we sometimes did. But during his illness he never questioned his beliefs. He'd say, "God's in control." But with everything seemingly so out of control, I had questions. I feared speaking those doubts aloud, especially in front of Stu. But whatever tentative belief in God I had turned hard and sunk deep inside me, lost inside thick muck of skepticism.

That day, with Elvis rocking to "Bosom of Abraham," Stu died. He just stopped breathing. Slowly. Each breath came slower and slower until they didn't come anymore. His hand had been cool to the touch a long while, but I held onto him, unable to let go. As the song crescendoed, building to a fever, Stu drifted into nothingness.

My life slipped out along with his. Everything I had, all my dreams, all my hopes, had been wrapped up with Stu. I'd taken his lead, as if we were dancing through life, content to hold on for the ride. But suddenly he was gone. And I was alone on the dance floor with no one to turn to, no partner, no music.

I wad the hotel's beige, rough towel into a ball, feel the misshapen weight in the pit of my own stomach. Of course, I have more than Stu. I can breathe and move, talk and think. So I stuff all my complaints and grumbling, stuff them deep inside so I don't hear them or look at them. But I know they are there, just as I've known Elvis lived in our attic all these years.

Now I step forward, tempted to shove the Elvis bust backward off the table. I imagine the broken pieces—thousands of them, jagged, cutting, sharp, blunt. Anger pulses through me. I wrap the towel around Elvis' neck, as if choking a statue can kill the pain inside me. But nothing eases these turbulent emotions. I'm not angry at the statue. Maybe I'm not even angry at Stu. Maybe I'm simply angry at God. It's irrational and unreasonable. Yet anger is like a broken guitar string inside me, loose and uncontrollable.

With great effort I smooth the towel around Elvis's shoulders, like one of his capes. The stark white studded collar stands above it. Then I cup his cold cheek with the palm of my hand, aching to feel Stu once again.

Chapter Ten

Little Sister

Overcrowded, the Jungle Room bar offers mostly carbohydrates like biscuits and gravy for breakfast. We load up Styrofoam plates with an assortment of muffins, bagels, and donuts. I grab a couple of bananas and an apple, then pour coffee into a disposable cup. Together we head for the Cadillac.

"There's a park not far from here," I say. We passed it on the drive to the restaurant last night. "We can eat there." I start the car, letting the engine idle a moment while I readjust the rearview mirror, which has a tendency to droop with the engine's vibrations. Without looking at Rae in the back seat I say, "Before we go, you have to tell us. You've kept us in suspense long enough." Then I turn and smile at her. "How did you meet Elvis?"

She sits back as if she's unconcerned. "You can ask . . ."

With lips pressed tight, I jerk the gearshift into reverse and back out of the parking space. After a moment I realize

I'm not so much perturbed with Rae, who withholds from sharing, but at my mother who never shared her heart with me. Drawing in a slow breath, I release the frustration.

A short drive up Elvis Presley Boulevard, I park the Cadillac along the street. Giant oak trees shade picnic tables along the edge of a small pond. The playground equipment looks as tired as the parents I imagine sitting around watching their children do what they are no longer able to do. Traffic noise surrounds us, but as we venture farther into the park, the honk of geese soon drowns out the car horns. As we carry our breakfast to a wooden table, a gaggle of geese and ducks waddles after us.

"Think they've been fed before?" Rae asks.

"We'll be lucky to get out alive if we don't give them some," I say, noticing a couple of small children and a frazzled mother swinging on the playground equipment.

"What's that?" Ivy asks. "An ice cream truck?"

A tinny noise reaches us from the far end of the park. I crane my neck and see a carousel, then recognize the familiar tune. It's Rae's grimace that catches my attention though. "What is it? Are you all right?"

"The carousel brings back memories," she says.

"Would you rather talk about Elvis?" I ask with a sarcastic smile.

Chewing on a muffin, Ivy settles onto the bench opposite Rae and myself. "We're not going anywhere till you tell us the story," she says.

I grin at Ivy's spirit this morning. Maybe her stomach is more settled. Our eyes meet. She gives me a tentative smile as if we've just joined the same team.

"So . . . ," I prod.

"It was nothing spectacular," Rae says.

"It had to be. Just because it was Elvis."

Rae glances at my watch as she spreads cream cheese on a bagel. "Shouldn't we try to beat the crowds to Graceland?"

"It's all up to you." Steam rises and curls upward from my coffee cup. I'm relieved I didn't spill any in the car as the hotel didn't have any lids.

Her mouth twists tight. A duck wanders too close and Ivy shoos it away.

"You told Stu," I prod.

"He was dying."

"So you're saying you'd have to kill us for knowing?"

She laughs.

"Neither of us has had the experience of meeting Elvis. I've never met anyone famous. Okay, Jason Robards. Years ago. Well, I guess I didn't really *meet* him. He was in a restaurant in New York. Stu walked over and said hello. I hung back and watched Stu talk to him like he was an ordinary guy."

"He was," Rae says. "So was Elvis. Ordinary and yet . . ."

"Tell us." Ivy reaches for half a bagel.

"We want to know what it was like. What *he* was like. Besides, I hate secrets."

"Secrets suck," Ivy agrees, borrowing Rae's plastic knife to spread butter on the bagel.

Rae makes a great show of pouring cream and sugar into her coffee. She sips it, scowls, then adds more. "Aren't you glad Stuart kept his experience with Elvis secret? You would have thought he was crazy."

"Maybe he was. But maybe if we'd talked about it, it would have spared me hauling Elvis to Memphis now and tracking down some mysterious owner."

"Have you known many secrets?" Rae blows across the top of her coffee.

"You're stalling," I accuse and flap my arms to ward off the encroaching duck-and-geese battalion.

"Yes."

"You know Mother . . . she did that, too. She never would tell me how Daddy proposed to her. And it drove me crazy."

"Why? What did it matter?"

"I just wanted to know. It was a momentous occasion in my parents' lives, and I just wanted to share it, to know what it was like for them."

"They were probably in bed," Ivy says, lifting her feet onto the bench. "They're coming closer!"

Ducks and geese are rushing us like Elvis fans trying to get to the King.

"Here!" I break apart half a bagel into pieces and toss them out on the lawn. The birds scramble over one another, their quacking arguments are deafening before they finally quiet. They peck at the ground, turning in circles. "Not my mother. My parents having sex before marriage," I laugh, "did not happen. Sometimes I wasn't sure . . ." I shake my head, laughing more. The wind stirs the napkins stacked on the table, and I slap my hand on them to keep them from blowing across the park. "Let's just say, sometimes I suspected immaculate conception got me here."

Ivy laughs, but Rae doesn't.

"More than likely my mother planned the whole wedding and just told my father, 'Be at the church at ten o'clock.'"

"It wasn't that simple." Rae places the second half of her bagel back on the Styrofoam plate. The hungry birds waddle toward us again. "We should go."

Ivy's up and walking toward the carousel before the flock reaches her side of the table. Rae carries her coffee and mine, while I dump our trash in a nearby bin. I catch up to them and say to Rae, "You know, then—how my father proposed?"

"Of course. I was there."

I glance back over my shoulder to see the lead goose turning and waddling down to the bank of the lake. Then I check the car, which sits alone in the parking lot. "You were there?"

"Guess it wasn't 'in bed' then," Ivy says.

"I probably shouldn't tell you this." Rae looks at me, but something tips her over the edge. "Beverly was twenty, and I was only fifteen. So I was still living at home. She was crying on the sofa. So was our mother. But she stood in the kitchen. And Dad . . . our father . . . well, he was fit to be tied."

"Where was my father? The groom to be?"

"Mike was there. Only very quiet."

"Why the drama?" Ivy asks.

"Your mother," Rae says to me as if we are the only two people in Memphis, "was pregnant."

"What?" I stop walking.

"She was. It happened. Happens today, doesn't it?" She looks toward Ivy for confirmation. "Although today it's not such a big deal. But back then it was a major crisis."

Ivy shrugs and keeps walking.

"Your mother," Rae takes my arm as we fall into step with Ivy, "was scared. Obviously. I mean, this was 1959." She glances again at Ivy.

"Wait a minute," I interrupt. "I wasn't born until 1963."

"I know."

I draw a shallow breath, my chest constricted with emotions. I sense this story will open a window to my parents' world that I'm not sure I want to look through.

Now the carousel's music is louder, and I realize we've reached the outside edge of the park. The woman running the ride has a wide, toothy grin. "A dollar a ride. Only one dollar."

I give a shake of my head to tell her we're not interested and turn to face Rae. "I don't understand."

"Your mother was horrified and never wanted anyone to know. But I tell you because I think you have a right to know the truth. Immaculate conception," she snorts. "I regret she didn't share more of herself with you. But that was her decision. This is mine, now that she's gone."

I nod, giving my consent, but I brace myself.

"As I said, she didn't want to tell our parents. But Mike knew it was the right thing to do. And so he did it. He told our father. Which, of course, created an uproar."

"What did Grandpa do?"

"He ordered Mike out of the house. But Mike would not leave. He spoke quietly but firmly. Very mature he was, even back then. He said he hadn't meant to harm Beverly. He loved her and wanted to marry her. Would want to marry her no matter if she was pregnant or not. So our father agreed and ordered Mike to ask her right then."

I imagine my prim and proper mother distraught with shame. Yet I can easily see my father determined and relentless. Pride fills my chest. He boldly stood up to his future father-in-law. I finally understand the tension I always sensed between the two men. They were always respectful of each other, probably because my father had behaved like a gentleman, but there had always been formality like a frost settled between them.

"So he did?" Ivy asks.

"Mike said he'd already asked, but Beverly refused. 'She won't now,' my father bellowed. And Mike got down on his knee, everybody weeping around him, even our father. But Mike only had eyes for Beverly. And he asked her again to marry him." Rae glances toward the carousel, something in her eyes darkens. "That music is annoying."

"What did she say?" Ivy seems caught up in the story. "She said yes, right?"

"Of course."

"That's cool," Ivy says.

"I don't know if it was or not," Rae continues. "But they married one month later. A quiet, private ceremony. Just our parents and Mike's. I was maid of honor."

"But the baby?" I ask, almost afraid to know.

"Ah, such a shame. She lost the baby not long after."

Ivy gasps. I must have, too, because Rae puts an arm around my shoulder. "Your parents loved each other," she says, her gaze steady. "You must know that."

"I do. But . . . all the rest, they never said . . . never spoke of it to me." That empty space in my heart pulses.

"And you didn't need to know. It might have caused doubt in your mind. It didn't matter by the time you came along. All that mattered was that they loved each other . . . and you."

I nod but feel hot tears sting my eyes. What Mother endured folds through my mind. Why didn't she tell me? If not before, then she could have told me when I lost my baby. When I was depressed and lost and hurting. Why didn't she tell me? Why did she hold back so much? Was it pride? Embarrassment? It would have helped to know that she'd survived a similar loss. It could have brought us closer.

But she'd watched in silence. Now the distance between us seems to widen. I feel a draft of coldness. Only because she chose to keep quiet and not reveal to me her own heartache.

Then I consider uncharted territory—that I could have had a big sister, instead of being an only child. The realization staggers me. What would it have been like to have someone else, a sibling to play with, to look up to, to understand and empathize, to shoulder the burden of caring for our mother.

"Why don't you like carousels?" Ivy asks Rae, interrupting my thoughts.

"I do," Rae says. "But they remind me of a difficult time. When I first lived in Oregon, I would go to a small zoo. There was a carousel there. I would watch the children laughing, riding the different animals. It had all sorts of animals, not just horses but elephants, zebras, a tortoise, even a triceratops. And I would think of my child."

I put an arm around Rae's waist, as she supported me. "That must have been hard."

She shrugs. "Shouldn't we be getting to Graceland?"

Ivy winks at me and tilts her head toward the carousel. Confused, I look from her to the carousel, then back. She steers us toward the grinning woman who's waiting for her first customers of the day.

"What about Elvis?" Ivy says. She pulls three dollars out of her hip pocket and says, "We'll ride."

"No, no," Rae says, trying to back up. But I have my arm around her waist and Ivy pulls on her other side.

"Come on."

Suddenly we're on the big platform, standing among a herd of painted horses, their bright colors as garish as the Elvis bust.

"This could give you motion sickness, Ivy," Rae warns.

"I'm fine."

"You gotta sit down before I can turn on the ride," the woman calls from behind us.

"Here." I urge Rae to sit in the chariot. She stumbles, and I hold her arm. Ivy climbs the nearest horse. When we're all settled, the carousel begins to turn. Ivy's horse rises and falls slowly. She twists in the saddle to look at us.

My hip is nestled snugly against Rae's on the bench seat that's built more for a parent and child than two adults. "Okay," I grin ruthlessly, "we'll have to ride until you tell us how you met Elvis."

With a sigh Rae spreads her skirt out along the bench seat. The carousel music drones on and on. The platform spins faster as Ivy's horse bobs up and down.

Taking a long, slow breath, Rae says, "Haven't we told enough family secrets for one morning?"

"Are there more?" My heart thumps in my chest.

She looks out over the park. From this angle I can see the car, and I know Elvis is safe. "There are things known and not. Elvis—I have not spoken of him in a long time. To Stu . . . but that was different."

"So you knew he carried your secret to the grave?"

"It's not a secret. No big mystery. I knew Elvis. It's difficult for me to speak of."

"Painful?"

"Heartbreaking."

I waver, then decide not to force her. After all, I would resent it now if someone asked me to speak of Stu . . . or the baby. Elvis, to me, is almost a mythical character; but to Rae he was flesh and blood, a person, a friend even. Maybe more.

In that awkward moment I forgive my mother for withholding her secrets, her losses. Maybe the pain of loss was too painful for her to discuss, like it is for Ben to talk about Ivy's mother. Maybe my mother couldn't find the right words either. Maybe she thought I'd be jealous of a baby always on her mind, forever in her heart. Maybe she wanted to hide what she considered a horrible sin. What she didn't understand was that, knowing, I would still have loved her. Maybe more. She would have been more real, less perfect, more human. What she didn't understand was that I simply needed to know it was okay to forever mourn a baby that I could never hold but would never forget.

I remember Mother flitting around, cleaning my house for me, bringing me raspberry Jell-O, sliced strawberries, and homemade chicken sandwiches. That was her way of trying to ease the pain when I came home from the hospital, my arms and womb empty—her way of helping me through those dark days when no words could have penetrated or healed the gaping wound in my heart.

"The tiny decisions we make each day," Rae says, her words somehow harmonizing with the carousel music, "they seem insignificant, silly even. But they can change our course. What's the saying about no controlling a bull, but put a little ring through his nose . . . ? That describes my life. And once God got a hold of me . . . once I let him have control . . ."

I'm not sure what she means. Doesn't God control everything? He's never asked for my consent. He certainly never asked my opinion on whether my father or Stu should live or die.

"But way before that happened," Rae continues, "I met Elvis. It was really nothing. Insignificant in Elvis's life, I'm sure of that. Of course, I knew who Elvis was before we met. Everyone knew about Elvis."

"Like Bono?" Ivy asks, her horse sliding up its pole.

"Who? Whoever," Rae waves her hand. "No, no. Elvis was . . . like a god. Everyone knew of him, young and old. You didn't even need to know his last name. Just Elvis. You either loved him or hated him. Very polarizing. Most parents didn't care for him at all. They believed he was a bad influence. He redeemed himself somewhat by going into the Army and serving his country. He was patriotic. Some folks thought he'd disappear from the limelight, being out of the public eye for so long. But the Colonel handled his publicity well, kept his memory alive. And then it was 1961 when I came to Memphis. The morals were different from today. Yet things were changing. Elvis had recently come back from Germany. Memphis was energetic . . . alive.

"I was young, restless. Just seventeen. I wanted to be away, off on my own. A friend of mine had an uncle who lived in Memphis who said he'd hire us to work in his office. What was her name? Hedda Winningham." Rae smiles to herself, as if lost in her own thoughts and memories. "We had such fun in high school." The fingers of one hand trace the shape of her nails on the other.

"So I followed her to Memphis. And we worked for her uncle, filing and doing secretarial things. I could type a little. We were foolish, looking for fun. She moved on to Nashville, I believe, and later married. Her name's . . . Polk now. Hedda Polk."

She pauses as if lost in her own memories. Her gaze drifts, and she stares off as if she's watching a movie we can't see. Ivy glances at me with a worried look, but I give her a quick smile of reassurance.

"Heddie became friendly with a man at a radio station in Memphis," Rae continues, her voice more mesmerizing than the tinny sound of the carousel song. "I believe he knew her uncle." She waves her hand as if passing over information that is unimportant. "He had a friend. I can't remember his name now, but he knew Elvis. I mean, really knew Elvis. They were good friends. Elvis used to drop by and talk to him regularly at the radio station. So this guy invited Heddie to one of the parties over at Graceland. She was excited. Who wouldn't have been? But she was nervous, too. Worried. She dragged me along. Not that she had to drag me at all. Who wouldn't have wanted to go to Graceland? In those days I was . . ."

"Bold?"

"Bolder than I should have been."

"So you went?"

"I did. And, of course, Elvis was there. It wasn't anything spectacular. No music sounding. No trumpets blaring." She pauses with a smile and glances at the speaker perched high at the carousel's center where the lyrical music tumbles out. "No bells. Yet it was magical. For me. He was beautiful. His eyes . . . and that mouth." She sighs like a young teenager. "He was cocky but also humble. Nice and cordial. But jittery. He seemed nervous, which astounded me. Then he showed us around. He seemed so proud . . . not in a 'look what I've got' way. More like amazement, like he still couldn't believe it himself. Like he feared he might wake up and find it was all a dream.

"I remember people were everywhere, crowding around him, laughing at everything he did or said, hanging onto his every word. It was kind of a disappointment actually."

"Hard to live up to the hype," Ivy says as if it's perfectly understandable. Maybe it is. How many times have I anticipated something, wanted something, only to be disappointed when I got it? Things that never lived up to the anticipation. Never filled the holes.

"Maybe that was it," Rae agrees. "Graceland was big. At least, in those days it was big. I'm sure there are bigger houses built now. But then it seemed extraordinary. And Elvis. He was big, too. Charismatic. My senses were on overload. I was out of my league. I felt . . . I don't know . . ." She gestures toward her stomach, her hand trembling. "Uncomfortable. I wanted to tell those people to go home and leave Elvis alone. In some ways Elvis seemed like a little boy who needed someone to protect him. That was my sense of it all."

"And that was it?" I ask.

"For that night. I went home. I'd met Elvis. What more could there be? I certainly wasn't a groupie. I wasn't looking to hang out at Graceland on a daily basis. And there was some dancer from Vegas hanging out with Elvis. And then later . . . maybe a week or so . . . he called."

"He called you?" Ivy asks, gripping her horse's pole. She's started to understand how big Elvis was with a hotel and street named for him and myriad souvenir shops stuffed with his memorabilia.

"No. The friend . . . Heddie's friend from the radio station. He called. Elvis wanted to see me." She puffs out her chest. "Actually, he'd rented a movie theater for that night. Elvis wanted me to come. Not Heddie. Well, she could . . . but he specifically wanted me there."

"And you went, right?" Ivy asks.

"No. I had a date."

"You didn't drop the guy for Elvis?" she asks, narrowing her gaze as if it would have been the biggest mistake Rae could have made.

Rae chuckles. "No. Of course not. He was more real than Elvis. Elvis was . . . like a dream. I didn't think anything could happen long term with a dream. Too surreal."

Ivy nods. I feel the carousel beginning to slow. I fumble with my purse and find three more dollars. I don't want the ride to stop and disrupt Rae's story. As we pass the attendant, I wave the dollars at her. She comes over and stuffs the bills in her pocket. Then the carousel picks up speed once again.

"I told him I was sorry but I was busy. Maybe another time. I didn't think I would hear from Elvis again. Turning down the King . . . well, it didn't seem like anyone turned down Elvis."

"And? Did he call?"

"The next time Elvis called. Himself."

Ivy leans over her horse as it slides downward along the pole again. "And you went, right?"

She gives a secretive smile. "Now you know my story."

"I don't think we've scratched the surface."

The carousel slows once more. The attendant shrugs as we pass. "The kids," she says, pointing toward a group of five waiting to board the carousel, "they want on."

"It's enough," Rae says. "Let's go to Graceland. You'll see who Elvis was. No ordinary man."

And she, I realize, is no ordinary woman either.

Chapter Eleven

Don't Be Cruel

Once back at the hotel, we walk across the street toward the graffiti-covered stone wall outside Graceland. I search surreptitiously for some enclave where an Elvis bust might be missing. Rae walks slowly, almost hesitantly. Ivy acts more like the tourists we are, her eyes darting all around as she gawks at the strange sights. She seems to feel better today after her high-carb breakfast, so I put my worries on hold.

When we finally reach the beginning of Graceland property, a woman with gray hair, openly weeping, writes a message to Elvis on the wall.

"What's with her?" Ivy asks.

"She loved the King of Rock 'n' Roll," I offer as explanation, although it seems pretty odd to me to weep over a dead stranger. But maybe she knew the King, too. Then again, I don't see Rae weeping and carrying on. Maybe it's only displaced grief the woman feels for Elvis. Maybe it's easier to weep over a legend, a tragic figure, than to face the pain in her own life.

Ivy keeps moving forward, but she glances back at the woman.

It takes only a few steps to reach the music-note gates, famous the world over. They stand open and seem smaller than I imagined. A guardhouse sits next to the entrance. The guard waves to a shuttle bus that drives through and up the lane toward the house. I get Ivy and Rae to stand in front of the stone wall and take their picture. The number of people milling around amazes me. How long has Elvis been dead? Thirty years? And still people clamor to be near him. I try to put it in perspective for Ivy.

"This many people aren't lining up to see Bruce Springsteen's or Paul McCartney's house."

"They're not dead," she says.

"All the more reason to go see their houses! I mean, you might catch a glimpse of them."

"Whatever."

"John Lennon . . . or Janis Joplin . . . they don't have this kind of following," I add, determined to show her how important Elvis was. "Maybe you don't know who Lennon—"

"I know."

"You know who John Lennon is?" Rae asks.

"Yeah," she says in that teen tone that means *duh*.

It's a hot June day, sticky with humidity, as we cross the street again to the tour shuttle. With the hotel suite I bought a package deal with tickets to Graceland. So we pass the line of fans, which are a mixture of young and old, and enter the strange and bizarre world of Elvis—and Rae's past. Before we board the shuttle, we're handed earphones and an audio system designed to dangle around our necks. It's a short drive to Graceland, where we get off the shuttle. We stand outside the front door on the driveway. There our fellow tourists take pictures of the house, the trees. One leans on the lion statue, but a staffer asks him politely not to touch. We're reminded to turn off the flash on our cameras.

"I don't know how," a woman beside me laments.

"I bet I can figure it out," a staffer says.

After a brief explanation of when the house was built and how Elvis purchased it for one hundred thousand dollars, we enter the house.

Rae walks slightly ahead of us, as if she belongs there, as if she's Priscilla Presley, with her chin tilted up, her expression closed, as if she expects someone to recognize her—or for Elvis to walk down the stairs and welcome her.

We stand in the hallway at the entrance of Graceland, jockeying for position to see the royal-blue dining room with its black marble floor and golden chairs. I imagine other famous stars sitting there with Elvis at the head of the table, enjoying the down-home cooking that he loved. On the other side is the living room with a long white couch and mirrored fireplace. At the end of the room are stained-glass peacocks bracketing a doorway that leads to the music room.

When our group begins to surge forward toward the kitchen, I touch Rae's shoulder. She turns, lifts one of her earphones. "Is it how you remember?" I ask.

"Some." Her brow crinkles as she looks over each piece in the living room. "It's not the same piano. I remember a white baby grand with gold trim." She rubs her hands together, making her charm bracelet jangle and her rings click against each other. "Things change." She speaks in a low tone as if she doesn't want anyone to hear her. "I didn't expect it to be the same. I have changed, too."

♪♩♪♩.♩♪♩

THE GREEN SHAG carpet on the walls and ceiling cause Ivy's jaw to drop with disbelief at the over-the-top decor. Rae has a wry smile curving her mouth and an occasional shake of the head. Nothing seems to surprise her though.

Ivy shrugs at the TV room. "What's the big deal?"

I'm sure she's seen more high-tech movie rooms in her friends' homes. Ben's big-screen TV can play more than one channel at a time. But Ivy doesn't realize Elvis was way ahead of the technological curve. Remote control wasn't even widely available then.

Someone brushes my shoulder, and I step out of the way while tourists angle their cameras for a quick picture. The flash goes off and someone calls, "Turn off your flash, please."

I keep looking for a giant pedestal where Elvis's bust could sit, like a king on his throne overseeing the throngs of admirers. A pedestal just waiting there vacant, expectant after all these years. I imagine a Grecian-style column, about waist high, broad and sturdy, made out of marble. A fitting place for a king. But there isn't a spot among all the outlandish decorations for the tackiness of the piece. It's an absurd anticipation but rather hopeful, or maybe selfish. I want the search for the bust's home to be over. I want to return to a normal life, whatever that is. For there is nothing normal or ordinary in what I'm doing.

"This is pimpin'," Ivy says.

I pause my audio. "What?"

"Pimpin'," she repeats, looking at the Jungle Room.

Surprised, I glance around, hoping others haven't heard. I can just imagine an ardent fan taking offense and starting a riot. "Elvis wasn't a . . ."—I lower my voice—"a pimp!"

I can hear Stu's outrage in my head and realize he would take offense, but there's no reason for me to be upset by her remark. Ivy simply blinks at me.

Rae joins us, taking off her earphones. "The seventies have returned, haven't they?" She glances purposefully at Ivy's bell-bottom hip-huggers.

"Take a picture, will you? Think Dad would let me decorate my room like this?" she asks.

"Doubt it." I wrinkle my nose at the garish decor as I snap a picture sans flash. "It's truly horrible."

"Don't be cruel," Rae sings softly.

"Pimpin'," Ivy says again, her head bobbing like she's jamming to some rap song in her head. Then she punches a button on her audio system and moves away from us.

"She means, it's cool," Rae explains at my stunned expression. "It's just a saying kids use now."

How does she know this? And how am I so out of touch that an older woman has to explain teenage jargon to me?

"Oh," I manage.

I would definitely not be a good mom to a teenager.

"Okay, well . . . I guess that's one way to say it."

WE TOUR MOST of the house, what's open to the public anyway. I catch Rae looking longingly up the great stairwell. But no one goes into Elvis's private residence.

"Were you ever upstairs?" I ask.

Rae lifts the earphone away from her ear. I can hear the automated guide talking. She fumbles with the audio player and finally stops it. I repeat my question.

"Of course. It was probably redecorated since I was here. Elvis stayed upstairs much of the time." She glances around at the crowd shuffling through his house. "Strangers . . . crowds made him nervous. There always seemed to be people everywhere. He'd stay upstairs and send someone down to see who was here, if it was safe for him to come down."

"In his own house?" I ask as we walk past a wall of gold records. It's a dazzling tribute to all that Elvis contributed to the music scene and our culture. Yet apparently the gates out front did not protect him. He may have been the King of Rock 'n' Roll, but he wasn't even the king of his own castle.

"Sometimes he liked to make a grand entrance. Coming down that staircase in style."

Ivy walks up to us in the carport. "I didn't see any place that could have been the spot for the bust."

"Of course, it's been years since it disappeared," I say. "They wouldn't have left an empty spot, would they?" I'm embarrassed now that that's exactly what I was hoping for—an empty space preserved with a framed marker explaining how the bust was stolen years ago and that there was still a reward for its return. A stupid hope.

"Should we ask?" Ivy suggests. "Like, hey, y'all been missing a butt-ugly Elvis head?"

I laugh. "Something like that. But who would we ask?"

Ivy waves toward a staffer.

"Ivy," I call, but she ignores me and walks over to a man who is wearing all black. "I'm not so sure that's a good idea," I say to Rae.

"It doesn't belong here," she says.

"How do you know?" I ask, still watching Ivy, who looks more like she's flirting with the staffer than asking about Elvis.

"I know."

"Then why'd we come?"

Rae smiles confidently. "Everyone should come to Graceland when they visit Memphis. It's like going to Mecca. Or the Wailing Wall."

"The wailing what?" Ivy asks, walking back over to us.

"It's considered a holy place, a shrine," Rae explains.

"There's been no bust stolen," Ivy says. "So are we done here, or what?"

"We have to see his grave." Rae steps toward the pool and the walkway leading toward the meditation garden. We follow after her. With a glance over my shoulder, I realize the staffers are watching us closely, as if we're looking to walk off with a piece of Graceland.

♪♩♪♩.♩♪♩

A RESPECTFUL, QUIET crowd has formed a line slowly moving past the grave of Elvis's grandmother. Once they reach Elvis's resting place and the eternal flame, they take pictures—flash photography is allowed here—and take their time reading the long epitaph written there. Some even whisper, "Good-bye," or, "I love you." Then they pay their respects to Elvis's father and mother, the line disbanding there as the guests linger, not wanting to end their stay at Graceland.

The woman ahead of us carries a bouquet of wilting flowers. Tears run down her face. The couple behind us in line giggle. Ivy keeps asking questions about the Moorish stained-glass windows we pass as we walk along the brick pathway, getting closer and closer to Elvis's grave. I glance at Rae, nervous for her seeing the site for the first time. But she looks calm except for a slight plucking of her sleeve.

I ask, "Are you okay?"

"Sure. It's not the same as you, Claudia."

"What do you mean?"

"When you visit Stu's grave, you mourn him. For yourself. You're in the midst of grief. I grieved for Elvis many years before he died. I grieved his loss of freedom. I grieved that I couldn't help him."

"I couldn't help Stu either."

She clutches my hand, and I realize she understands my loss more than I ever imagined.

"Jeeze, it's hot." An overweight man ahead of Rae swipes his forearm along his face. "I gotta get me a beer. Are you ready, Betty?"

Betty elbows him in the gut. "What a tragedy." She wipes tears from her eyes and lays a bouquet of flowers along the wrought-iron fence. "So young."

"Boy, did I love him." A woman behind us smacks gum. "I did. He loved me, too."

I glance back at the woman with an old-lady hairdo sprayed into place. Others start looking at her too.

"He did," the woman argues with the silent accusations. She readjusts her fanny pack around her wide waist. "In 1970, I saw Elvis in Houston."

"Where?" someone asks.

"At the Astrodome." She lifts her chin indignantly, as if irritated her story has been challenged.

"In concert?"

She props her hands on her ample hips. "Well, I weren't there to see football."

"He said he loved you?"

"Sure 'nuff. I was up on stage. Yes, sir, I was. Crawled my way up onto the stage. The guards didn't take kindly to that. So they grabbed me and started carrying me off. I hollered for Elvis. And he looked over, saw me, and did that kinda secretive smile of his. I yelled, 'I love you, Elvis!' and he said, 'I love you, too, baby.'"

Her story silences those around her into submission. Apparently, none of the others saw Elvis in concert or had the nerve to jump on stage to get close to him. I nudge Rae, wondering what all these people would say if she told them she'd actually *known* Elvis, spoken to him. I notice she's smiling secretly to herself. But I know she won't share her story. Some secrets are best kept private.

The brazen woman's companion readjusts his baseball cap. "I didn't care much for his music."

The Elvis attacker glares at him. "Well, I never!"

"Sissy boy, is what I thought." Another man postures beside them, already edging toward the exit.

"He weren't no sissy," pipes up a burly man wearing a leather jacket like it isn't pushing 90 degrees in the shade. "He had a black belt."

"Two," someone else says.

Then I realize Rae's standing at the foot of Elvis's grave. The splashing of water falling in the fountain behind the semicircle of four graves swallows the words of those chattering around us. I give her room, remembering when I stood beside Stu's grave for the first time. I read the engraved stone over and over as if that would make me finally believe. But the impact of losing him came at night when I crawled into bed alone, when I ate meals alone, when I wanted to tell Stu something and realized he was gone. I imagine Rae's loss was felt long ago when something happened and Elvis no longer called, no longer remained in her life. Loss, I'm beginning to understand, comes in many shapes and sizes, but the emptiness throbs with the same beat.

Those behind us grow restless, coughing, clearing throats, whispering, and edging forward. I want to give Rae the time she needs, but obviously the others want their own time with Elvis.

"Rae?" I whisper, reaching out to her. Slowly Rae turns toward me, her face a closed mask. But she reaches out and takes my hand.

♪ ♩ ♪ ♩. ♩ ♪ ♩

THE HOUSE REFLECTED the sixties and seventies in all their gaudy fashions, but the museums of Elvis memorabilia, from cars to costumes, reveal more of the man. By the time we reach the last elaborate jumpsuit, I'm thinking someone should have said, "Elvis, are you sure you want to wear this? Maybe we should rethink this." So it wouldn't surprise me if Elvis had a bust of himself commissioned, as his tastes seemed to grow more ludicrous during the years of the heavy gold jewelry and intricately beaded jumpsuits. But nothing gives me a clue as to where the bust came from.

Tired from walking, we stop for a burger and fries at an old-fashioned diner near Elvis's plane, Lisa Marie. It's more of an early dinner than a late lunch. I give Ivy several quarters for the jukebox, but she comes back and says, "It only had Elvis music."

"Well, maybe we'll hear some different tunes when we go to Sun Records this afternoon."

We decide to take the Cadillac rather than the shuttle to the historic recording studio. We take the ten-dollar tour, and I find myself standing next to the microphone used by Elvis Presley, Johnny Cash, and Jerry Lee Lewis. I wonder if Stu ever came here. Rae buys a T-shirt for Ivy and a CD of Sun's hits for the car. At this point anything is welcome if it's not Elvis.

By 5:30, I plop down into one of the chairs in our joined living area. The Elvis bust holds its own secrets as easily as Rae. I wish he could speak, tell us where he came from, where he needs to go. I remember feeling a similar desperation after Stu endured his first brain surgery. I wanted to shake him in recovery, see his eyes flutter open, talk to him again, know he was going to be okay.

"What do you want to do now?" Rae asks.

"I want to find where Elvis belongs and go home."

"I'm gonna call Dad." Ivy heads to her room and closes the door behind her.

Before the trip I searched the Internet, googled for anything relating to an Elvis bust. But I found nothing. No old newspaper articles. No conspiracy theories on a fan's

Web site. And now I don't know what else to do. "This is like looking for a needle in a haystack."

"He's a bit larger than a needle."

I start to laugh but can't summon the energy.

"I haven't been there before, but I've heard . . . Well, I think it's our only option." She settles her hands in her lap.

"What do you mean? Where?"

Rae stands and slides her bare feet back into her clunky sandals. She wears a silver bracelet around one ankle. "It's a club. Not far from here, I think. On Beale Street."

That's close to where we were earlier at Sun Records. "A club. You mean, a bar?"

"Something like that."

I hesitate, glancing at the closed door to the girl's room. "What about Ivy?"

"What about her?"

"Will they let her in?"

"Of course. You're her guardian."

"Ben's going to kill me."

"It's not a strip club. It'll be fine."

Reluctantly, but having no other suggestions, I knock on Ivy's door.

"Yeah?"

I twist the knob and peer inside. Ivy swipes her arm over her eyes. I'm not sure if she's been crying or is simply tired.

"How's your dad?" I ask.

"How should I know?" She's lounging across the bed. Her tone implies she doesn't care.

"He wasn't home?"

She shrugs. Maybe she simply needed an excuse to get away from us for a while. I can imagine what it must be like to troop around with two older women all day. Exhausting for a teenager.

"Oh. Well . . . are you okay? Your stomach still doing okay?"

"Yeah."

"Good. We're going to a club to look for clues." I think. "To find where Elvis belongs." I hope.

"Okay." But she doesn't move to get up. Her foot swings back and forth along the side of the comforter.

"Leave in five minutes?" I ask.

"Y'all go ahead. I'm gonna stay here. I'm tired."

"But—"

"I don't need a babysitter." Her tone takes on an edge.

I tread carefully. "Do you feel okay?"

"I'm not five."

"I know." I glance back at Rae. She shrugs her thin blade of a shoulder as if she's unconcerned. "We won't be long. You'll be all right here?"

She gives a heavy sigh, like she's bored.

I don't know what to say. I'm not sure what to do with a teenager anyway. Just this morning we were a team, or so I'd thought. Now I feel distanced from her. It would simplify matters if she stayed in the suite. That way I won't worry about taking a juvenile into a bar. I turn back to Rae. "How long do you think we'll be gone?"

"It's not far," Rae says.

"Okay, we'll be back in an hour . . . maybe two. Will that be all right?"

"Whatever."

"We could go to a movie after. Or maybe get ice cream."

"You don't have to entertain me."

"I know. I just thought it might be fun."

"Whatever."

"You're sure you'll be all right?"

"Positive."

"Okay. Call me on my cell if you need anything. You have the number, right?"

"Yeah." Her tone becomes huffy.

Reluctantly, I leave Ivy in the room alone while Rae and I go on an adventure of our own.

Chapter Twelve

Devil in Disguise

Steel guitar and smoke make the air in the bar fairly sizzle as we enter Double Takes. Elvis, a real flesh-and-blood sort, stands on a small stage at the front of the club, surrounded by tiny tables and ardent listeners. On a neon sign outside, the club boasts the "Best Elvis Impersonators, Better than Vegas." I check my embarrassment at the door.

At least I'm not screaming and offering the Elvis wannabe on the stage my hankie to wipe his sweat. Some other woman does that. She's obviously had too many of the drinks the male waiters—dressed in Elvis-esque jump-suits—have to offer. Although Rae is much bolder than I, I can't imagine her behaving in such a way, even with the real deal. Maybe because she wasn't so ardent, Elvis was more intrigued by her.

After being seated in a booth toward the back, I'm grateful for the distance from the stage. The impersonator looks more like the Elvis of the seventies, with thick black sideburns and rounded belly. He struts and karate-kicks in a silver-and-gold-studded white jumpsuit with white fringe dancing about him. Sweat flies with each move, making me cringe. If someone—and I don't care if it was Elvis, the Dalai Lama, or even Stu—handed me a sweat-soaked hankie, I'd hold it by the tips of my fingers and drop it in the nearest washer.

I still have too many memories of Stu hugging the toilet as I handed him washrags. And the nosebleeds . . . there were too many sodden rags, too many damp sweaty pajamas, too many horrors. Once when Stu was far into his chemo treatments, he lay on the bathroom floor and joked, "I'm goin' out like the King."

Rae touches my arm. "A different world, isn't it?"

I glance at the dark walls, flashing lights, and eager fans. "Definitely."

A wry smile touches her lips, then broadens as the waiter in a jumpsuit open to his navel arrives. We place our order and the waiter says, "Thank you. Thank you very much."

"Does this bring back memories?" I ask. Or nightmares?

"Some. Not of Elvis. The Elvis I knew . . . well, he wasn't on stage. I wasn't in this environment much. But I'd seen him on television, watched women swooning when they saw him."

I lean forward, propping my elbow on the table, my chin in my hand. "So was he worth swooning over?"

Her eyes twinkle. "He was beautiful. His eyes . . ." She sighs. "And he had a fabulous mouth. And that voice . . . well, it could melt you from the inside out."

I smile, wishing I'd had someone who had melted me that way. But I suppose Elvis was one of a kind. Not everyone had an Elvis in her life. And it didn't mean I hadn't loved. I had. Stu just wasn't a celebrity with heavy-lidded eyes, pouty mouth, and a voice to die for. But I'd loved him. I still love him and will always, with more of a real love than most of these women have an opportunity to experience with Elvis. I wonder if he ever had anyone truly love him.

Stu's life was cut as short as Elvis's. "Elvis was forty-two," he'd said. Forty-two. He'd accurately predicted his own death at the same age. Even though we hadn't had riches or an extravagant lifestyle, Stu had claimed he had no regrets at the end. I wonder if Elvis was so fortunate. Stu had died with me beside him, holding his hands, with friends and family who loved him, but no ardent fans. Elvis had died alone on his bathroom floor. The stark contrast cut me to the core.

The impersonator finishes the song with a flourish and begins what's famously known as the American Trilogy. I've heard Stu play it often on his stereo. The sweat on the tanned impersonator's skin glistens like diamonds in the spotlights.

A woman wearing a sixties-looking outfit walks around carrying a case of CDs, photographs, and memorabilia. When she stops at our table for us to peruse her wares, I ask, "Do you carry bigger souvenirs?"

"What did you have in mind, honey?" She winks.

"A bust." I keep my eyes from straying to her large, overly exposed one. "You know, of Elvis's head. Do you carry things like that?"

"No, but you might find one in a shop here on Beale Street, or even over on Elvis Presley Boulevard."

"Really? Are they common?"

"Money can get you whatever you want."

It's not the answer I'm looking for. And I doubt money can give anyone the elusive things most of us want, like love and security. Wasn't Elvis proof of that?

"Is Howie working tonight?" Rae asks.

"Howie who?"

"Restin."

"Oh . . . you mean Howard." The girl beams. "Oh, sure. You know him?"

Rae nods. "Can I send him a note backstage?"

"Sure."

Rae scribbles a note on a paper napkin. I peek at the message. It reads, "The original Devil in Disguise." Rae sends it along with a ten-dollar tip for the girl.

"Who's Howie?" I ask when the waitress has moved two tables away.

"You mean Howard?" She grins. "Many things change, yet nothing does. He's an old friend. I knew him when I lived here in Memphis. He worked for Elvis for a while."

"And what did the note mean?"

Her eyes widen.

"I'm sorry; I shouldn't have read it. But—"

She laughs, tilting back her head and letting her long hair fall in a silvery wave. "I was hell on wheels back then, and Howie was sweet on me. A year or so after I left, I wrote to Howie. It was pre-cell-phone days. Before e-mail, too. Letters went back and forth between us for a while. After

Elvis's song 'Devil in Disguise' came out, I signed my letters to Howie that way."

The lights on stage flash and swivel around in psychedelic colors. The Elvis impersonator swaggers about while singing "Rubberneckin'." Rae taps her fingers to the rhythm and laughs.

A few minutes later the busty woman comes back. She leans forward, revealing more of her cleavage than I care to see. Her eyes are fringed with what I guess are fake lashes. I wonder if everything in this place is a facade. "After the show," she says, "Howard says to come on back. Just walk around the back alley and come through the stage entrance."

Rae thanks her and sips her Coke. She sings along with the entertainer, her voice low and husky.

"I guess you were right," I say. "He does remember you." How, I wonder, could anyone, even Elvis, forget Rae?

♪♩♪♩.♩♪♩

NIGHT HAS NOT yet arrived, but the sun is setting, shadows growing longer, and the light taking on a peach hue. We walk through the alleyway, past a dumpster and several dark doorways. The thick smell of stale beer and grease surrounds us. Music pours out of doorways. Depending on where we're standing along Beale Street and what store or restaurant we're near, we can hear B. B. King, Johnny Cash, or Jerry Lee Lewis. Right now "Great Balls of Fire" rocks the air around us. Rae sings along, giving a little shimmy with her shoulders.

My nerves tighten and my heartbeat quickens. I remember Ben's story of Stu's encounter with an Elvis impersonator on a dark road, and I glance over my shoulder. I wonder if Stu was nervous or scared. Knowing him, he'd have been wired to be around anyone or anything remotely Elvis. Rae doesn't seem nervous. She never does. Her confidence amazes me. But I tighten my grip on my purse and keep close beside Rae.

"A drink, sister?" a voice from a concrete stoop beckons.

I almost jump out of my skin. "I'm sorry but—"

Rae grabs my arm and pulls me away. I glimpse a figure hunkered down behind the garbage dumpster. The rest of the way down the alley, I can hear our footsteps on the asphalt clipping along with the rapid beat of my heart.

"This is it," Rae says with confidence.

"Have you been here before?"

"No." She stumbles to a halt.

I look past her shoulder and see two persons in close conversation. They are partially hidden by a stack of crates. The man is shorter than the woman, who has long dark hair. Their low voices mingle with Jerry Lee jamming on the piano keys. Rae clears her throat, once, twice, then loud enough to wake the real Elvis from the dead.

"Hey, what's the big idea?" a gruff voice asks. The woman turns. It's then I realize that she's a he, dressed up like Priscilla Presley with a bouffant hairdo straight out of the sixties. And she, actually he, is talking with an Elvis wannabe, a skinny short guy with a wig that's tipped slightly off center.

"Excuse us," Rae says. She breezes between them to reach the door.

The alley door to Double Takes has no handle, just a place to put a key.

"If you want in," Priscilla says in a voice more suited for football huddles, "knock loud."

"Thanks," I manage.

Rae bangs on the metal door. Nothing happens. So I reach around her and pound harder, jarring the bones in my hand, in hopes the sound makes it through to the other side. Slowly the door opens with a creak and a groan.

"Yeah?" asks a woman with a voice as rough as the lines on her face. Her heavy eye makeup reminds me of the sixties before the art of blending came into vogue. "Elvis has left the building."

I laugh.

She narrows her gaze on me.

"But has Howie?" Rae asks. "We're here to see him."

"Howie?" She grunts. "Hang on." She slams the door closed and leaves us waiting in the alley with Elvis and Priscilla moving away from us. I hear Rae breathing softly next to me. I imagine all the creepy things that could happen in an alley. Once again I glance over my shoulder. "Maybe we should go—"

The door opens again, and the woman steps aside. "Come on."

Looking back, I notice Elvis and Priscilla have slipped away into the shadows.

Backstage another Elvis puffs on a cigarette and downs a beer. "You wanna autograph?"

"Oh, uh . . . thanks but . . ." I sidestep after Rae.

She moves along like she's the real Priscilla. "We're here to see Howie."

Elvis nods toward his right. "In his office."

I grab Rae's elbow and steer her in that direction. We step over cords taped to the floor. "Nowhere to Run" blares from the speakers in between the Elvis sets. When we reach a door with a sign stating "Office," Rae doesn't bother knocking. She pushes it open and steps into a small room.

"Howie, you going to keep me waiting forever?"

A low whistle escapes the man sitting behind a crowded desk. The man, who looks like an overinflated turtle, plops down a thick cigar into an Elvis ashtray and pushes his chair back from the desk. His eyes tilt down at the outside corners, and his nose hooks downward to a sharp point. "Rae! Where the blazes have you been for forty years?"

"Here and there. Mostly there." A full smile crinkles her features, revealing her age while at the same time taking years off her face.

He comes around and hugs her, lifting her off her feet. It's an intimate embrace, and I feel like an intruder. "Been too long," he says, "too long."

Rae, still smiling, moves away but pats his shoulder. He ushers her into a wooden chair and hollers out the door, "Polly, bring us a chair." He sets up a folding chair for me beside Rae. "Here you go." He sticks out a hand toward me. "Howie Restin."

"Claudia McIntosh," I say, shaking his hand.

He looks at me for a moment, sizing me. "You Rae's—"

"She's my niece," Rae interrupts.

He peers closer, studying my features. "Huh. Well, good to know you. Rae, whatever happened to—"

"We need your help, Howie," she says without preamble.

"Oh?" He squints his bloodshot eyes at me. "You Irish? You don't look Irish."

I laugh. "No. My husband was. Or someone in his family was once."

"Catholic?" he asks.

"No." I shake my head, amused by his intensity.

"Good. Don't trust Catholics. Church of Christ myself. But that's what I was raised. If it was good enough for my mama, then it's good enough for me." Then he snaps his fat, yellowed fingers. His attention shifts abruptly to Rae. "I took you to church once."

"A lot of good it did me," she laughs, "or you."

"Ah, but that's where I learned your secret."

"Secret?" I ask.

He nods, his gaze caressing Rae. "You ever sit in on one of them jam sessions with the boss?"

"A few," she says.

"I bet he ate your voice up. Why didn't you ever tour with him?"

"I don't have a gospel sound."

"You ain't black, that's for sure. But you got soul." He looks at me then. "This little lady," he waves a finger at Rae, "could sing the horn off a rhino."

"Yes," I agree. "I've recently discovered that."

"And the boss . . . man, oh man, he could really get to the soul of them gospel tunes. Still can get me right here." He thumps his fist against his chest. Then he sniffs loudly. "Have a seat, have a seat." He waves at me and returns to his desk. He plops into his own chair, almost tipping it over backwards with his weight. "You gals wanna drink or something?"

"We're fine," Rae says.

Howie rocks forward then back in his chair, clasping his hands over his large belly. "Rae. It's been ages."

"Bet you didn't expect to see me again." She grins.

"I thought you'd already gone heavenward. If I'd known you were still livin', I'd have looked you up after my divorce."

"From Glenda?"

"Polly." He sucks on the end of an unlit cigar, swirling it this way then that and making popping sounds with his lips. "Nah, Glenda and I never married. She went off with some yahoo to Nashville, wanting to sing. But I ain't never heard her on the radio, have you? No, and you're not likely to. She didn't have it. But Rae here, she could have been like Loretta Lynn or Trisha Yearwood. You was something." He waves his arm as if dismissing his own thoughts. "Nope, Polly and I hitched up after that. Had a couple of kids. But she took a shine to Rance Skye, one of our Elvises. Looks just like the boss. And I should know. But you know me, not one to hold a grudge. They both still work here. And I married Roxanne. She used to be a showgirl. We hooked up in Vegas, and she moved here. But that's enough about me."

He props his seventies-style boots on the edge of his desk. "What ever happened to you? Ol' Joe Dixon and I were tossing back a few beers not too long ago, reminiscing 'bout old times, and he asked, 'Whatever happened to Rae Picard?'"

"Not too much," she says. "I've lived a quiet life."

Howie laughs, a full-blown belly laugh. "You, quiet?"

I feel the urge to laugh with him. My aunt is anything but quiet. She walks into a room and draws attention without even speaking a word. She lives life in a big, bold way.

"I changed," she says softly. "Do you think you can help us? We're—"

He waves away her question with the flick of his wrist. Flecks of cigar ashes fall on the desk. The acrid smoke chokes me, and I swallow a cough. "You ever marry? Have kids, 'sides that one—"

"No," she says, her tone icier than normal. "I never married."

"I bet you had a few offers though." He chuckles and looks to me. "She could wrap a man around her little finger in a heartbeat. But she was always aloof. Hard to get. But which one of us didn't try? The boss woulda married you. We all thought so. After you left, we were all lookin' for you."

"Howie," she interrupts his wandering comments, "we're looking for infor—"

"Oh, sure, sure. You in trouble, darlin'? Need some money?" He plops his feet on the floor and leans forward to grab his wallet out of his back pocket. "I'm a bit low at the moment. You know how things are in the biz—flowing one minute then dry as a nun's—" He stops himself, coughs, and turns a watermelon red. "You can have what I got here."

Rae puts out a hand to stop him. "No, Howie. I don't need your money."

"Howie," I attempt, "we don't need any money, although you're very generous to offer. We simply need some information."

"This is a very delicate matter."

"Oh!" His bushy eyebrows rise. He rests his forearms on the desk. "So tell me."

"It has to do with Elvis," I venture.

"What doesn't around here?"

"We've . . . ," I decide it's best not to divulge all our secrets, "there's some memorabilia that we're trying to—"

"Yeah? When did it go missing?"

"Around 1987."

He frowns. "Well, I don't know nothin'—"

"Of course you wouldn't."

His head jerks to the side, then gives Rae a broad wink. "You wantin' to sell some memorabilia? Some pretties the boss give you? I don't handle that stuff. But I always have my ear to the ground. I know a fellow—"

"Could he tell us the value?" Rae ask.

"Oh, sure. He's honest as they come."

I squelch a laugh. Dealing with red-hot Elvis artifacts, Howie's friend couldn't be too honest.

"You 'member Baldy, Rae?"

"I don't think so."

He leans back in his chair, making it squeak and groan in protest. "Matt Franklin ring a bell?"

She makes an inarticulate sound that neither confirms nor denies.

"Well, no never mind. He's got a place across town. Here I'll write the directions."

I notice how he knows it off the top of his head. He scribbles notes onto the back of his business card that boasts five shows a day at Double Takes. "You tell him I sent you. He'll take care of you right fine. Just takin' care of business; right, doll?"

Rae takes the card. "Thank you. For everything. Especially your discretion."

"'Course. No problem. You need anything else, just come see Howie." He coughs. "Howard," he corrects himself. "It's Howard now. Roxanne thinks it makes me sound more professional. Come on in for a show anytime." He stands and rocks back on his heels, his Elvis-sized belly protruding. "I got a new Elvis comin' next week. And he's better than ol' Rance. Reminds me of the boss back in the fifties. He's young and can swivel them hips like there ain't no tomorrow." Howie does his own version of free-wheeling hips. "I'll give you both a free drink."

"It's a tempting offer." Rae gives him a quick hug and a kiss on his cheek.

He keeps an arm around Rae's waist. "The boss was upset when you left." His voice turns soft. "I figured he missed you. But I hadn't heard you'd . . ." He glances at me, then back to Rae. "Well, no never mind. Now you wanna sell some of his stuff? That's cool. A girl's gotta take what she can get. Believe me, my ex-wife took what she wanted. But whatever you got, Rae, you deserved more. You be careful, Devil."

"I'm always careful. Thank you for your discretion. Take care of yourself, Howie."

"Oh, sure, sure. Roxanne doin' a fine job of that." He pats his rounded belly. "Makes me biscuits and gravy every mornin'."

Rae gives him a gentle smile.

"Where you livin' nowadays? You ain't back in Memphis now, are you?"

"No," Rae and I say simultaneously. We glance at each

other and smile sheepishly. By the time we hit the alleyway again, we're laughing, our arms interlinked. She hugs me as the door closes behind us and laughs until her eyes glitter.

"I can't believe you knew that guy," I say.

"I've known a few characters," she says, walking beside me.

"But Howie. What a trip."

"He was not quite so humorous back in the old days. Mostly he was a good friend when I needed one."

"And now he thinks you stole stuff from Elvis?"

She shrugs. "An easy assumption. Many did. But I know the truth. As you do. That's all that matters."

♪♩♪♩.♩♪♩

IT'S GETTING LATE, later than I anticipated, when we arrive back at the Heartbreak Hotel. The lobby is like a graveyard, and I wonder if Elvis's contemporaries and fans are too old now to stay up late and party. Together Rae and I ride up in the elevator to our floor. I push the plastic key into the door, and we enter the darkened hotel suite. The noise of the television greets us. Elvis lights up the screen. He's in black leather, sitting in the midst of a screaming group of women. A few of his band sit with him on a small circular stage. He's singing "That's All Right, Mama." But Ivy isn't in the main sitting room.

"Ivy?" I call out, assuming she's in her room or bathroom. "We're back!"

"I don't know if it's safe," I say as soft as I can, so as not to disturb Ivy, "for her to go with us tomorrow. I mean this could be another club or some kind of a racket. If this guy . . . Baldy is dealing with stolen items, then it might not be safe. And I'm responsible for Ivy."

"Matt's harmless," she says. "No trouble there."

"How do you know?"

"I know him."

"You do? But I thought you told Howie—"

"It's best not to reveal too much."

"I suppose. So is this his house, you think? A club? Warehouse? What?"

"If I know Matt, then it's safe. I should have thought to go to him first. I regret I didn't. Howie will be telling everyone he knows that he saw me."

"It's okay," I say. "There is no way he could know about our problem." *My* problem. I jab my thumb in the direction of Elvis who sits on the table in the living area. My stomach coils in a hard knot. I'd expected Ivy to be watching television or talking on her phone, not sleeping. I hope she's not sick again. "I better check on Ivy."

Rae nods. "It wouldn't hurt."

I notice a red light blinking on the phone. "I think we have a message."

Sitting on the sofa, I dial into the hotel phone system to retrieve it.

"You girls having a hunka, hunka burnin' night?" Ben's voice comes through the phone. "Tried calling Ivy on her cell but couldn't get her. Just wanted to know how things are going on your search. Hope you got Elvis returned to sender." He laughs at his own joke. "Call me back."

Shaking my head at his attempts at humor, I place the receiver back on the phone's base. "Hmm."

"What's wrong?"

"Ivy didn't answer when her dad called."

"You know teenagers. The last person they want to talk to is their father."

"I guess. I just worry about her. You know?"

"Have you checked her bathroom," she lowers her voice, "for drugs?"

"No, I didn't want to be intrusive. But maybe I should."

"There's time."

I place my hands on my knees, reluctant to go snooping around like a concerned parent. I'd rather be Ivy's friend. "So when do you think we should go tomorrow? Do you think Baldy . . . Matt has regular business hours?"

"Always takin' care of business," Rae says in a thick imitation of Howie's accent."

"You're sure?"

"We can ask for directions from the concierge."

"Okay." I stand and walk to the closed door leading to Ivy's bedroom. I decide to hold off searching the bathroom. It feels too dishonest. "I better let her know what our plans are."

"I'm going to bed," Rae turns toward her own room. "Good night."

"Rae?"

She turns back toward me.

"Thank you for your help today."

"Of course."

"I don't know if we're any closer to solving this mystery, but I had fun."

"Me, too." She looks at me for a long moment, and I feel something I don't understand. If for no other reason than it's brought us closer together, I decide this trip has been good. I understand her better. And my mother as well. Yet at the same time I'm not sure I understand either of them completely. She turns and enters her bedroom, softly closing the door behind her.

Turning back toward Ivy's room, I knock on the door. I wait but there's no response. I knock again. Then louder.

Rae comes out of her bedroom. "Is there a problem?"

"I don't know." Cautiously, I open the door to Ivy's room and peer into the darkness. After my eyes adjust, I realize the bed is empty, the covers rumpled where she lay on it earlier. "Ivy?"

There's no answer.

"Ivy?" I call louder.

Rae touches my back. "She's not here?"

"Apparently not." I feel my spine stiffen as my heart slides down it, landing with a heavy thud in the pit of my stomach. "Where could she have gone?"

"Let's check the bathroom," Rae says. "No reason to panic."

But Ivy isn't in the bathroom or anywhere else in the hotel suite. And neither, we discover, is her suitcase.

Chapter Thirteen

Why Me, Lord?

"What do we do now?" A ball of panic surges up from my heart and wedges itself in my throat.

"Maybe she was hungry and went to eat." Rae's voice is a calm, soothing source of reason to hold onto. "Or to work out or swim."

Logical assumptions. Good. Yes. Let's think logically. For a moment there's a rim of light, then just as quickly it fades and my thoughts remain dark. "With her suitcase?"

"I admit that would be odd." The lines around her eyes seem deeper, or maybe it's my imagination. "But there's no reason to panic either."

My nerves snap with irritation. "Because you're not responsible for her. I am."

I begin pacing, my breath seemingly racing my footsteps in the small sitting area. Rae sits on the sofa, her ankles crossed.

"Let's think this through. We know she didn't take the car. She didn't take Elvis either."

I glance back at the bust, cloaked in shadows. I'm not sure that's a source of relief. I want to shake the bust until he tells me where Ivy has gone, what he saw and heard while we were away. As ridiculous as that sounds, I feel desperate enough to try it. I wish Stu were here. He'd know what to do. Actually, I stop myself because he wouldn't. He always said, "I don't know how Ben does it with Ivy. I wouldn't have been a good dad. Not like Ben." Disappointment rises like bile in my throat.

I wonder if Priscilla cursed Elvis for his absence when she was trying to raise Lisa Marie alone. I rub my forehead, pushing against the headache gathering behind my eyes like a storm.

"Maybe she needed more drugs," Rae suggests.

"You're not making me feel any better."

"Sorry."

"You think she'd know who to contact for something like that? I mean, a drug dealer?"

"They're not difficult to find."

I'm not sure that would be the case for me, although I have to admit I've never tried to find one. Ivy doesn't seem as inept as I am, which only pushes my concerns closer to the edge of fear.

"Or she—"

"Cell phone! I bet she took hers." I race across the room to my purse. Pushing aside the Memphis map and Graceland brochure, I fumble with a tube of lipstick, half of a leftover apple tart, a pack of gum. My hands shake. Finally, I dump the contents out on the sofa and paw through the pile until

I locate my cell phone. I arrow down the keypad where I plugged in Ben's number along with Ivy's, just in case.

Doubt gives me pause. Should I call Ben first? But what if there's a simple explanation? Tightness seizes my chest. What if there isn't? What if Ivy started to feel worse and went to the hospital? But what if she's down the hall getting ice? Taking her suitcase along? My thoughts zigzag to different possibilities. I feel trapped in indecision and confusion, fear and panic. I don't want to cause Ben worry for nothing. But I also don't want to delay seeking help when every minute might be crucial. Drawing a shaky breath, I release it with a pathetic huff of frustration.

Cursing myself for going against my better judgment and leaving Ivy in the room alone, I dial her cell phone number then wait, tapping my finger against the ear piece.

"Well?" Rae stands next to me, crossing her arms over her chest.

One ring. Two. Three. I glance toward the bathroom, closet, bedroom, hoping, wishing, praying she'll appear suddenly, mysteriously, miraculously. Four. Five. Six. Then over the line comes, "It's me." I recognize her overtly perky voice, which is not her everyday tone. "Leave a message and I'll call you back. Maybe."

Maybe.

Would she call me back? I suck in a break, hoping for the courage I lack. "Hi, Ivy," I say into the phone as cool and casual as I can manage, even though my heart pounds like U-2's drummer. "Rae and I got back from the club." I attempt a laugh that sounds fake. Rae arches an eyebrow at me. "You should have been there. You would have gotten a kick out of the Elvis impersonator. Anyway, uh, we're back at the hotel. Where'd you go? We're kind of hungry and thinking of grabbing a bite. So we'll, uh, wait for your call."

I press the *end* button and snap the phone closed. Now what? Suddenly I'm cold. Very, very cold.

"That's called putting a positive spin on things."

"We can't leave the room," I say, my thoughts frantic, my nerves tightening with every second. I chafe my arms. "What if she returns or calls?"

"But what if someone in the lobby saw her?"

"You're right." I walk toward the door, then back. Crazy, irrational thoughts swoop in on me like vultures. "Okay, you stay here. I'll run down to the front desk and check. See if anyone saw her leave." I grab my camera, which holds pictures of all of us at Graceland. I can show a picture of Ivy to the person at the front desk. This is good. Movement. Activity. A plan. Good. We'll find her. "Maybe she's at the pool. Or in the Jungle Room bar." Or not.

Fifteen minutes later I'm back in the suite. When I ask if Ivy has called, Rae answers no, the lines around her mouth definitely deeper and more strained. For the thirty-third time I check my cell phone to be sure I didn't miss her call. Nothing. No calls. No Ivy.

This time I dial her cell again, more determined and more frightened with every unanswered ring.

"Ivy," my voice quavers and I bite my lip, taste blood, "I really need you to call us. Okay?" My voice gains strength, sharpens with anger. "We need to know you're okay. So call me, okay?" Again, I repeat my cell phone number.

Clicking shut the phone, I ask, "Now what are our choices?"

"When can you call the police?"

A shiver ripples through me. "She's a minor, isn't she? I don't know. Yes, yes, she is. Anytime, I suppose. Do you think we should? I mean, do you think she's really missing? Maybe I should call her dad first.

"Oh, God." I sink into the nearest chair. "He's going to kill me. And I deserve it. What if I upset Ivy talking about her mother?" I brace my head with my hands. I would rather be dead myself than face the possibilities. "Why did I say all that to her? I should have just told Ivy to talk to her dad."

"You didn't say anything wrong. More than likely Ben's going to kill his daughter for pulling a stunt like this. That is, when we find her." She puts a warm hand on my shoulder and squeezes. "And we *will* find her."

"Where could she have gone?"

♪♩♪♩.♩♪♩

AT A QUARTER to eleven, completely out of options, I phone Ben. My nerves are a jumbled knot of possibilities and fears. How can I tell my friend, my boss, that his daughter's gone? I remember calling him the day Stu died. "Ben?" But I couldn't say more. He knew. I thought that was the worst phone call, besides calling Stu's parents. But it wasn't. This is worse. Much worse.

"Had a late night rockin' and rollin'?" Ben asks when he picks up.

"Hi," I manage before my throat closes. I look to Rae for support.

She sits beside me, takes my hand in hers. "Want me to tell him?"

I give a slight shake of my head. "Uh, Ben . . . Ivy is, uh . . ." I can't find the words, much less speak. Tears swell in my throat, choking me.

"She's not giving you a hard time is she?" he asks. When I don't answer, he says, "Put her on, I'll talk to her."

"When was the last time you did?" I ask.

"What? Talk to her? I don't know. This morning. Before y'all went to Graceland. Why?"

"Because . . . uh . . . she's not here."

"Have her call me when she gets back. Where'd she go?"

"That's the problem." I try to put my words together logically, follow the time line as I explain the situation to Ben, but things keep getting jumbled in my head. Rae corrects me a couple of times. "Ben, I think we should call the police."

There's a pause, as what I've told him sinks deep and spreads more fear. I can only hear the pounding of my heart. Ben makes no sound. No breath. No curse word. No reply.

"Ben? Are you there?"

"Okay. Okay. Yes, do that. I've got to make a couple of calls. Friends of Ivy's I want to talk to. See if they know anything. Then I'll catch the next flight to Memphis. Don't worry about picking me up at the airport. I'll rent a car. Call me on my cell when you talk to the police or if you hear from Ivy. I'll be in Memphis as fast as I can." He rattles off a list of instructions as if somewhere in his brain he's registered this emergency. But having worked for Ben for years, I know it's how he operates. He's a take-charge kind of guy.

"Okay. Um . . ."

"What?" He sounds as if fear has jump-started him with a blast of energy. My brain can hardly keep up.

"Ben, I'm . . . I'm sorry." A sob breaks in my throat. "I really am."

"It's not your fault." His tone is flat, serious, but not reassuring either. Nothing could reassure me, make me feel any better at this moment. Guilt resides squarely on my shoulders, weighs me down.

I'm responsible. I knew something was wrong. I should have said something, warned Ben, tried harder to talk to Ivy. I click *end* on my cell phone, go to the bathroom, and vomit.

♪ ♩ ♪ ♩. ♩ ♪ ♩

THE POLICE PUT out a bulletin on a missing teen, but they don't seem as concerned as we are. Ben's called me about twelve times since the first time I spoke to him, keeping me posted on his flight information and that he's been talking to a friend of Ivy's. He offers to e-mail pictures of his daughter to the police station, but the police have already downloaded pictures off my digital camera.

The police say it happens all the time. There are millions of runaways from one coast to the other. I remember hearing the same thing from others when Stu was diagnosed with cancer.

"It happens all the time," the doctor said.

"Lots of men get cancer and survive," a friend said.

"Look at Lance Armstrong," someone else suggested.

The hope their words instilled had kept me going at first. I had believed. We'd looked into drinking carrot juice and cod liver oil and envisioning a blue healing light inside Stu's body devouring the cancer cells like Pac-Man one by one. I'd believed as best I could. But maybe I hadn't believed enough; maybe my lack of faith failed Stu. I scrambled for something, anything, to believe. To avoid falling into a depression, I stayed busy. But the months dragged on, first one surgery then another. Stu grew weaker with each chemo treatment, and the doctor's words became more dire. What little hope I had left withered.

So now I find it hard to believe we can find Ivy easily, quickly, safely. It's better to face it from the beginning than to believe, to hope, and be slammed with reality later on. Accept things. Handle it.

But it's harder to control my emotions, knowing I'm at fault.

I stare at Elvis and think of Stu lying in the satin-lined casket, the white roses rounding over the base eliciting a sickly sweet scent, and I picture Ivy there. Too young. Lost forever.

Chapter Fourteen

I Feel So Bad

Armed with pictures of his daughter, Ben arrives at the hotel at 7:30 the next morning. He spent half the night at the airport and took the first flight available.

"Ben," I hug him close. "I'm so—"

With a tight squeeze he stops any apologies or excuses, lame though they might be. When he releases me, his eyes are red rimmed. Fatigue stretches his features. "The first thing I want to do is talk to the police."

"They discovered Ivy took the last shuttle to the Sun Records Studio tour last night. Right after we left her for Double Takes."

"What's over there?" Ben asks.

"Not much," Rae answers. "We took the tour yesterday, and I don't think she went back for a second look."

"Then what?"

"It's not a far walk to Beale Street."

"What's on Beale Street?"

"A jumpin' place at night. Bars—"

"There's a mall not far from there with lots of shopping."

"Perfect for a teenager," Rae adds.

Ben's frown deepens. "I think we should split up and start searching the area, showing her picture around to the shops and stores. Somebody had to see her."

"That's a good idea. But what did her friends say? Did you talk to them before you left?"

"I spent over an hour at Kerry's house. She and Ivy have been friends since third grade. She wouldn't say anything at first, not wanting to betray Ivy. But she finally told me Ivy wants to find her mom."

"Her mom?" My knees feel weak, and I sit on the sofa.

"When I went home," Ben says, "I started digging through her room. I found a letter from Gwen—"

"Ivy's mom," I explain for Rae. "When did she—"

"After Gwen left, she wrote me a letter. I'd hidden it in my desk drawer and forgotten about it. But I guess Ivy found it. The return address was Memphis."

"So that's why she was so eager to come on this trip."

"And could explain the car sickness," Rae says.

"What?" Ben asks.

"She could have been nervous about this reunion she was cooking up with her mother," Rae suggests.

"What did the letter say?" I ask.

"Not much." Ben rubs the bridge of his nose. "Gwen wasn't much of a writer. And she didn't want to say why she left. Why she wouldn't come back. I guess I'm glad for that now, for Ivy's sake. She just said she couldn't handle it, couldn't be a mother."

"How awful," Rae breathes.

"Poor Ivy." I reach sideways for a solid form, needing Stu's strength. It's something I've always done, reach out in my sleep for him, reach out when I need reassurance. But my hand touches cool plaster. It's Elvis, not Stu. Anger thrums inside me. If Stu hadn't sent us on this wild goose chase, then I wouldn't have taken Ivy away from her dad. And I wouldn't be responsible for her disappearance. She wouldn't be on the streets alone. Lost. Maybe even . . .

"Can you imagine what Ivy must think? That her mother didn't want to be a mother to her. That it's her fault!" I understand how it feels to be emotionally abandoned by a mother, separated by death from a spouse. Neither brushed me aside on purpose, yet the loss is the same. But I also know all too well how guilt eats away at the soul.

"Not to mention if she knows the truth." Ben curses.

I lift an eyebrow in question. But when he doesn't answer, I ask, "What do you mean?"

"Doesn't matter now. But I was wrong. This is all my fault. I should have told her. I should have—"

I reach toward him, wanting to help but not knowing what to say or do.

"We've got to find her."

"Could Ivy's mom still be here in Memphis?" I ask.

His jaw tightens. "No."

"We should tell the police. Just in case."

Rae looks at me, then back to Ben. "Do you know where her mother is?"

"Yes." His answer sounds curt.

"Do you think she'd meet with Ivy?" I ask. "Maybe you should call—"

"No." His word slams the door on that idea.

"Did you ask Ivy's friend, this Kerry, if Ivy was having any other problems?" Rae asks.

"What do you mean?"

I try to stop Rae with a slight shake of my head. I suspect where she's headed. "Rae . . ."

"What is it?" Ben's voice sounds tight.

"Does she have a boyfriend?" Rae asks. "Has she used drugs?"

"Drugs?"

"Rae!"

"It's a possibility." She looks pointedly at me.

I gulp, feel the weight of Ben's stare. "We don't know that for a fact."

"Forget it." Ben grabs the door handle, then turns back to face us. "My daughter is not a drug addict. She's an A—okay, B student. Now are you going to help me find her?"

I glance at Rae. Without another word we go in search of a hurting young woman in need of a mother.

♪ ♩ ♪ ♩. ♩ ♪ ♩

WE SPLIT UP, checking in by cell phone periodically, and spend the day traipsing up and down Beale Street. The sidewalk is uneven and awkward, perfect if you're drunk and off-kilter but not so great if you're stone sober and in a hurry. I've tripped more times than I care to admit today. Music spills out of doorways. Each building is playing a different song. It's like walking through a life-size jukebox, the songs changing constantly.

Anyone I see, I show them a picture of Ivy. Sad,

curious, and concerned eyes meet mine. I hand them a flyer with Ivy's picture that Rae thought to have made up and move on to the next pedestrian or shop.

Pushing noon I find Ben near Dyer's, a famous burger joint that boasts of using the same grease year after year. He's speaking with the police, and I wait until he's through. "Any news?"

"None." His fatigue has turned into a haunted look. "Where could she be?"

"Have you eaten?"

He looks at me like I've just asked him if he wants to dance.

"Come on," I take his arm and drag him into the burger joint, which smells of smoke and grease. The floor is sticky, as if someone spilled a soda on the brick-red tile. "If you fall over, it won't do Ivy any good."

He frowns at me. "I'm fine."

"Well, I'm hungry." But I'm not. I think putting a bite of anything in my mouth will be like swallowing rocks. I hand Ben a menu and push him into an open booth. He pushes his arm outward, then toward himself, squinting down at the tiny words.

"Do you just want a burger?" I ask.

"Whatever," he sounds like his daughter and tosses the menu to the side. I order us both burgers, fries, and Cokes. When I put my wallet back in my purse, I realize Ben is staring out the plate-glass windows toward the street. I can only guess what he's thinking. Probably running through the possibilities the police began checking: the Peabody mall, twenty-four-hour restaurants, highways for hitchhiking, the airport, bus stations, hospitals . . .

"What?" he says when I put my hand on his arm and give him a straw. "Oh, here. Let me . . ." He reaches for his wallet.

"It's taken care of." I push my straw into an icy drink and notice he's still holding his. I unwrap the straw for him and stick it in his cup. The cold drink tastes good. "It must be pushing a hundred degrees out there."

"Where's Rae?"

"She walked over to the mall."

Ben glances toward the door. "I don't have time—"

"Yes, you do. Collapsing on the sidewalk from heat exhaustion and starvation won't help Ivy. You need your strength."

He's staring at nothing, his gaze distant. "Ben? You okay?"

He nods. "I was praying."

I wonder why I hadn't thought of that. But then I know the reason: Prayer didn't work with Stu.

When our burgers are served, Ben eats as if on autopilot. The greasy meat lands like a boulder in my stomach. But I force-feed myself in hopes Ben will keep eating. He pushes his plate away first, half a burger and most of his fries left.

"I should have talked to her. Like you said."

"Ben," I put my hand on his arm, feel my throat tightening, "you can't beat yourself up over that. You'll have that talk when we find her."

"What if we don't?" His Adam's apple works up and down as he fights the emotions that threaten to overwhelm us all.

I slide out of the booth, around the end of the table, and onto his bench. "Hey," I put an arm around his broad shoulders, "we're going to find her. You've got to believe."

"Is that what you told Stu?" he asks.

Guilty, I look away, stare at the paper napkin he threw on the table. The truth lodges in my throat.

"Do you really believe it?"

Shifting, I wrap my arms around him. He lays his head against my shoulder. We sit that way for a minute or two, then his arms tighten. It feels as if he might squeeze the life out of me.

I remember being in the hospital waiting room, watching other patients' family members pace and make phone calls. Ben sat beside me. When the doctor came in wearing his scrubs, Ben stood, but I couldn't. The doctor knelt in front of me, told me Stu had made it through the surgery but that he couldn't be sure he'd gotten all of the tumor. Right beside me, Ben was there. I hadn't felt it then, but I remember now his arm was around my shoulders holding me together. And so I hold onto him now, trying to be strong for him.

But all my doubts and fears, all the possibilities, darken my thoughts. I knew after that last surgery that Stu couldn't fight off the cancer that so wanted to eat him alive. I knew. And yet I'd said, "You can beat this." I'd tried to be positive. I'd lied. Because deep inside I remembered the doctor saying, "We couldn't get it all." Those optimistic lies choke me now.

The sounds of the burger joint creep into my conscious thoughts, and suddenly I'm aware of others glancing at us. My arms tighten around Ben's shoulders. I want to shield him from the pain I felt when I lost Stu, when I lost my own child.

Maybe that's how Mother felt when I lost my baby. Did she remember how her own heart broke? Did she try normalcy to fend off the dark waves of depression that threatened to pull me under?

Feeling Ben's heat press into me, I smooth my hands over his shoulders and back. The hair at his nape is soft, curling at the ends. It's been a long time since I felt a man's arms around me. I feel the muscles along his back, the dampness of sweat. His scent is a mixture of lingering soap and the heat of the sun. I notice his neck is sunburned and remind myself to buy sunscreen for all of us braving the heat of the day.

"It's true what they say," Ben pulls away, sniffs, pulls himself together.

"What's that?"

"You never walk alone."

Even though I've felt alone in my own grief, I realize others—Ben, Rae—have been there with me. "That's right. I'm here."

A wry smile tilts the corner of his mouth. "I know. But I meant God. I feel His presence in this."

A knot tightens around my throat, choking off any response.

Ben swipes his hand over his face. Then together we leave the shop, separating in search of his daughter.

♪ ♩ ♪ ♩. ♩ ♪ ♩

ABOUT THREE O'CLOCK I hand a Japanese couple a flyer about Ivy, then enter a souvenir shop. In the window are coffee mugs with Elvis's face on all sides, a Russian matryoshka doll in Elvis's likeness, a ceramic frog with a pompadour and leather jacket, foot-tall busts of B. B. King, even Elvis and Priscilla salt and pepper shakers. In the corner a small bust of Elvis catches my eye. Its similarities to the one in our hotel room cannot be ignored.

Johnny Cash sings "Walk the Line" as I enter the open door. The store smells musty. Along one wall are old magazines, newspapers, and record albums. Covering the walls are posters of the young, svelte, hip-swinging Elvis in a suit right alongside those of the weight-battling Elvis in a form-fitting jumpsuit. A rotating display case holds a wide assortment of Elvis-styled shades. I should have brought some of Stu's souvenirs and sold them here. Maybe at least I could get an idea about what some of his things are worth. Stu has a pair of sunglasses the King himself supposedly wore.

Waiting for the clerk, I glance at a record from the movie *Roustabout* with a whopping price attached. My mouth actually drops open. Blinking, I look again and shake my head in disbelief. I consider taking pictures of Stu's souvenirs and posting them on eBay to sell.

"Looking for something specific?"

I turn toward a woman with an Aunt Bee hairdo. "Actually, I'm searching for a young girl. A teenager. Her name's Ivy." I show her a picture. "She's been missing since last night. Have you seen her?"

The woman studies the picture carefully. Most people only glance at the picture and turn away, not wanting to get involved. Or else they start asking nosy questions. But this woman really looks at the picture as if she's memorizing Ivy's features. Hope billows inside me as if a wind of change has taken hold. I hold my breath and wait.

"Sorry. I'm pretty good at faces, but I haven't seen her. I know a gal who's psychic if you're interested."

"I'll let you know." I'm desperate but not that desperate. Not yet anyway. But if we decide to hire a psychic to find Ivy, maybe the psychic would give us a two-for-one deal and lead us to the owner of the Elvis bust.

I notice a rotating stand with reading glasses perched on little spiky arms. Smiling to myself, I pick up a pair that has tiny red fake stones spelling out "Elvis" across the top and buy them for Ben.

"I'll post that picture in my window with the girl's description if you want," the woman suggests, "and I'll keep an eye out for her."

"I'd appreciate that." I turn toward the door, purchase in hand, but pause when I see the small replica Elvis bust looking out the store window. This bust has Elvis wearing a blue jumpsuit, not white like the one Stu found. "Excuse me?" I glance at my watch, knowing I should keep moving. The more people I talk to about Ivy, the better. But I have to know about the bust. "Could you tell me about that bust in the window?"

"Which one? B. B? I get lots of requests for that one. And the frog."

"Elvis. In the corner."

"That's my favorite." The woman smiles proudly. "It's a copy."

"Really? Of a famous one?" Interested, I walk across the store to take a closer look.

"Elvis. You've heard of him?"

I try to get a read on her if she's joking with me or serious. "I think I have heard of him. Singer, right?"

"Oh, an actor, too." She laughs and lovingly caresses the top of Elvis's head. "They're really a dime a dozen. You can find them most anywhere. They don't make too many anymore. Not in much of a demand."

"No one wants Elvis on their coffee table?"

"I suppose. Folks buy them more for gag gifts nowadays."

"I'm sure." Is that what the bust is from Stu? A gag gift?

"There was a rumor way back that the ghost of Elvis had been seen stealing old souvenirs like this. People will believe anything."

This from a woman who believes in psychics. But I've been desperate enough to believe in the unbelievable. And now I see that desperation in Ben. "Yes, they will." I need to get back out on the streets. "Well, thanks."

"Sure thing. Good luck finding that girl." She waves the flyer of Ivy. "You know . . ."

I pause at the door. "What?"

"There's a chapel near here. Friends of mine own it. Real nice folks. Down-home, you know? They mean well anyway. Their doors are open 24/7. They've offered help to the homeless and destitute. Just good folks wantin' to help those down on their luck. Lord knows there are enough of those to go around."

I nod, thinking it's worth a shot, wondering if Ivy would go into a church.

"They got it all decked out with Elvis stuff. Play his music day and night, too. Not the rock or country stuff, just the pure gospel. Gospel is the only music Elvis won a Grammy for, don't you know?

"And where did you say this place is?"

"Oh, it's just down the block. Turn right on Third

Street and you can't miss it. Right there. Like I said, it's open day and night. Faithland Chapel."

"Faithland?" My heart skids to a halt. Stu wrote "Faithland" in his note to me. Maybe it wasn't a mistake. Maybe he meant Faithland, not Graceland.

"Well, I wish you luck. I'll be praying that girl's safe. And if you wanna call my friend the psychic—"

"Thanks," I say with a wave as I rush out the door. Reaching for my cell phone, I head in the direction of the chapel. I redial Ben's number. "Any news?" I ask when he answers. "There's a chance—"

"I'm at a place called Faithland. Ring any bells?"

"Yeah. I just heard—"

"Get here. Fast."

Chapter Fifteen

Crying in the Chapel

I call Rae's cell phone and explain where to meet us at the chapel. The wood-and-stone chapel is squeezed among dilapidated buildings and blues bars. A stained-glass window depicts a man kneeling in a church, crying.

From the street, Elvis's "Crying in the Chapel" competes with Jerry Lee Lewis's "Whole Lotta Shakin' Goin' On." Radio stations played the heartbreaking tune incessantly the week Elvis died. Only thirteen at the time, I wished they'd played something, anything else, especially by Andy Gibb. Stu asked for the same depressing song to be played during his funeral. I agreed but refused to listen. Instead I played my own version of "The Hustle" loud inside my head to keep from curling up on the church pew and covering my ears. I realize now there are a lot of things I did for Stu, things that made me uncomfortable, things he wanted. Was that how it was? Me bending my needs to meet his?

A carved stone above the arched doorway displays the name of the chapel. Faithland. I never imagined it was an actual place. I thought it was just another mix-up in Stu's failing recall.

Could Ivy have come here? Stumbled onto this place? Recognized the name from Stu's note? I draw a steadying breath, swipe the sweat off my brow with my forearm. My skin feels grainy. I heave open the heavy door.

"I'm calling the police right now!" Ben is punching numbers into his cell phone.

"Sir, please!" An older man, with his hair pulled back in a gray pony tail, tries to calm him. "Listen to me."

"Ben?"

His gaze swerves toward me. His eyes widen with fear, anger, disbelief. "She's here! They so much as admitted it. But they won't let me see her. My own daughter!"

"Did they say why?" I place a hand on Ben's arm, feel the tension in his taut muscles, the heat of panic on his skin. "Hello," I say to the older man who's wearing jeans and an Elvis T-shirt. "I'm Claudia."

"Guy Larson." He holds out a hand. His handshake is firm, his palm callused. Light from the variegated windows splotches his face with unexpected colors, but his expression seems open and friendly.

"His wife's back there with Ivy, but the door's locked!"

"It's our safety precaution," Guy explains. "Sometimes we get women who've been abused. They need a safe place from—"

"I have not been abusing my daughter!" Ben yells, his voice filled with rage like he might start abusing some latent hippy any minute.

"Ben, he didn't accuse you of that. It's a precaution. It's for Ivy's protection, too."

"Yes," Guy says, "you can call the cops. We've already spoken with them. We've worked with them many times with runaways. They were about to contact you when you burst in here."

My gaze shifts toward the front of the chapel, and my breath catches in my lungs. It's just as I imagined it would be. At the front of the chapel sits a shrine with silk flowers in the shape of a guitar. A deep-set impression in the wall arcs like the stained-glass windows in front. A pedestal holds the place of honor. It's empty, yet large enough to hold an Elvis bust.

"Of course, it's just a precaution," Guy says, picking up on my comment. "Myrtle, my wife, is makin' sure your daughter is okay. We wanna know she ain't gonna run again. We don't want her goin' anywhere. She's safe here. We're gonna get all this straightened out and get her the help she needs. You're gonna have to trust me, sir."

"*Why* would I do that?"

"Because you don't have a choice." His frank, open manner is disarming. "Now if you want me to call the cops on you, sir . . ."

Ben steps back, but the tautness remains. His cell phone rings. He answers, speaking tersely into the receiver. "Okay. I understand." When he disconnects the call, he looks drained. "That was Detective Berringer. He said you've handled these situations before."

Guy nods.

"You better know what you're doing."

The door near the raised dais opens, and a woman with

short, spiky red hair enters the chapel. She's wearing a tight-fitting white shirt and snug jeans on her overly curvaceous body.

"Now don't you worry, Daddy-o." Myrtle, I guess, waves her hand as if shooing a lazy fly. "We're doing just fine back here. Just fine. Ivy's calm now. I actually got her to eat a little something." She winks and smiles, showing a gold eye tooth. "Popcorn. Works like a charm with teenagers." She sees me and stops. "Are you mama bear?"

"No, just a friend."

"How-do. I'm Myrtle."

"Claudia. Could I see Ivy?"

"Not right now." Her answer is firm.

The front door opens, and we all turn as Rae breezes inside, her hair loose around her shoulders in a carefree way. "You found her?"

I nod and make quick introductions. Focusing on Myrtle, I ask, "How is she?"

"Oh, she's better. She was a pure mess last night. But she managed to sleep a little this morning. She wouldn't tell us who she was or where she come from. That's why we hadn't contacted you personally. Besides, we always contact the police. They know us. When these things happen, and they have many a time, we like to make sure our guests are safe and comfortable first. Then we try to find out what has happened to cause them to run away. Sometimes they're a bit reluctant to say. Sometimes they're more open, desperate to talk."

"And Ivy?" Rae asks. "Was she reticent?"

"Actually no. She's very open about her situation." She waves her hand toward the pews lining the chapel. "Why don't we all have a seat?"

"I want to see my daughter."

"Of course you do, Mr. Moore." She pats his arm. Ben's frown deepens. "And you will. You will." She moves toward the front pew and sits on the front step leading up to the altar and empty shrine.

I want to ask about the pedestal, what went there, if it was an Elvis bust, but I don't dare. Ivy is more important than the Elvis bust. Still, I can't help staring at the blank, empty spot that reminds me of the hole Stu left in my life. I suppose Ivy feels the same hole in her own life, the one her mother left behind.

"Mr. Moore," Myrtle says, "Why don't you tell us what's been happening with Ivy lately?"

Ben slumps in his seat, seeming deflated. "I don't know." He taps his thumbs together between his knees. "I really don't. For so long it's just been Ivy and me. Her mom left when she was three." He shrugs. "And I thought we were doing okay. You know?"

He looks first to Myrtle, then to me, as if seeking confirmation. I offer him an encouraging smile.

"I'm sure things were just fine," Myrtle's voice soothes like a hot cup of tea. "But Ivy's growing into a woman. When did you first notice some changes?"

"About six months ago. Her grades started to slip. She became kind of sullen. Not as talkative as she used to be."

Rae nods as if she suspected as much, and I can almost hear her thinking, *Drugs*. Or is that my mother speaking inside my head?

Myrtle listens, her head tilted to the side as if she's heard it a thousand times before—not in a jaded, callous way, but knowledgeable. "Yes, yes."

"When this trip came up, I thought it might do Ivy some good. To get away from me for a while, to be around other women, you know, mature women who might be maternal toward her."

"Very solid thinking," Myrtle says.

"But I'm just a dad. I don't know anything." He pulls an envelope out of his hip pocket and unfolds it. Age has yellowed it. He turns it over in his hands. "Then I find out she's wanting to see her mom. I thought I handled all that the right way. Years ago the counselor said to wait until she was old enough to understand about her mom. But . . . ," he rakes his fingers through his hair, "she's been impossible to talk to lately.

"What's going on?" He leans forward, bracing his forearms on his thighs. His eyes darken and his gaze shifts sideways toward me, then Rae. Finally he looks back at Myrtle. "Is it drugs?" His voice is almost inaudible. He drags his fingers through his thick, wavy hair, leaving tracks like unanswered questions. "God, what did I do wrong?" Then his head snaps upright. "She had a boyfriend. Could he have gotten her to use cocaine or—"

"I don't know," Myrtle says. "We asked her about drugs and she denied taking, smoking, or snorting anything. I even searched her bags when she was asleep. I hate to do that, but we have to be careful, too. Can't have illegal drugs on the premises, you know. Besides, if it is an addiction, then we can only do so much. She'd need professional help. But I think you're right, Mr. Moore. Ivy needs a mother. She's a young woman with a lot of questions right now. She's needs that maternal guidance."

"Which she didn't find with us," I say, feeling guilty and helpless.

"Now I wouldn't say that," Myrtle tsks. "I'm sure you did the best you could. What Ivy wants is her real mother. Her own. Not a substitute. She said she looked in the phone book but couldn't find her. She called directory assistance—"

"Her mother's dead," Ben states matter-of-factly.

It feels as if Ben's words suck all the air from my lungs. "What? Gwen?"

Ben and Gwen married not long after Stu and I. We'd talked many times about wedding things—flowers, rings, mothers-in-laws. I remember sitting in the church, watching them take their vows. Stu stood next to Ben, supporting his friend the way Ben had weeks earlier championed Stu during our wedding. Together we rejoiced with them when Gwen became pregnant. We visited baby Ivy in the hospital the day she arrived.

When Gwen left their little family, we grieved with Ben, feeling resentful and betrayed ourselves as if she'd duped us all. We asked all the same questions, starting with *why*. But I'd always imagined her living somewhere alone, maybe, or starting another family, pursuing some dream. I never thought, believed, or hoped for her death.

Hearing Ben say it now feels like a rebreak of an old injury, the throbbing pain more penetrating, the bruises fresh and swelling, the anger screaming inside my head. I can barely speak when I ask, "When?"

"The year after she left. I–I didn't say anything because she was gone already. And I thought it would be harder. It was hard enough. I couldn't talk about it. But Stu knew."

"He did?" Once again I feel outside the loop, oblivious of the undercurrents sweeping around all of us. Why did Stu keep the secret from me?

"Then," he says, "I simply blocked it out. Ivy was too young to know. I knew someday I'd have to tell her. We'd have to talk about it. But I waited—I guess too long."

I touch his arm, trying to understand, suspecting how painful it must have been, the deep resonance of his loss. He'd dealt with it alone. Tears press against my eyes. "I'm so sorry, Ben. So sorry."

Words feel inadequate, but Ben accepts them.

"What happened?" Rae asks.

Ben leans back, his shoulders look weighted down with exhaustion and worry. "She killed herself."

I slump suddenly back against the pew. Tears spill over. Now I understand. Or think I do. Had shame kept Ben silent? Regret? Guilt? Sorrow so deep it couldn't find words? "Oh, Ben."

Moving toward him, I wrap my arms around his shoulders. He puts a hand on my waist. He doesn't turn toward me, but he doesn't turn away either. It's as if he doesn't need the comfort, but he offers what he can to me, as if he's tried to shelter all of us from this news.

"Ben, I'm so sorry. I don't know what to say."

"There isn't anything to say." He lifts a shoulder, not suggesting he doesn't care, just an uncomfortable shrug that no words can convey. "She wasn't happy. And I couldn't make her so. She left because she was lost. I think it ate her up even more. But she couldn't find her way back emotionally. So she ended it all. I couldn't tell Ivy."

"Of course not. I understand."

"She'll have to know now," Myrtle says.

"I don't know how I'll tell her."

I can't speak for the tears clogging my throat. Laying my

head against his shoulder, I offer the only comfort I have—warmth and closeness. I remember Gwen fretting over her wedding dress. "Is it beautiful? Will Ben like it? How do you know Stu really loves you?" Her words float back to me.

Was her insecurity her undoing? Did Ben make her feel unloved? I can't imagine that, although I don't know what went on between them behind closed doors. But I remember how Ben looked at her with eyes shining, how he would watch for her when we would meet after work at a restaurant, saving a seat beside him, uneasy until she arrived. Even during all these years suffering her absence, he kept any disparaging comments to himself. I realize there are no answers for the questions churning inside me.

"Ivy has something pretty difficult to tell you, too," Myrtle says, interrupting our quiet grief.

Ben stiffens. "What?"

"She's scared. It's one of the reasons she ran away. Why she needed her mother. She was scared how you'd react. She didn't know what else to do."

"She's pregnant," Rae says.

Her words fill the room like a loud heartbeat.

"Yes." Myrtle confirms.

Silence descends on the chapel like a prayer. I don't know what to say or feel. Then Ben erupts. He jumps up from the pew and spews language I've never heard Ben use, much less in a chapel.

"Ben!" I reach for his arm.

Myrtle waves me back. She watches him, not flinching at his words. Maybe she's wise to let him blow all his anger now. Better than in front of Ivy, which would not do any good.

"How old is Ivy?" Rae asks when Ben, mottled face and sweating, sits back down as if he has no steam left.

"Fifteen," I answer.

Ben leans forward, resting his elbows on his knees and holding his head in his hands. He looks defeated, the way Stu looked when the doctor told him to contact hospice, that there was nothing else to be done for him. My throat tightens with words I want to say, should have said, but they can't get through. Finally I put my arms around Ben again and just hold on tight. He did the same for me when Stu died. Then I hadn't known who was holding whom together. But I suspect now he doesn't need me.

Ivy's news is not tragic, not like a death. I believe Ben knows that. But for a father it is the death of his hopes and dreams. Life will never be the same or as simple again. But has it ever been simple for Ben?

Knowing Ivy is pregnant answers a lot of questions Rae and I asked during the drive to Memphis. It explains her acute car sickness that never stopped, her mood swings, and her sudden yearning to find her mother. Did she seek the answers to the questions that haunt her, answers that might help her make the right decision concerning her baby?

"It happens all the time," Myrtle says. "It's not the end of the world. Things can be done if she's not too far along. Although we don't promote that here. We like to preserve the sanctity of life. There are no mistakes, we believe, only consequences. And so, there are choices she can make. There's no stigma these days."

She continues talking about young girls raising their own babies, adoption, and so many other things that make my head feel woozy. I know Ben isn't hearing any of it. He's in his own dark world of grief, a place I know well.

"College," he says in a rough voice. "She was supposed to go to college. She had good grades . . . such potential."

Myrtle moves with lightning speed and kneels down in front of Ben, her hand on his knee. "Now you listen here, mister. She still has plenty of potential. She's a very smart girl. And she can still go to college. This is a little detour on that path. This doesn't have to change anything. Especially the way you feel about her."

Ben bristles. "What do you mean?"

"Your daughter is back there, terrified that you will hate her, disown her."

"She's all I have."

"Then she needs to hear that from you. Not all that filth you were tossing out earlier."

His eyes widen, as if he's suddenly seeing he's in a place of worship. Elvis decorations aside, it's still a house of God. "I'm sorry. I shouldn't have—"

"You should. And it's perfectly justified. You've had quite a shock. That's why I didn't stop you. You need to get it out, not stuff it in." She looks at the rest of us. "Bad for the heart and indigestion to stuff emotions, you know." She peers up into Ben's face. "Don't let her hear or see it. She needs your support. She needs your love."

"I don't know if I can."

"Why? Because you're angry? Embarrassed? Morally discombobulated?"

"What if I don't have what it takes? What she needs? I mean, I haven't been much of a father up to now. Isn't that how we got here?"

"Ben!" I slap his shoulder in rebuke. "You have been an adoring father, supportive, loving. Not permissive. I've watched you from the time Ivy was born, and you've done a great job. These things happen to girls from broken homes, to girls from all walks of life. To my own mother!" Reality sinks into me. "No matter their economic status, no matter their family background. Mistakes—"

"Ah-ah," Myrtle waves her finger at me. "No mistakes. Consequences. She made a choice. A choice to be intimate with a young man. How many of us can boast we haven't done that? None of us are any better, none of us any worse. Just a choice. The Bible don't say anything bad against loving somebody. Who was it, honey?" She turns to Guy who's been leaning against the white grand piano and watching the whole scene dispassionately. "Who was against foolin' around?"

"I believe it was the apostle Paul."

"Yes. Good advice, that's for sure. I mean, diseases, unwanted pregnancies, all sorts of problems. But it happens. Has since the beginning of time. And we all know that's true."

"Elvis didn't invent it," Guy says with a chuckle. "Sex, I mean. Although there were plenty of pastors and parents who acted like he did back in the fifties. Said he'd put sex in the mind of all those young innocents. But the fact is, the good Lord made us with all those surgin' hormones."

"That's right," Myrtle pipes in. "So we don't promote sex before marriage, but we don't condemn it either. But heavens, it certainly complicates matters when it ain't done God's way."

Once again the room grows quiet except for some piped-in Elvis music—the King singing "Amazing Grace."

I hadn't noticed the music until now. It has a soothing quality and somehow makes the chapel complete.

Ben nods, as if resigned, as if he's tidying up his emotions like tightening shoelaces on his running shoes.

"I had a baby when I was nineteen," Rae says.

No one speaks, but all eyes turn slowly toward her once again. She lifts her chin a notch as if challenging anyone to condemn her for it. I wonder if anyone had.

"You weren't married?" Ben asks.

"No."

"What did you do?"

She met his gaze without shame or remorse. It's then I realize her own experience helped her piece together Ivy's mysterious behavior. "I had the baby. But I gave her up for adoption. Then I tried to put my life back together."

I want to ask if that was what she'd been running from, the memories, the pain, but I decide to wait until later. If it's the reason, it won't help Ben to know that now.

"I didn't tell you for the shock value," Rae says, "or for sympathy. I just wanted you to know it happens and life goes on."

"It's all about life," Myrtle says.

Ben leans back. "So now what? What do we do?"

"I need to talk to Ivy again. Tell her you know the truth, that you love her, and convince her to come out."

"Will she?" He looks hollow eyed, shaken but steady. This is a serious blow to him, but he's survived worse. I've only now realized how much worse.

"I don't know," Myrtle says.

Chapter Sixteen

You'll Never Walk Alone

The track of Elvis spirituals loops around again. I'm growing weary of "Crying in the Chapel." But there isn't much to do but wait and hope.

I bought an assortment of sodas for everyone at a nearby general store, along with cookies and chips, and brought them back to the chapel. It's given me something useful to do. But now it gives me something to hang onto while we wait.

Ben paces the floor. Rae tinkers at the piano. I sit in a pew, wondering and thinking through the surprising things I've learned about my friends and family over the past two days. What next?

"What are you doing?" Rae asks, looking at my hand.

I realize I'm tapping on the top of my Coke can, way over the three-time requirement. "Sorry."

"Why do you do that? The tapping thing?" she asks.

"It's supposed to keep it from spewing Coke all over the place."

Ben stops his pacing and looks at me.

"It works," I say, defensive.

"Who told you that?" he asks.

"Stu. He said it diffused—"

"Figures."

Is the tapping another practical joke courtesy of Stu? I sigh and pop the lid on the can. Bubbles spill up and over the top. As fast as I can, I slurp them down and manage to avoid a mess on the red carpet of the chapel.

Shaking her head, Rae turns back to play the piano, her fingers moving agilely over the keys. The irony strikes me then that Rae had a baby out of wedlock and my own mother got married because of a pregnancy that ended too early. I wonder what it would have been like to grow up with an older brother or sister. What would it be like to have a sibling in my life now? Would it have changed anything? My personality? Would it make my life, especially life without Stu, easier? No. But it might have eased the loss of my parents. But my one sibling did not survive the womb, so it's a moot point. But somewhere I have a cousin. In Oregon? California? New York? Here in Memphis even? I wonder if Rae knows where her child is.

The tinkering of the piano keys draws my attention. I wonder if Rae felt the same way, ill equipped to care for someone else. Did that help her give her baby to another family?

I watch her back, so straight as she sits at the piano, toying with the keys. Age has crept into her silvery hair and formed graceful lines around her features. She's younger than my mother but is now at the age when my mother died.

"You play?" Guy asks Rae, leaning on the white piano.

"Not much. Not anymore." With her pointer finger she picks out a tune that sounds familiar but which I can't place. "When did you open this chapel?"

"'Round seventy-nine," he says.

She nods and keeps playing, her fingers moving rhythmically and skillfully over the keys. Occasionally she hesitates, as if trying to remember the notes. "I lived in Memphis in the early sixties . . . but haven't been back since."

"We were here then, too. Fact is, Myrtle grew up here. I'm from Georgia. Things have changed since the sixties. Then again, not so much."

She smiles an obscure remembering smile, like she's caught in her own memories. "I know what you mean. What made you want to open a chapel with an Elvis motif?"

"Well, I knew him. See?"

She misses a note but recovers.

"Myrtie and I knew Elvis, knew he was hurtin', but there wasn't much could be done. We couldn't help him. When he died, it affected me deeply. I wanted to be a help to others who are hurtin', to do something. I figured there were a lot of folks out in the world that had lost their way, needed help finding their way back to faith, to believe its yours for the taking. So we just decided one day."

Rae smiles with her lips closed, still listening, still fooling with the keys.

"Kickin' around names, of course we thought of Graceland."

"But that's already been taken."

He laughs. "Sure, sure. But it wasn't about grace. The grace was already there. Folks, I figured, needed faith, to find their faith again. You gotta have faith to receive the grace."

"Isn't it a free gift?" I ask, moving toward them.

"Sure, sure." Guy gives me a welcoming grin.

Rae moves over and makes room for me on the piano bench.

"But," Guy says, "if you don't know a fancy car is sittin' in your drive with a big red bow on it, what good does it do you? You gotta take the step out the door or peek out the window to see it. If I gotta big wrapped gift box for you, you gotta reach out and take it. It's still free, but it takes an action of faith. See what I mean?"

I think back to what Ben said, how he trusted, how I couldn't.

"Maybe." Rae's fingers loosen up, scattering over the keyboard in a rambling fashion.

Guy and I watch her a moment. He grins and winks. "I think you still know how to play that thing."

Her smile broadens.

I close my eyes, listening to the notes climbing and descending the scales. Then I look at Ben, sitting slumped in a pew, thumbing through a Bible. I wish I could help him, but he seems trapped in his own private thoughts. I know that place. Sometimes I need to be alone to get my bearings and find my own way out. Or maybe he's praying again. Something inside me envies his ability to pray, his unquestioning belief. Inside I know the ugly truth about myself. It's easier for me to sit back now and do nothing but watch and empathize with Ben, especially when I don't know what to do to help him. Besides, I know there's nothing I can do or say to make the situation better.

Alone I carried the burden for nursing first Mother, then Stu. I've always been grateful I could help them, love them, care for them. But I also know this terrible fact about myself now: I don't want to take care of anyone else. It sounds selfish, but I can't help the way I feel. I'm tired. Exhausted from loving, from losing too much.

I wonder what Ben will do about Ivy's predicament. I don't know how he feels about abortion, if that will be an option, although it makes my stomach tighten into a hard knot. Will Ivy even want to have the baby? Will she raise it? Give it up for adoption?

Ivy's situation makes it easier for me to understand the predicament my mother was in. And Rae. I ache for all of them. I want to reach out to Ivy, but I'm not sure she will accept my compassion. I don't know what to do or say anyway. A part of me, a part I'm once again ashamed of, wants to turn and walk away.

Seeing the bag with the glasses I purchased on the pew, I carry them over to Ben. He stares at them. "I thought you could use these."

"You're kidding, right?"

"You need reading glasses. And these, well, I thought they'd remind you of Stu."

"They do that." He laughs but then puts them on. I admit he looks ridiculous. But when he looks down at the Bible, he says, "Hey, I can read the words now."

"Good." I pat his shoulder.

The door where Myrtle disappeared earlier opens. Rae's

fingers pause, resting on the piano keys. Guy looks over his shoulder. Only Ben speaks as he takes off the Elvis spectacles. "Well? Can I see my daughter?"

Myrtle nods.

I move over to Rae and tap her shoulder. "Maybe we should leave. Let this be a private family matter."

She stands with me, closing the piano as I give Ben a hug. "It'll be all right," I whisper in his ear. "It will."

"Ivy wants you two to stay," Myrtle says.

"But . . ." Ben hesitates. I sense he wants to be alone with his daughter.

Myrtle's eyes deepen with sympathy. "It was her request."

Ben motions for us to all sit down again. I move a few feet from Ben and settle back onto the pew. I don't want to be intrusive. Rae sits back on the piano bench.

"Okay," Myrtle says, opening the door again. "Come on, it's okay."

Ivy walks through the door, wearing the same thing she wore yesterday when I last saw her. She looks tired, her face mottled red and streaked with black mascara. My gaze automatically moves to her abdomen, where she has her hands clenched tight, but I can't detect any roundness or slight baby bulge. A part of me hopes she's mistaken, but remembering our constant stops on the drive to Memphis, I know she's not.

Ben walks toward her, his motions stiff and awkward. He holds out his arms to her. Then he waits, lets her make the next move. She glances at Myrtle, who gives a slight nod, then back to her father. Her eyes fill with tears that spill over to her cheeks.

"Oh, baby," Ben says, his voice hoarse.

"I'm sorry, Daddy. I'm so sorry."

He enfolds her in a tight embrace, rocking her from side to side as I've seen him do since she was a baby. But now he can lay his cheek on the top of her head. He shushes her.

"It's okay. It's going to be okay. I don't want you worrying about anything. Anything at all."

♪♩♪♩.♩♪♩

EVENTUALLY BEN LEADS Ivy to a pew and settles her under the shelter of his arm. Rae stays at the piano, with Guy leaning on the upright. I sit next to Myrtle on the steps leading to the altar.

"Was it Heath?" Ben asks.

"Dad!" Her tone is that of a normal hormonal teenager.

I notice Ben's hands clench and every muscle tenses.

"Now Ivy," Myrtle says, interrupting, "your father is going to have questions. That's natural."

Ben gives her a nod of thanks, but his jaw flexes in an effort to withhold his riotous emotions.

"But maybe we could focus on a neutral topic," Myrtle suggests. "For now."

"Like the weather?" Ben asks. He peers down at his daughter, his brows pinched together. "Does he know?"

Ivy looks down at her hands. "Yes."

"And what did he say?"

She shrugs. "He . . . he said it was my fault. That I was stupid."

"We'll just see about that."

Ivy places a hand on her father's leg. "Dad. Please don't. Just let him go."

"She doesn't want anything to do with the baby's father," Myrtle says.

"Well, what are you going to do? Deal with this alone?" Ben asks, frustration sharpening his tone.

Ivy hides her face in her hands and starts crying. Ben's anger melts. He glances at me, looking helpless.

"Ivy," I say, "you're not alone. We're here to help you. And—" the words catch in my throat. I can't say what Ben said, that God's right there helping. I can't. "You know," I add, "there are lots of options. But nothing has to be decided today."

Ivy snuffles. Rae brings her a tissue, but the girl keeps her face averted.

"Ivy," I say, "we just want you to know we're here for you. We care about you. And we'll be with you through this."

Each of the adults surrounding Ivy murmurs agreement. Then the room grows silent, except for Elvis singing "I Believe."

"Rae had a baby out of wedlock," Ben says.

Ivy looks up then, stares at Rae, as the rest of us do.

"It's a bit old-fashioned to say it that way." She shrugs. "But it's true."

"I'm sorry," Ben says, "I shouldn't have—"

She waves her hand to stop his apology, her charm bracelet jangling. It's then I notice one of the charms laying flat against her wrist. The silver sparkles. It's in the shape of a baby's bootie. "It's all right. It's the truth."

"How old were you?" Ivy asks, curious yet wary.

"Nineteen."

"Oh."

"But this was forty years ago. So I was very naive. And times were different. It's more accepted now. It wasn't then."

"What did you do?" Ivy asks.

"I had the baby. I had no choice there. Then I gave it to someone else to raise, someone who had a home, who was ready for a baby, who needed a baby. I never had that need. Although sometimes in the years since I've had a longing. But need . . . is different. I was too young, too stupid to raise a baby. I would not have been a very good mother."

"How could you do that?" Ivy glares at Rae. "Just walk away!"

I hold my breath, expect Rae to put the girl in her place. I sense Ivy's anger should be directed at her own mother. But Rae is the closest target.

"It wasn't easy. But I couldn't imagine myself as a mother," Rae says. "I knew my limitations better than anyone. And I had to think of what was best for the baby."

Ivy wraps her arms across her stomach.

My heart contracts, thinking of two girls, pregnant, trying to make the right decision. And so young to make such a grown-up one.

"It's the hardest thing I've ever done," Rae says, her voice cracking, her gaze sliding toward me.

Ben gives a small shake of his head, as if he's still coming to grips with the news. I suspect he hopes for adoption, for Ivy to give up her baby. But I give him credit for not having asked that of her yet.

In my bones I feel Rae's loss, as I lost a baby of my own but not of my own accord. At least her baby had a life to live. But I know the agony, the emptiness that never goes away.

"My mother thought like you," Ivy says, her tone bitter. "She didn't want to be a mom."

Ben leans away from his daughter to look at her face. "You don't know that."

"She left, didn't she?" Ivy's tone is jagged with anger.

"There's a difference," Rae says, "in not wanting to be a mom and in not feeling capable."

"I'm not going to abandon my baby!" She covers her belly with her hands. "I'm not! Ever." She glares at Rae. "No matter what any of you say."

♪♩♪♩.♩♪♩

"IT'S TIME TO GO," Ben says. "We're all tired and we need some rest."

My heart feels heavy as I look at Ben's defeated expression. He's wise not to respond immediately to his daughter's challenge.

Myrtle and Guy seem pleased with the results of the reunion. Guy retrieves Ivy's backpack and suitcase from the back room and hands them over to Ben. Myrtle gives everyone hugs.

"Thank you," I say, with her arms wrapped around me. "Your kindness will not be forgotten."

"You help them, okay?" Her gaze pierces me.

Even though some part of me flinches and I want to withdraw, how can I not help? I love them both. Yet how can I promise such a thing? What will it demand of me? Will I even have anything to give them?

"You have much to give," she says, then hugs me again.

Then Myrtle moves on to Rae, saying to her, "You have wisdom to share. Hard earned. Share it now, you hear?"

Finally Myrtle enfolds Ivy in her arms, whispers maternal things in her ear. The girl crumples into her, tears staining the thin white material on the older woman's shoulder. "You're gonna be just fine. Just fine. You keep in touch with us, all right?"

"Yes ma'am."

Myrtle laughs and hugs Ivy close again. "I like a girl with manners."

Turning to Ben, she opens her arms. "All right, Daddy-o."

Surprising to me, Ben almost falls into her arms, hugging her close. "Thank you," he whispers. "Thank you for giving my baby back to me."

She pats his shoulder. "Oh, fiddle. We do like happy endings. Everything is going to be all right. You just keep remembering that."

He nods, his throat working up and down.

The silence on the way back to the hotel throbs. How can I argue with Ivy's sense of rightness, the desire to do the opposite of her own mother? I felt that in my early years. My mother acted stiff and undemonstrative, self-righteous. I yearned for more. Did I choose Stu, a very physical male who liked to touch and hold, to help me be the opposite of my mother? Or was it something I yearned for deep inside? Was I looking for some kind of fulfillment? Did I depend on Stu the way Ben leans on God? The way Stu held to his beliefs no matter what?

Piled into the Cadillac, I'm halfway back to the hotel when I realize I forgot to ask Guy or Myrtle about the shrine to Elvis and if it's missing a bust. I flip off the stereo as I've had all I can stand of the King. The thrum of the engine sounds like a lion purring.

I park at the back of the hotel. I grit my teeth at the sound of Elvis singing some rockabilly song that surrounds the hotel. It's another reminder of what I haven't yet accomplished with the bust.

Together we troop upstairs. None of us slept the night before, and the strain and fatigue show in our faces. I wonder how families survive when a child disappears for years or is never found. For the first time in a long while I have something to thank God for, and I offer a silent, hesitant prayer of gratitude.

Since none of us is hungry, and Myrtle fed Ivy earlier, we separate to our own rooms, our own thoughts. Ivy closes her door first. Ben settles on the sofa with a pillow and blanket I found in a closet. With his head and feet sticking off the ends of the sofa, he looks like one of those pigs in a blanket my mother used to fix on Sunday mornings before church.

"Maybe you should sleep in my bed," I suggest, then realize how that sounds. "I'll sleep here."

"No way. I'm not going to put you out any more than I already have. I'll get a room tomorrow."

I pat his shoulder. "You'll stay here with us."

"Thanks," he whispers.

Tears fill my eyes and I swallow hard, then sniff, "It's going to be okay."

"I know. Although it doesn't feel that way now." He leans back into his pillow and closes his eyes.

I don't understand his unwavering faith. Stu had the same, but it didn't work out for him. It wasn't all right.

Ivy's door opens then. Ben practically leaps off the couch. "What is it? Are you okay?"

She stands in the middle of the sitting room, her hands on her hips. "Where is my mother? I want to see her. I don't care what *she* wants. I need to see her, to talk to her."

Chapter Seventeen

Love Me Tender

Ben steps toward his daughter. "Come here." His voice is gruff but tender. He takes her into the sitting area. "I should have told you a long time ago."

Ivy stares up at him, a mixture of defiance and aching need. She crosses her arms over her chest. "So, where is she? If she wants—"

"We'll just . . ." I back away, knowing this needs to be between father and daughter. But the nearest bedroom is Rae's, so I take her arm and move in that direction.

"Stay," Ben says.

"Tell me where my mother is! Do you even know? Do you care?"

"She's dead, Ivy." Ben pauses but holds his daughter's shocked glare. "She—"

"You're lying!" Ivy's outburst shatters the room.

Rae squeezes my arm.

Ben looks stunned, hurt, as if she slapped him. "No, Ivy. I'm not. Your mother died the year after she left us."

"I don't believe you! It's not true."

"That's your choice."

"But . . ." Tears choke Ivy's words. She looks at Rae and me then back to her father. "How? Why?"

"I don't know why, Ivy. I wish to God I did."

Ivy's shoulders begin to shake. Her whole body trembles. I know that feeling so well. I reach out to her but stop when she says, "How? How did she die?"

Ben looks away.

"You can tell me. I'm not a baby."

He nods, his mouth a pencil-thin line. "I know. It's . . ." He looks down at the floor, his face reddening, tightening with emotion, then back at his daughter. "She killed herself, baby. I don't know why. But she did."

Ivy starts to back away, bumps into the corner of the wall, then wheels around and stumbles toward her room. The door slams shut. Through the thin hotel walls I can hear her choking sobs.

Ben sits down hard on the coffee table. I go to him, put a hand on his shoulder. His cotton shirt is damp with sweat.

"You did the right thing," Rae says. "She'll mourn, but she will heal."

"Did I?" Ben looks up at me, his eyes rimmed red, the green irises darkened with unshed tears.

"Yes," I say. "Let me go to her. Okay?"

He nods, unable to speak. I embrace him, putting my arms around his shoulders. In spite of the painful moments, he feels sturdy and strong.

♪♩♪♩.♩♪♩

"IVY?" I KNOCK on her door. "I'm coming in, okay?" I can hear muffled weeping, and I open the door and enter the darkness of her room.

She's sprawled across the bed as if she simply collapsed there. She clutches a pillow to her, has buried her face in it. Her whole body jerks and shakes with sobs.

I put a hand on her back as I sit next to her. I can feel her trembling. Slowly I smooth my hand along her black hair, down her back, over and over, the action comforting me probably more than her. Her snuffling, congested sounds fill the room. Her grief consumes her, penetrates the defenses I've built. Suddenly I taste my own tears. I cry for Ivy, for her pain, her loss of never knowing her mother, and for Gwen who will never know the beauty of her own daughter.

I'm not sure how long I sit there beside Ivy, but eventually there's a shift in the grief tide. She reaches out a hand to me. Then suddenly this young woman is in my arms and I'm holding her, rocking her, feeling her tears and grief pour out. I mutter useless, senseless words, knowing nothing can ease her pain. The tears will bring acceptance and eventually healing. Or so I hope. Over the past year I've grieved not only Stu but also our dreams. Ivy is now grieving her little girl dreams, dreams so basic—the need for a mother. Her cries claw at the wounds in my own heart.

When she finally collapses back onto the bed, I hand her tissues as I blow my own nose. There's a washrag on the bedside table, probably the one I brought her when her stomach was upset, and I use it now to wipe the tears off her face.

Suddenly she sits up, stares wide-eyed. "I'm gonna barf!"

"Okay." I grab a trash can and hold it with one hand in front of her as she heaves up her grief. With my other hand I pull back her hair. "It's okay. Don't worry. You're okay."

When she slumps back onto the bed, I set the trash can near the door, my nose pinched from the rancid odor. "I'll get you some water and be right back."

Out in the hallway, the lights are off but suddenly Ben is there. "Is she—"

"She's fine. I'll stay with her tonight. In case she needs anything."

"Did she . . . ?" He looks at the trash can.

"It's okay, Ben. She'll be okay." I empty the trash can into the toilet. Then I gather more tissues, a glass of water, a wet washrag.

Back in Ivy's room, she sips a little water then falls back on the bed, exhausted and spent. I bathe her face and neck. She whimpers some, tears seeping from her closed eyes. But eventually even that stops and she sleeps. Folding back a corner of the comforter, I cover her. Then I move Ivy's iPod and backpack out of the armchair beside the bed and curl myself into it.

It's lumpy and too small, but exhaustion eventually overwhelms me and I sleep, waking periodically through the night to check on Ivy.

♪ ♩ ♪ ♩. ♩ ♪ ♩

THE DREAM COMES in waves, like the foamy surf creeping onto a sandy beach, filling my subconscious from I don't know where. I wonder if dreams are a figment of our imaginations or if those who've died before us visit us through dreams.

My mother sweeps into mine. She wears a swirly blue dress that ripples about her like sea grasses rolling with the gentle sway of the ocean. We simply look at each other as underwater divers might through masks. When she begins to fade, drifting off, slowly, slowly, slowly, I feel my insides rocking like the wake of a boat. It's then I realize she carries a baby with her, curled against her shoulder. Is it mine? Or hers?

I awaken crying.

I lie in the darkness, listening to the hum of the air conditioner and the snuffled breathing of Ivy as tears run down the sides of my face into my hair. I remember the hope, confidence, and joy of knowing a baby was growing inside me. Does this young girl feel that now? Or is she naive about the changes, the great responsibility? Or overwhelmed and frightened? Despite the burping and the bloating as my body began to change, accommodating a new life, I was delirious.

Stu acted more like a opossum out for its nightly stroll along a Texas highway, seeing the light bursts of a car and freezing, eyes locked on the headlights of change. Would he be a good daddy? He'd asked, "What about our lives? How can we pay for college? What if the baby's a girl? Then we'll have to pay for a wedding, too."

"Yes," I told him. "Our life is going to change. For the better."

After all, we'd seen Ben in action as a father, changing diapers, rushing home from work, rarely working late, buying baby paraphernalia and formula by the truckload. Then watched him as a single father, shouldering the burden of parenthood alone, taking Ivy's temperature, burping, consoling, loving his little girl. We'd marveled at his abilities, seen his joy and sorrow, all made richer and deeper by the sheer existence of his daughter. Were we ready for that roller coaster?

I was. But I was never sure about Stu. Oh, I figured by the time the baby arrived, he'd come around. After all, we'd planned the pregnancy. We'd read books on when to conceive, how to prepare, how to conceive a boy or a girl.

Stu always joked he wanted to name his son Elvis. At least, I'd hoped he was joking. He'd finally said, "Let's call the baby Elvis . . . or Priscilla, whichever is appropriate when we find out if it's a boy or a girl."

"But everyone will think—"

"Exactly." He winked and grinned. "Then we'll surprise them with the real name when he or she arrives."

Relief had washed through me. "And what is that real name going to be?"

"Elvis." He laughed. "Kidding. Only kidding."

Remembering the hope swelling within me when the baby began to grow, I could never have given up my baby voluntarily. It amazed me that Rae survived that. Not in a condemning way but in awe of her strength. Knowing my own weakness, I can't suggest that Ivy give up hers. After learning about her mother, I have no idea what she will do.

THE HOTEL ROOM seems as quiet as Elvis's grave site when I venture out of Ivy's room. With everyone else still sleeping, I pace along the end of the bed in my own room. My limbs are stiff and sore, my neck aching from sleeping in the chair all night. I look at the ads in the yellow pages left on the bedside table. The sky outside my window remains dark with heavy clouds. I can't get the image of my mother and the sleeping baby out of my mind. I can't escape the memory of Ivy's weeping.

I thought I'd mourned our baby. The miscarriage happened years ago. I'd had other things to mourn since then. But maybe Ivy's pregnancy, maybe the drama of learning about her mother, exhumed the pain within my own soul.

"Why?" I whisper. "Why?"

I realize I'm asking this of God. It's not the first time I've asked that question. Still there's no reply. No answer.

With my insides unsettled, my mind restless, I finally venture out into the joining area. Ben's awake, sitting at the table. At first I think he's talking to Elvis, who is still but ever alert and watchful. Then I realize Ben has his cell phone to his ear. I laugh at my own foolishness, and he turns.

"How's Ivy?" he asks as he clicks off his phone.

"I think she'll be okay, but it's going to take time. Was that about work?"

"I'm trying to figure out how much of a donation I can make to Faithland . . . as a thank-you for all they did for Ivy."

I remember the sign in front of the chapel saying their services were free but they accepted donations. "I'm sure anything you could give would be appreciated." Then an idea occurs to me. "Why don't we hook up your nonprofit with theirs in an effort to help families in need in the Memphis area."

"It's a thought. When we get back to Dallas, let's work on it. I'll put you in charge." He pushes against his knees and stands. "Now, I'm starving."

"I could probably eat. How long will the others sleep?"

"Rae's up," he says. "She's getting dressed." He looks toward his daughter's closed door. "I can wake Ivy. She needs to eat, too."

But before he can, the bathroom door clicks, then the shower spray swooshes.

"Thanks," Ben says, "for helping her."

"I didn't do anything—"

"Yes, you did."

A warmth spreads through my limbs. It feels good to be useful. "She's going to be fine."

♪♩♪♩.♩♪♩

THIRTY MINUTES LATER we take the elevator down to the lobby, only to learn that breakfast in the Jungle Room ended twenty minutes earlier. So we pile into the Cadillac and go in search of a café. Ivy wants an omelet and pancakes. Ben is determined to get it for her. She seems somber this morning, quiet but rested. Mostly hungry, which is a good sign.

When we're settled in a large round booth, we study the menu. Ben pulls the Elvis spectacles out of his shirt pocket. I hide a laugh.

"What are you doing?" Ivy asks.

Ben looks up. "Reading the menu."

"But where did you get those?" His daughter's nose wrinkles with disgust.

"Oh these?" He tugs off the glasses, then puts them back on and grins. "Great, aren't they?"

"Uh, no." She shrinks down in her seat.

After a few moments we greedily order coffee and fresh-squeezed grapefruit juice, bacon and sausages, pancakes and hash browns, along with omelets and eggs over easy, scrambled, and fried. We eat like we haven't eaten in days.

Rae quietly gives Ivy tips on eating during pregnancy. "Avoid grease. Eat healthy, wholesome foods—grains, fiber, lots of vegetables and fruits."

"That means no French fries," Ben says, sliding a piece of bacon in his mouth.

"Yogurt," Rae adds. "It will aid your sluggish digestive tract."

Ivy wrinkles her nose, then slaps another pat of butter on her pancakes. "Whatever."

"Eat a little bit, several times a day," Rae continues as if her advice is being absorbed with relish. "Having something in you will settle your stomach."

Silverware clinks against the plain white plates. The attentive waitress brings more coffee, then a basket of hot-out-of-the-oven biscuits.

Eventually Ivy's the first to surrender. "I'm stuffed."

We laugh. Not that her comment's funny, but it provides relief for all of us. Our manic eating slows, and we nibble on bits of biscuit, a last swipe of pancake through thick syrup, broken pieces of bacon.

"What are the plans today?" Ben asks.

"Maybe we should do something just for fun," Rae suggests.

"A movie?" Ivy asks.

"I thought we'd head home," I say, more than ready to abandon this journey that has been too difficult already.

Everyone stares at me for a minute as if I've spoken treason. Then the excuses shoot out of them, overlapping one another.

"But," Ben said, "what about—?"

"It's not possible," Rae imposes.

"No," Ivy says, "we can't go yet. What about Elvis?"

Why did it always come back to him?

"Stuart asked you to return it," Rae says.

"I think it was his final joke on me," I return.

"No, it wasn't," Ben argues.

"How am I ever going to find where Elvis belongs? It's crazy. You all should have stopped me back in Dallas. It's insane."

"I know," Ivy says.

"See! Even Ivy can see the absurdity of it."

"No," she says, leaning forward, "I *know*."

"Know what?" Rae asks.

"I know where Elvis belongs."

"You do?" Ben asks. "Where?"

"The chapel. Faithland."

"That pedestal did look the right size," I say, "but that's no proof. And I am not about to go back and ask Myrtle and Guy if they're missing," I lower my voice to a whisper, "a big head of Elvis."

"Yes, but I *know*." Ivy sets her napkin beside her plate. "Myrtle already told me."

"She told you she was looking for a bust of Elvis?" I ask, my heart beginning to pound.

"She told me the story of how the bust disappeared."

That bit of news causes my eyebrows to lift in question, or doubt, or both. But I lean forward, elbow on the table.

"What did she say?" Rae asks.

Ivy gives a secretive smile, as if she has us all right where she wants us. "It was on the tenth anniversary of Elvis's death. The city was crammed with Elvis fans, right?"

Collectively we nod. Not something a teenager who hadn't even known who Elvis was before coming to Memphis would comprehend. So I figure Myrtle told her that much.

"That's the night the bust disappeared."

I look at Ben to see if the information lines up with what Stu told him, if that had also been the right time for their college football game. He nods his affirmation.

"You mean, stolen," I correct. After all, we know the bust didn't vanish into thin air. It's sitting in our hotel suite. It was in my attic for twenty years. I have a sinking feeling Stu's guilty conscience weighed on him near the end of his life. Never before would I have believed my husband was a thief, but considering his obsession with Elvis, I suppose anything could have happened. Especially in his younger, wilder days.

"Stolen by Elvis," Ivy says.

"Oh, please." I roll my eyes in disbelief, then smile at how Ivy has rubbed off on me. "Not another conspiracy theory. Was he abducted by aliens? Or is he living in the Caribbean under an assumed name?"

"No!" she protests. "I swear. It's true! More than one person saw Elvis that night. Plain as day. But not Elvis . . . you know, alive. This was a ghost. Myrtle saw him. She was coming back to the chapel after a candlelight vigil."

"Uh-huh." Disbelief saturates my tone. But I notice Ben and Rae remain silent, listening . . . maybe even believing what my father would have called "hogwash."

"It's true, I'm telling you!"

"They knew Elvis, too," Rae says, her voice husky. "Guy and Myrtle knew him. She'd recognize him."

"Okay, okay. It's true." But I don't necessarily believe it. Under my breath, I whisper, "What was Myrtle smoking that night?"

"She was not high or hallucinating," Ivy defends her friend.

"Okay, let's just pretend this is all true. If Elvis is floating around Memphis, then why would he care about some bust? Wouldn't he be more concerned about his daughter marrying Michael Jackson? Wouldn't that have been a good time to step forward and say, 'Here I am! I'm stopping *this* wedding!'"

Ben laughs. With his arms crossed over his chest, he looks as skeptical as I feel.

But no one offers an explanation, which to me is proof they're all loony tunes for even contemplating the possibility of a ghost. Ivy's young, gullible. Rae's nodding her head. She's not young. Far beyond gullible. So what's her excuse for believing? Is she eccentric enough to believe in aliens or ghosts?

"Stu saw him, too," Ben reminds me, making me wonder whose side he's on.

I glare at him. "Oh, sure, how could I forget that?" Has everyone lost their minds but me? "So why would Elvis stop Stu on some lonely back road and ask him to help steal the bust?"

"Even ghosts have their reasons," Rae says quietly.

I toss my napkin beside my plate. "You know what I think? I think some people are desperate enough to believe Elvis is alive, well . . . around in some form or fashion, only because they need it somehow to validate their own existence. After all, Elvis had it all—looks, talent galore, money, fame. Yet he died. You can't accept that. But I can. I know how someone can be struck down in the prime of life for no reason other than life sucks sometimes. People die. We all die. Even Elvis!"

"Is that why it's so easy for you not to believe?" Rae asks.

"This obsession with Elvis has to stop. Stu wanted to be cool like Elvis. He must have wanted to believe Elvis was alive—"

"That's not true," Ben says.

"What?"

"Stu didn't want to be cool like Elvis."

"How do you know?"

"Because we talked about Elvis. Many times."

I'm struck dumb for a moment. Something else my husband didn't talk to me about. I feel a dull ache in my heart. Did he not trust me? I swallow back the bitter tears. "Then why?"

"Stu identified with Elvis."

"What?" We weren't rich. Stu couldn't even sing a note. "How?"

"Elvis personified all of our struggles with right and wrong. Elvis had a love for gospel music and all his beliefs about God. Yet he had this wild, rock 'n' roll side that he couldn't tame."

Rae nods. "You're right. He did. Except that Elvis's struggle was always splashed across tabloids and newspaper headlines."

"Exactly," Ben says. "Our struggles, Stu's struggles, are usually on a smaller scale and more internal."

"Some hidden." Rae straightens the charms on her bracelet.

"Like my mother's," Ivy says.

"Yes," Ben agrees.

"Others not so hidden." Rae lays what looks like a diploma charm flat against the underside of her wrist. Then she looks at me. "It's your struggle between belief and disbelief."

Unable to answer, I shove back from the table, my chair legs screeching, and stand on suddenly shaky legs. My heart pounds. With as much dignity as I can muster, fighting tears all the way, I walk out of the restaurant and wait for the rest of the group in the car.

♪ ♩ ♪ ♩. ♩ ♪ ♩

WITH EVERYONE'S STOMACH full, we ride silently back to the hotel. The car idles at the curb, a rough-and-tumble shaking, making everything in the car jiggle. When I pull up to the front entrance of the hotel, Rae gets out with me. Ben slides behind the wheel and drives off with Ivy. They've been requested to appear at the police station to unfile their missing person's report. I imagine Ivy has a few explanations to make.

Together we waddle to the suite. I need space, some time to process Ben's revelations and Rae's accusation. But

I stop in the doorway, suddenly thirsty. I pour myself a glass of water, sip it, then *thunk* it on top of the television. I can't seem to settle into one place, so I pace the floor in front of Elvis.

"Sit down, Claudia. There's nothing to do but wait." Rae flips open a magazine, *Nightlight in Memphis*.

"You think she'll be all right?" I move to the window and look out over the parking lot at the footbridge that leads to Elvis's planes and an assortment of museums and souvenir shops.

"Of course. Ivy's strong. Resilient."

I nod, embarrassed to say I wasn't even thinking about Ivy. Why can't I believe like Stu, like Ben? Is my disbelief what kept others from talking to me, confiding in me? Questions surround me, and no ready answers surface.

It's actually easier to focus on Ivy. What will she decide to do about her baby? Will Ben pressure Ivy to give the baby up for adoption? I think about Rae and the decisions she had to make as a young woman. "You're strong, too."

Rae shrugs. "Maybe now. But not always."

"How so?"

"You face what you have to. Do the best you can. Just as you've done."

"I suppose."

"As you did with Stu's death."

I scoff. "I didn't handle it gracefully."

"Grace has little to do with death. I don't believe there is a right or wrong way to handle such things." Rae crosses her legs, making her skirt ripple outward. She kicks her leg forward and back, a slow, rhythmic motion. "I haven't always handled situations with aplomb."

"We all make mistakes."

"I didn't say they were mistakes necessarily." Rae jerks her chin. "But I ran from tough situations."

"I can't see you running from anything. You seem so strong, so confident, like you've always believed."

"Belief isn't natural or a guarantee. It's a choice."

"What do you mean?"

"I mean you have to choose to believe. Even when nothing makes sense. It's easy to turn away. It's easy to give up. It's not always easy to make the choice to believe."

"But maybe it's belief in a fantasy. Or something false. What if it's folly to believe?"

"It depends on what that belief is then."

I sigh. "What about God?"

"Do you believe God is folly?"

"Don't make fun of me."

"I'm not." Rae closes the magazine and lays it on the coffee table. "I'm asking what you think, what you feel in your heart."

"I thought I did. I went to church as a kid. Mom made me. I did all the things our church said to do, you know? I prayed the prayer. I was baptized. But I don't know anymore."

"That's honest, and that's a start. Just remember, Claudia, running isn't necessarily a sign of weakness. That's Hollywood's take on it. Intelligence and wisdom—that's what I used. It was probably misinterpreted as fear though."

"What did you run from?"

"Motherhood."

"I imagine giving up your baby was very difficult."

"It was the right thing to do. That has brought me comfort over the years. But it was the hardest thing I've ever done. And if Ivy must . . . or does, then it will change her forever. You'll be there for her and help her through it."

Skepticism makes me doubt I'm capable. "Motherhood," I say, "whether she keeps the baby or not, will change her, too."

Rae nods.

"Have you ever tried to contact your child?" I ask. "She must be grown now."

"Yes, she's all grown up." A wistful smile softens her features.

"And you've never looked her up?" I lean forward, resting my elbows on my knees.

"I didn't say that."

"You have then? Or has she found you?" I sit back suddenly, as if preparing myself for the unveiling of another family secret. "I'm sorry. It's none of my business." I stare at Rae's charm bracelet, notice little ballerina slippers and a Girl Scout charm. So many activities we shared, and yet I'll probably never know my cousin. "I was just curious about my cousin. I don't have any, not on Mother's side. And Dad's family lived far away. We've had very little contact over the years."

"Of course." Rae reaches over and touches my hand. The charms brush my arm. They hold Rae's body heat. "She's well. That's all I needed to know. I don't want to intrude too much in her life. She's not looking for a mother. I'm content. But Ivy—"

"Do you have grandchildren then?"

Rae waves her hand as if shooing away an irritating fly. "I hope," she straightens the lines of her skirt, "that Ben will let Ivy make her own decision about her pregnancy."

"She's just a kid though. You were nineteen."

"She was old enough to conceive, right? She's old enough to decide if she wants to be a mother . . . or not."

"I don't know. It's a big decision. Can a fifteen-year-old girl make a good decision, see the big picture, the far-reaching effects?"

"Wisdom knows no age. You'll help guide her."

I shift in my chair, uncomfortable with this new role as guidance counselor. "Her decision will impact the baby's whole life. Along with her own."

"Ivy will have to grow up in ways she never imagined. Her father must give her that room. But I sense that in Ben. He's a good man, kindhearted."

"Yes, he is," I agree.

"And Ivy," Rae says, "she loves her father. You can see that. Their bond is solid. Not easily severed.

"But can a father understand a girl's heart? How can he understand how a pregnancy, or termination of one, will change his daughter, body and soul? Or how giving up her baby might fracture her heart permanently?"

"I wish I could help them. I love them both, Ivy and Ben. I've known them a long time. And this, well, it's going to be rough on them."

"Your love will buoy them when they believe they're sinking."

"Was there someone like that for you? When you were pregnant. Helping you? Loving you through it all?"

"Your mother." She smiles, but tears gather at the corners of her eyes. "Why do you look surprised?"

"I always thought you two didn't get along, that you'd had a fight or something a long time ago."

Rae shakes her head, denying my assumption. "I told

you there wasn't a fight. We loved each other. Respected each other."

"But you didn't talk. For my whole life. I don't mean *you* so much as both of you. No phone calls. No letters. Nothing. Just silence."

Rae wraps one hand around her other wrist, capturing all the charms of her bracelet under her fingers. "Silence isn't always the result of anger. It *can* be the deepest form of respect. Even love."

Chapter Eighteen

All Shook Up

Ben and Ivy arrive back at the hotel suite. Ivy collapses onto the sofa next to Rae and lies with her knees curved over the arm of the sofa and her bare feet dangling off the side. Rae hands her a pillow. Ben looks as flushed, restless, and agitated as I was earlier.

"How'd it go?"

He gives me a dark look that makes me wish I hadn't asked.

"Anybody hungry?" he asks.

We all groan. Then silence stretches between us, fragile as a glass bridge.

"We need to make a decision," I finally say. "I need to tell the hotel what our plans are. I suppose we could still start back to Dallas this afternoon. Or we could wait till morning." I'm hopeful they'll see the trip to Memphis has been pointless. A mistake of gigantic proportions on all our parts.

"It's too late today," Ben says. "Let's wait until tomorrow at least."

"I'm bored," Ivy says. At that moment her cell phone spews a succession of beeps—some tune that seems familiar yet I can't place it. She rolls off the couch and runs to her room.

"Everything go okay?" Rae asks Ben.

"Sure. Since she's a minor, they had to make sure she wasn't being abused or coerced or anything. But apparently Myrtle spoke with the police. They've worked with her before and value her opinion. They also gave Ivy a strong warning about what can happen to a young woman who runs off like that."

A shudder passes through me.

"No young person thinks anything bad can happen to them," Rae says. "It's the strength and weakness of youth."

He collapses into a chair near Elvis, who seems to be observing us with a bemused smirk. I wonder if Stu is somewhere . . . watching . . . hovering nearby, laughing at us. The thought makes me want to knock the bust off the table.

The slump of Ben's shoulders outlines his fatigue and melancholy. "I never thought driving too fast would end in a car wreck. Or drinking too much in college . . ." His voice trails off. "But I never ran away either. I was never that—"

"You were never a young girl," I say. "Even if you had . . ." My voice trails off as Ivy comes back into the room and flops back onto the sofa.

"Was that him?" Ben asks, unable to disguise the vehemence in his voice.

"Dad." She turns the one syllable word into two.

"I need to know what's going on with him. And you."

"It's none of your business." She crosses her arms over her chest.

"None of my—" His hands clench, as if he's ready to do battle for his daughter's virtue. Which would be a little late at this point. "He gets my daughter preg—"

"Shut up! I'm not listening to this!"

The room seems to freeze for a slow second, as if time stops then bolts forward. Ben blocks her retreat from the room. "Yes, you will, young lady. If he's not going to be a part of this, fine. Better, even. But he's going to have to sign some papers saying he gives up his rights. Then you can make your own decision. But I need to know—"

"I've already made my decision." Her voice is calm but high-pitched. "I'm keeping my baby!"

"A sixteen-year-old does not need a baby. What are you going to do?"

"I'm not running away like my mother!"

Ben looks as if he's been slapped. He takes a shaky breath and releases it. "You have to think like an adult, Ivy. How are you going to take care of a baby? How will you afford all the things a baby needs? Do you even know how much a baby costs? How can you go to school, take care of a baby, work—"

"I don't know!" She turns one way, then another, looking for an escape route. "I haven't figured out all that stuff—"

"You better think about it," he grabs her arm, "because—"

Ivy jerks away from him. "I don't have to listen to you! This is my life! My baby!"

She slams the door to her room. The wake of silence

remains. I glance at Rae. She's experienced this all before and lived to tell about it. I sense she's sided with Ivy, thinking the girl should keep her baby if she wants. But it seems a selfish decision, a childish one. I realize in that moment that I want Ivy to decide for herself, but in the end I, too, hope she'll give her baby up for adoption.

Ben stares out the window, tilts his head, and cracks his neck. "I'm glad I handled that well."

His self-derision makes my heart ache. "Ben . . ." I don't know what to say to make the situation more tenable. "It's—"

"I know. Sorry about this. Life can be pretty messy and ugly sometimes. Especially mine, it seems."

I shake my head. "It's no different from anyone else's."

"Sure seems different." He shoves his fingers through his hair and jams them in his back jean pockets. "I don't know how to handle this. Is there a book that gives incompetent dads like me the right dialogue?"

"You're not incompetent. You're a great dad. And you'll muddle through this. It'll take some time for all the raw emotions, on your side and hers, to settle down."

"Although," Rae says, "her hormones will not allow those emotions to settle for some time."

Ben makes a half attempt at a chuckle that turns into a grimace. "I know she doesn't want to be like her own mother."

"Of course," Rae says. "And she won't be."

"How do you know?" Ben asks. "She could have the baby, keep it for a while, then change her mind."

"And that would not be so horrible," Rae said. "The baby wouldn't know much different. It's hard to know what it'll be like to have a baby and juggle life at the same time. She will learn."

"I want to spare her that. And the baby."

"Of course you do, Ben. You never wanted her to get pregnant at fifteen. But you can't protect her from this. Sometimes life hands us a raw deal. We just have to deal with it the best we can."

"We," he scoffs. I know what he means. He wasn't being condescending or ridiculing my remark. He simply knows he has to deal with this alone, just as I ultimately had to deal with Stu's death alone. Just as Ivy has to deal with the pregnancy herself. No platitudes of "God is with you" can make it easier. "You just gotta believe" doesn't work either. Sometimes, I've learned, no amount of believing is enough.

I remember sitting in the doctor's office with Stu, listening to the doctor rattle off big words I'd grown accustomed to because I'd learned to look them up on the Internet. Then Stu asked, "So what does all this mean, doc? Boil it down for me."

"There's really nothing else . . . nothing the medical community can do. I wish there were."

Stu swallowed hard. He gave the doctor a terse nod, squeezed my hand, then shook the doctor's. After we left the office and were in the quiet of our car, I said, "We'll manage. Together."

We. But Stu had the heavy burden to carry. He had the end of his life to face. I only had to pick up the pieces and try to carry on.

At the funeral, four months later, I stayed after everyone had left, stayed so I could watch Stu's casket lowered into the ground. The funeral director wanted me to leave. But I couldn't. "Do it now," I said. "I'm okay."

But I wasn't.

Ben stayed with me. "You're not alone in this, Claudia. We'll get through this."

We. That's when I understood how little my words had meant to Stu yet how much they meant at the same time. Ben had to face the loss of his best friend. But his loss was far different from my own.

"What if Ivy gets depressed . . . like her mother?" Ben voices his deepest concern, drawing me back to this crisis, this dilemma, this heartache.

"Then we'll watch for the signs and get her help. So much more is known today about postpartum depression . . . if that's what Gwen had. You can tell her doctor, so we can all be watchful." There's that *we* again.

And maybe there's comfort in that. I'm not sure I would have made it through the last year without Ben or Rae. Even though I tried not to turn to them, I felt their strength. Some days knowing they'd be calling if I didn't show up at work or didn't answer my door, their presence got me out of bed, kept me moving forward. Maybe their belief kept me going.

♪♩♪♩.♩♪♩

AFTER I CALL the front desk to inform them we'll need the suite another night, I turn back to Rae and Ben. I feel antsy, like we need to do something. I'd prefer driving back to Dallas, rather than sitting here, waiting and doing nothing, even if it means carrying Elvis all the way home again.

I'm not exactly in the mood to visit the Elvis car museum. Our options seem limited, especially considering the circumstances and the tempers involved. "Now what?"

"Lunch?" Ben asks.

"No thanks," Rae declines.

I put a hand on my unsettled stomach, which could use some Pepto-Bismol after our full, greasy breakfast.

"Graceland?" Ben says.

"Been there, done that," I smile, which feels more like a contortion.

"I can't believe I'm going to say this to three women, but . . . shopping? I'm sick of this room and need to get out."

"It's okay with me, I guess." It would be something to do. "Would Ivy be interested?"

"I'll ask her." But Ben stares at her closed door, foreboding as Mt. Everest.

"I have an idea," Rae offers. "We still have a mystery to solve."

"The mystery of the missing Elvis bust." Ben claps Elvis on the shoulder. "Could be the title of a new novel."

No one laughs.

Rae's eyes dip downward at the corners as if weighted by disappointment. "Don't you want to know what Stu meant?"

"No." Suddenly I'm trembling all over. "Yes. I don't know. There doesn't seem to be a likely solution."

Ben sighs heavily. "It's not a joke. But it bothered Stu . . . up until the end. We owe him."

I feel a wire snap loose in my brain, and the electric current zaps my heart. Anger shoots through every fiber.

I don't owe Stu *anything*. I gave him everything I had. Why does he want more now when I have nothing left? "It's too much." Tears burn my eyelids. I tilt my head into my hands, push my fingers hard against my forehead. "Too much."

Ben kneels beside me, clasps my hand with his. A hand touches my shoulder, and I look up at Rae.

"You don't have to do this alone, Claudia."

"We'll help."

We.

"Elvis weighs more than I thought," I try for a joke, but it lands flat.

Rae nods her understanding. "I've been thinking about this. Elvis isn't alive. I'm certain of that. Whatever Stuart saw—"

"You're saying Stu saw a ghost? Frankly, it doesn't matter to me if Elvis is a ghost, alive, or operating as an undercover CIA agent. The point is Stu stole the bust, obviously his wild side at work. And that clashed with his belief system at the end, leaving him with guilt. No wonder he identified with Elvis!"

"It wasn't stealing," Ivy protests, suddenly standing in the doorway to her room.

Ben looks toward his daughter, a smile curving his lips.

"Did it belong to Elvis?" I challenge. "Did it belong to Stu?"

No one answers my questions. Silence hums between us.

"Then," I say, flinging my arms out wide, "there you are! Stealing. Burglary. Breaking and entering."

"The chapel is always open," Ben reminds me.

Exhausted by this discussion, I roll my eyes in exasperation. Ivy laughs at my teenage impression.

"Okay," I say, "let's pretend it happened the way you're implying. Some ghost appeared to Stu, got him to drive to the chapel," the absurdity almost makes me laugh, "to steal the bust. He's still an accessory to a crime. A crime!"

"Myrtle and Guy didn't even file a police report," Ivy says. "It really creeped Myrtle out. Scared her. She believes she saw a ghost."

"I'm beginning to think *you're* 'all shook up.'"

Rae chuckles. Ben rubs a hand over his face, hiding a smile.

Ivy simply blinks. "I don't get it."

"It's a song of his, Elvis," Ben tries to explain my remark. "It was a joke." His gaze slants toward me. "A poor one."

"Did you tell Myrtle and Guy we have the bust?"

"No." She crosses her arms over her chest with a look that says she's not stupid. "They were just telling me about the legend. It's pretty famous around here."

"So who did Stu want me to return it to? The chapel?" I pause for effect and alter my voice to sound spooky. "Or the ghost?"

"We should find out," Rae says, surprising me.

"We could call Myrtle and Guy and simply ask them," Ben suggests, reaching for his cell phone.

"Not yet," Rae says.

"Please don't tell me you want to hold a séance."

She starts to smile, then simply shakes her head. "We should go see my friend Matt Franklin. He's more than likely awaiting my arrival."

"Who?" I ask.

"Baldy," she gives me a wink. Oh yes, Howie's "honest" friend who deals in hot-ticket Elvis souvenirs.

"But . . ." I want to go home.

"Baldy will know."

"Know what?"

But Rae never answers my question.

Chapter Nineteen

Impossible Dream

"Are you sure we're going in the right direction?" Ivy asks from the back seat. The uncertainty in her voice irritates me and ratchets the tension in me even tighter.

"So the directions say." I turn down the volume on Elvis singing about Dixie but keep a firm grip on the wheel, which overcompensates at the slightest touch, much as I seem to be doing.

Earlier at the hotel, I put an arm around her and asked how she was doing. She said, "Okay," but she's been quiet most of the day. My gaze darts from the winding road to the canopy of oaks.

"I guess if you wanted to do anything illegal, this would be a good place."

"Illegal?" Ben asks. "What do you mean illegal?"

"Maybe we should go back?" Ivy's voice is shaky.

Howie had hinted in his office about black-market

peddling of Elvis stuff. I imagine Baldy as some mafia type with dark glasses and a swarthy complexion.

"Oh, it's nothing," Rae says from the back seat. "Matt—"

"Otherwise known as Baldy," I interject for Ben's benefit.

"—has many interests. He's a good man, trustworthy."

"More than Howie?" I ask.

Rae laughs. "Certainly. I trust Howie as far as I can throw him. He's always been kind to me, but Baldy . . . I would trust him with my life."

I note the deepening shadows around us.

"Believe me, whatever happened, whatever is being said, has been said, or whatnot," Rae continues, "he will know."

"In other words, he'll know if Elvis is alive. Or haunting Beale Street." I drive under low-lying tree branches. One scrapes the Cadillac's canvas top. Stu wouldn't be happy about that. I wonder if this is the type of road he was on when he met Elvis, or whoever it was, on that long-ago night. Even though it's early afternoon, the heavy foliage blocks most of the sunlight that speckles the blacktop road.

Barely hearing Elvis's voice coming through the speakers as he sings "A Little Less Conversation," I can't put my faith in a ghost any more than I've been able to put my faith in God. Most likely it's some impersonator giving that impression.

"How much longer?" Ivy asks, her tone whiney.

I glance sideways. She looks pale. "Are you sick?"

"Here," Rae rummages in her purse. She pulls out a lemon drop. "This will help."

"Let me know if you need me to pull over," I add, hoping she won't throw up in the car.

Ivy plops the fat yellow candy in her mouth and nods.

Ben leans forward in his seat to get a better look at his daughter. "What's wrong?"

"I'm okay, Dad," she says in that irritating teen tone every parent despises.

His mouth thins. "Myrtle and Guy could have hired someone to steal the bust."

I toss a smile over my shoulder to show my gratitude for his solidarity with me on the anti-ghost issue. Encouraging this line of thought, I ask, "To give the chapel more of an aura?"

"Could be."

"That's not true!" Ivy's outburst doesn't surprise me. For her sake I hope they haven't done anything shady. They seem like an honest, sincere couple. Hiring an impersonator to steal the bust and concoct some weird legend seems underhanded and undermines the good they're trying to do at Faithland.

Spotting a bent metal post with a street number attached leaning into the shadows, I slow the car to a crawl. Out of habit I turn on the left blinker even though there's no traffic. However, it alerts those in the car that we're almost there. Everyone seems to lean forward, anticipating I don't know what. We jounce over roots and ruts in what becomes a dirt road that rocks us from side to side.

"Are you sure about this?" Ben asks, bracing a hand against the side door.

"No." I clutch the wheel as well. Ivy has to hang onto

the dash. We drive deeper into no-man's-land, or so it seems; I doubt any of our cell phones will work out here, much less be able to call the police if we need help. "Aunt Rae, you sure this . . . this guy . . . this place is safe?"

"Matt will help us. You'll see."

The road veers left, then back to the right. I no longer know if we're driving north or south or in circles. I stop at a wide puddle, unsure of its depth. I worry the Cadillac will get stuck. No tow truck will ever find us out here.

"What do you think?" I peer over the steering wheel. The puddle takes up almost the entire road, which is bracketed by tall, leafy trees.

Ben shrugs. "See if you can pull to the side. You might make it around the left over there."

I turn the steering wheel hard to the left and inch the car as close to a tree as I dare. "Stu would have a cow if he knew what I was doing to his car."

"You're okay." Ben's voice is calm as he leans forward to look out the windshield at the puddle. I wonder if he's anxious to get his hands on the wheel. "Keep going."

The car dips to the right, toward the small lake in the middle of the road. Suddenly one tire rolls through the edge of muddy water, making a big splash that leaps above the side door. Before I brake or decide to back up, we're on the other side. I breathe easier, until I realize we'll have to pass it again on our way back to the hotel.

Up ahead, the road widens and the woods end. We drive out into a clearing, the sun almost blinding and making my eyes water. I'm shaky all over and want to get out and walk around.

"Looks like we're late," Ben says.

We drive into what looks like a makeshift parking lot in the middle of an open field. A dozen or so cars are parked in orderly yet uneven rows.

"Maybe we're in the right place," I maneuver the Cadillac around another major rut and pull alongside a pickup truck that looks almost as old as the Cadillac.

"We're in good company," Ben comments.

I laugh, needing levity for my nerves.

Just beyond the parking lot sits an old metal trailer. Rounded on the ends, it looks like a silver hotdog with antennae sticking out in all directions like toothpicks.

Ben turns off the stereo, cutting off Elvis's "Viva Las Vegas" and rolls down his window an inch from the top. From the outside comes a booming voice over a crackling sound system and squawking microphone. I kill the engine but still can't make out the speaker's words.

"Are they having an auction, you think?" I imagine all sorts of Elvis paraphernalia set out and bidders poised and raising paddles to up their bids.

"An outdoors Christie's?" Rae asks.

"Only one way to find out," Ben says.

Rae opens her car door. "Let's go." Before I can blink, she's out of the car and walking through the field, lifting her knees high through the tall grass and brushing weeds away from her skirt.

"What do you think?" I hesitate.

"We can't let her go by herself." Ivy opens her car door and follows.

"Okay." I sigh. "Maybe we should have brought the bust. We could at least sell him to the highest bidder."

Ben laughs. "Or maybe we can find it a matching twin."

I groan.

In a long, scraggly line, we follow our fearless leader through the field and around the trailer. The booming voice pulls us in its direction, but I can't siphon out the static to hear what the man's saying for concentrating on not turning my ankle along the rocky ground. The voice sounds deep, with that Southern cadence that Elvis was famous for. Sticker burrs grab hold of my jeans and won't let go. One pricks my skin around my bare ankle. I feel a sharp jab and pause. Ben takes hold of my arm. I pause to brush off a sticker that has hitched a ride on my tennis shoe.

As I round the end of the trailer, I see a stage set up along its backside. Old, faded Christmas lights, several bulbs missing from their designated sockets, have been strung along the edges of the stage. The rest of the bulbs try their best to glow merrily; the colors are faded and give off a halo of light against the trailer's silver siding.

When I pass the stage, I notice a group of around fifty people from all walks of life, not all bunched together but spread out in little groups like patches on a patchwork quilt. A few gazes veer away from the speaker toward us, and they give polite nods of welcome before darting back to the man on stage. I pass a man in a wheelchair who listens in rapt attention. A young family in lawn chairs sits behind the wheelchair, the little ones crawling over each other.

I finally reach Rae, who's stopped walking and stands at the back of the crowd, her attention focused on the speaker. My breath comes in tiny huffs, and sweat dampens my forehead as I step beside her.

"What on earth is this?" I whisper.

But she only grabs my hand to silence me.

The man on stage has stark white hair, wide sideburns, and heavy jowls, but it's his speech that reminds me most of Elvis. I wonder why impersonators choose the older version of Elvis to imitate and not the younger, handsomer version.

Bits of what he is saying begin to pierce my thoughts. Before it had just been noise, loud and booming, but now his voice filters down through the open air, and I focus on what he's actually saying and not the crackles of the sound system.

". . . and it's time. T-time, do you hear?" he sounds like an old-fashioned, Bible-thumping preacher. "Time for us to help others, not takin', takin', takin'." He grabs at the air. "Who are you lookin' at, takin' from? When you should be givin' back?"

I glance at his audience. Most nod their heads up and down, in rhythm with his speech. A black woman walks along the perimeter of the group, pacing back and forth, her head bent as she listens.

"W-w-we got to bring folks together, not separate 'em. In my old life, my sin life, I was looked up to, admired even. Seein' me now, you probably c-c-can't believe that. But I was! I was a big shot. Now I'm just," he pauses to pat his belly, "big."

A murmur of laughter ripples through the crowd.

"But I kept trying to point folks to the higher one, to the only one that mattered." He jabs a fat finger at the sky. "A-a-and . . . I was just gettin' in the way. I was tearin' people apart." He pauses, eyes the audience, and wipes his face with a handkerchief.

"The Good Book says a wise man builds his house. Builds it! But fools tear it down. They ain't really meanin' to tear down their house with their bare hands. No, the Lord is talkin' 'bout things we do and say, things that knock others down rather than building them up.

"What you say to your brother, your daddy, your mama, your sister lately? Good buildin' things? Or tearin'-down things?"

My eyes meet Ben's as he stands beside me. He arches an eyebrow. I'm not sure if he means we've entered the Twilight Zone or if he regrets the things he's said to Ivy. I know there are things I regret, things I wish I could change. Maybe I came to Memphis for more than Elvis and Stu's request. Maybe it's my way of asking Stu to forgive my thoughtless words or careless actions.

I focus on the speaker again. If he's Baldy, then where'd he get the name? He is, however, large, his girth hefty. He paces back and forth along the small stage. He wears a startling white three-piece suit that accents the albino hair. He yanks his red tie from around his throat, and it dangles loosely against his rounded belly. Sunlight glitters off the beads of perspiration dotting his hairline.

"That should give you a-a-a something to think about this week. A-a-and I'm gonna do some ponderin' myself. I-I-I'll be back when I got more to say. Thank you. Thank you very much." He slurs the last words together into one, Elvis-like.

An equally large black man vaults onto the stage, claps the preacher on his back, and takes the microphone. The white-haired man all but collapses in a nearby folding chair and covers his face with his handkerchief. Unaccompanied and in a slow rhythm, the black man at center stage begins to sing "Working on the Building." Those in the audience stand and rock back and forth, matching his rhythm even when he picks up the tempo. Those in front of us start clapping, nodding their heads. The preacher raises his face toward the blue sky and sways in a Ray Charles fashion, as if he sees nothing but his own image of heaven.

Then I notice Rae. Her eyes are closed and she's moving with the music as if she's entered her own world and blocked out everything but the music.

The black man, who is bald, changes the tempo yet again with "Known Only to Him," a song I recognize from the Elvis gospel album that Stu listened to more and more toward the end. It's then, I realize, the preacher has disappeared from the stage.

I elbow Ben. "Where'd he go?"

"Who?"

"The guy who was preaching earlier." The guy who looked like an old version of Elvis, much older than forty-two.

Ben shrugs. "How should I know?"

As suddenly as the music started, it ends. The crowd pulls out baskets of sandwiches and fried chicken. Rae doesn't motion to us or anything; she just steps forward through the crowd, toward the stage. I attempt to follow but am stopped by a man with long, gray hair tied in a braid, his beard straggly.

"How y'all doin'?" he asks. I imagine him as a bouncer in a bar. His muscles bulge, bunching the sleeves of his T-shirt into his arm pits.

"Fine," I say. "And yourself."

"Not too bad today. Nice day. No rain." He rolls his arm and pops his shoulder. "No arthritis."

I nod, looking past him to Rae, who has reached the stage and is giving the black singer a hug. They're laughing, and I'm anxious to catch up to them. Ben and Ivy stop beside me. Ben and the man shake hands.

"How'd you folks learn about us way out here?"

"A friend." I use the word loosely in reference to Howie. Is the preacher, I wonder, one of Howie's older, retired impersonators?

"A friend," Ben agrees.

"Someone here?" The man looks around.

"We know Baldy," I say, hoping Baldy is the name he goes by rather than Matt and hoping it's the black man that Rae's conversing with.

"I see. I see. Well, glad to know you. Come back anytime."

"Thank you," I say, inching by him with Ben and Ivy in tow and moving toward the front of the crowd.

"That chicken smells good," Ivy says.

I laugh and wrap an arm around her shoulders. "We'll get you some food soon."

Stepping up beside Rae, I glance at the curtained windows along the back of the trailer and wonder if the preacher has disappeared inside.

Rae's saying, ". . . that time we sang in the bathroom."

The black man rocks back on his heels and laughs. He has a big, toothy grin that splits his face into sunburst lines. "The acoustics were good though."

"It was the police who didn't understand." She laughs.

He rubs his jaw. "Well, there were some ladies who wanted their privacy, I expect."

"Matt," she says, "I want you to meet some friends of mine. This is Claudia, Ben, and Ivy." With her hand still on Matt's shoulder, she adds, "This is Baldy."

Smiling, he rubs his hand over his bare head. "Want me to tell your nickname, sugar?"

"Not today." She matches his smile.

"You all come all the way from Texas?" he asks.

I grin and shake his hand. "All the way."

Ben grips his hand then. "We heard you might know—"

"This is an amazing place," Rae interrupts. "When did you start this congregation?"

I exchange glances with Ben, who shrugs and keeps his question to himself.

"Oh, well, 'bout five years ago. You'll probably be the talk of the day, seein' we don't often have visitors."

"Is it supposed to be private?" Ivy asks, her eyes wide as if we crashed a funeral and didn't know the deceased.

"No, no. Don't you worry, miss. Ain't nobody but us interested in our ranting and raving way out here. We're a small group, but this is all some of us have for family. Don't like meetin' Sunday mornin'. Sometimes it's hard to get up after a Saturday night of fun, you know what I mean? So we meet out here toward evening every Sunday. Unless it's rainin'. What with the microphone and such, we don't want to set off those kinda sparks."

"And the preacher?" I ask, curious about the man who looked too much like Elvis for my comfort.

"Oh, Aaron. Well, he comes when he's got something to say."

"Where'd he go?"

"You's welcome anytime," he nods to Ivy, ignoring my question, which makes me even more suspicious. "Anytime. You bring that baby of yours when it comes, and Aaron will baptize it for you."

"Is he a real preacher?" I ask.

"Ordained by God," he says.

But not by a school of divinity, I surmise.

Ivy stares at the man as if she's been struck dumb. "H-how did you . . ."

I wonder how he knows she's pregnant since she doesn't have a big tummy yet. I doubt Rae would have mentioned it to him before introducing us.

"Know?" Baldy finishes her question. "I knows things. Don't know why. Just do."

"Always has." Rae touches his arm. "You knew about me, about my . . . before I even knew."

"That's right!" He slaps his leg. "I'd forgotten that. My momma said I had the sight. The vision. Some folks call me psychic, but I don't hold to that. Ain't spoken about well in the Good Book, you see? I just knows things sometimes. And then other times, I don't think I know much at all." He rocks backward on his heels and laughs, like he's sharing a joke with the Almighty.

I don't know if this man can help us, but I like him. And I know now why Rae never forgot him. She slides her hand down Baldy's arm and clasps his hand. Neither seems aware of it, yet it seems like a natural gesture between the two.

"If I'd known you was comin' today," he says, looking down at Rae, "I would have had you sing with me."

"Oh, no. I haven't . . . not in a long while. I'm out of practice."

But I remember her singing in the car, her hands covering the keyboard at Faithland.

"Some things," he continues, "you can't forget."

"That's true." Rae shares a look with him, something that excludes the rest of us.

"So what brings you out here? You wantin' to talk to Aaron? He don't usually—"

"We came to see you," Rae said. "I didn't know about Aaron. Is he okay?"

"Sure. He goes off after he's done preaching. Needs some peace. He's spent after he spills it all out like he does."

"I'm glad you've remained friends all these years," she says.

I stare at Rae. She knows the preacher, too? I can't wait to ask her a few questions when we're alone.

"Oh, you caught us on a good day. We must be mellowin'. We ain't had a fight in a year or two now. 'Course, now that you're here, we might fight over you."

She laughs, then her smile fades.

"What's wrong?" he asks.

"Howie thought you might help us."

"About the bust?"

My jaw drops. Did Howie call? No, he couldn't have known about the bust. "How'd you know?"

He shrugs, holds his hands out as if he's showing he has

no cards up his sleeves. "This the bust that disappeared . . . a while back?"

"Do you know who it belonged to?" Ben asks.

"Some things don't belong to nobody. They not of this world."

I doubt that. The plaster is certainly of this world. Not from Mars. "My husband wanted me to return it to its owner. It was his last request."

Baldy rolls his thick lips inward and contemplates the situation. "Not sure that's possible."

"So it was him, wasn't it?" Rae asks.

"Some answers can't be known. It takes faith." He looks at me then. "You's questioning, I know. But don't. Just believe."

"What if I can't."

He laughs a deep rumbling laugh. "Oh, sure you can. Everybody can. It's a choice. But you gotta *want* to believe. Then you'll see. Gotta take that first little step."

I don't want to talk about me and my lack of faith. I want to clarify things. "You're saying my husband saw and met Elvis? The King? Elvis Aaron Presley?"

Remembering Elvis's full name, I glance at the trailer and feel a jolt deep inside me. Did they mean . . . ? Was the preacher Elvis? He went by Aaron, didn't he?

"Ah, well, who or what your husband saw ain't the important thing here." Baldy rubs his jaw and glances at me sideways.

"Was he alive or dead?" Ben asks.

"Her husband?" Baldy asks.

I sense he's toying with us.

He cracks a smile which then fades into a long, somber look. "No, you's missing the point. Pay attention now."

We all lean forward.

"Elvis ain't the king."

"How so?" Ben asks.

"Just is. Ain't right. Aaron said last night . . ."

A movement of the curtain in the trailer's window grabs my attention. I lose track of what Baldy is saying. When he pauses, I ask, "So you think my husband helped a ghost?"

"You folks sure is hardheaded." Baldy scratches his head. "I can't say for sure what your husband done or who he helped. But if you got that Faithland bust, then the best thing you can do is get rid of it. It's—" He glances over his shoulder, rolls his thick lips inward as if he's changed his mind about saying anything else.

"Is the bust haunted?" Ivy asks.

"Nah. But all the same, drop it in the river or take a hammer to it. Anything."

"I have to return it."

"Maybe it ain't meant to be returned to nobody. Maybe your husband wanted you to let it go. Let him go. Ain't it time?"

Chapter Twenty

Return to Sender

Shaken to my core, I climb back into the Cadillac, the hot seats searing my backside. I stare through the now dusty windshield at the silver trailer and the dispersing crowd. I roll down the side window to release the hot air trapped in the car.

Baldy struck a raw, exposed nerve that throbs with resentment. But he's right. I need to let Stu go. I've been hanging on, clinging to him, his memory, his things. My life can be divided into three parts—pre-Stu, Stu, and post-Stu. Before I met him, I felt as if I was waiting for something but wasn't sure what. With Stu, I came alive. Without him, I feel as if I've died.

But how can I sever the cord that binds us? I don't know anything to do but to keep moving forward, slowly, slowly, in the opposite direction from him. Which means living. I hope at some point the cord between us will snap in two.

How long will it take for that to happen? How will I respond? Will I have moved so far down the path into my own life that I won't even notice? Will I simply awaken one day, go about my business, and realize when I come upon an old picture of Stu that I haven't thought about him in minutes, hours, days?

"That was interesting." Ben settles into the back seat beside Rae.

"Pimpin'," Ivy says, making me wonder again if that's good or bad. She slams the front passenger door shut. "Can we come back?"

Rae remains silent in the back. Is she lost in her own thoughts, her own past? Is she remembering her younger days, her friends in Memphis, Elvis?

I can't stop thinking of him. It's as if Elvis and Stu have merged into one being. The questions formed during the sermon rise within me as I stick the key in the ignition and crank up the air-conditioning. Hot air blasts me in the face.

"Aunt Rae," I readjust the vents, "who was that Aaron?"

"A friend."

"But—"

"I knew him back in my Memphis days."

I figured that much. But his resemblance to Elvis, his mysterious behavior, and the strange references to a previous, affluent lifestyle fit together like puzzle pieces. Is he the King of Rock 'n' Roll? Not according to Baldy. But then he'd cover for his friend, wouldn't he? It's easier to believe that Elvis is still alive than to believe his ghost wanders around Memphis searching for a butt-ugly bust, as Ivy likes to call it. I swallow back any embarrassment and let the most obvious question fly.

"Is your friend Aaron really Elvis?"

When I turn around to look at Rae, she stares back as if trying to absorb the question and understand it. "Elvis?"

"Are you talking about the preacher?" Ivy asks. When I nod, she adds, "Kinda weird and freaky."

"He looked a lot like Elvis. What Elvis might look like at the age of seventy. If he was still alive." My gaze slants toward Rae. "Is he?"

"Definitely Elvis impersonator material," Ben agrees. "Had his nose. Even the same mouth. And that awkward stutter."

"Dad! You were staring at another guy's mouth?"

I laugh at Ben's comical expression.

"I was being observant," Ben defends himself.

"Thank you. Thank you verra much," I say in my best Elvis impression.

Ben snaps his fingers. "What was Elvis's brother's name? Didn't it start with an A?"

"His dead twin?" I ask.

"Yeah."

"Aaron? No, Aaron was Elvis's middle name, wasn't it? His twin had something similar. What was it? I saw something at Graceland about him. I remember Stu telling me there was some controversy over the spelling of the name, whether it was two *A*'s or one. Which made some conspiracy fanatics believe Elvis took on his brother's persona rather than dying."

Ben chuckles.

"So that was Elvis's dead brother?" Ivy asks. "Gross!"

"The preacher was not Jesse Garon Presley," Rae says in a slow, methodical cadence as if to make clear to the slow-witted. She waves her arm and the tiny charms on her bracelet tinkle like bells. "Nor was he Elvis."

"But he wouldn't talk to anybody. He just disappeared," I argue. "And—"

"He talked about being rich. Highfalutin'," Ben adds, "before some life change."

I laugh. "Highfalutin'? You've been in Memphis too long."

Ben grins like a little boy. "His words, not mine."

Rae sighs as if frustrated with us. "He's Aaron Wise."

"Who?" Ben asks.

"The preacher."

"Yeah," I say, "but what was all that talk about him being a big shot way back when . . ."

"He was an attorney. He thought he was a big shot, better than anyone else. Like most attorneys. But then he had what you might call an attitude adjustment."

"What happened?" Ivy asks.

Rae looks down at her lap, rubs a thumbnail along a line down her palm. "I wasn't here at the time. Happened in the early eighties, I think."

"When all tragedies were known to occur," Ben jokes.

"Fashion tragedies were in the seventies," I say.

He laughs. "I remember some from the eighties. Remember *Flashdance*? Madonna . . . ?"

"Cindy Lauper, Boy George." I make a face. "Robert Palmer—"

"Now, he was cool."

Rae clears her throat.

I share a smirk with Ben, like we're in college once again. Then I feel guilty for interrupting my aunt. "I'm sorry, Rae. Please go on."

"Aaron was hit by a bus. By the way, you forgot Calvin Klein jeans."

"Nothing wrong with Brooke Shields in her Calvins," Ben says.

"Dad, that's disgusting."

"Okay," Ben says like he's conducting a business meeting, "so Aaron met a Greyhound up close and personal, huh? I guess that would get your attention."

"It did. He was in a coma for four months. Rehab for a year. Or so I'm told."

"And now he gets messages from the Almighty?" I ask.

Rae shrugs. "That is open to interpretation."

I glance out the windshield toward the hot-dog-shaped trailer, the silver shell glinting in the late afternoon sunlight. "Do you think we should talk to him? Think he might know about Stu's Elvis?"

"He doesn't see anyone. We should forget about the bust."

Rae's words stun me. She's been adamant about following Stu's directive.

"Claudia," she continues, "you should keep it if you want . . . or sell it. I don't think there is any place for you to leave it here in Memphis. Although you might get a fair price."

I shake my head. "That's not true. I think it belongs to Myrtle and Guy over at Faithland."

"But," Ivy protests, "it'll destroy everything, all the mystique of the chapel."

"Mystique? A church needs mystique?" I ask, then focus on Rae. "Or did Baldy tell you something before we caught up with you?"

"I don't know what you mean," Rae says.

"You were talking to him alone. Had you already told him about the bust?"

"You're being paranoid."

"I'm going to take it back. If it belongs to Myrtle and Guy, then they can put it in the attic or behind the altar or smash it. I don't care." I want my life back. "They should have the choice of what to do with it."

"I don't know," Ben says. "You might be messing with more than you realize."

I glance at Rae. Her features seem closed, as if she holds her own secrets. I shake my head. "This is crazy. It's a bust. Plaster and air. It's probably hollow on the inside."

Ben whistles the theme to *The Twilight Zone*. I laugh. Ivy looks heavenward. Rae cocks her head and looks at Ben as if he's slipped off his rocker.

"Maybe there's something inside the bust." He licks his lips, puckers again, and whistles the familiar refrain from *Raiders of the Lost Ark*. "Maybe we should crack it open and take a peek."

"That's gross." Ivy leans back against the seat and crosses her arms over her chest.

"It's not like an autopsy," I say. "How would we do that without destroying it?"

"X-ray?" Ben grins at my exasperated look. "We'd simply—"

"We can't do that anyway," I disagree before Ben can finish. "It would ruin it. And it's not ours. Remember?"

Ben whistles a strange eerie tune. "It's Elvis's. He'll come back for it. You wait. You'll see."

With a snicker of laughter behind me, I shift gears into reverse. I'm more determined than ever to find an ending and move on with my life. Even if that means simply returning to the life I know in Dallas. Alone. Without Elvis.

♪♩♪♩.♩♪♩

I STARE AT the bust. Elvis sneers back at me. I want to take a hammer and bash in his head, see if there's some treasure inside, some reason for all this fuss.

Ben crosses in front of me and picks up the bust. Heavy as it is, he tilts it this way and that. Leaning close, he says, "I don't hear anything . . . no old coins jingling around . . . no rattling of diamonds."

"What about heavy gold chains?"

He laughs and puts it down on the table with a satisfied *clunk*. "I think it's hollow. Or maybe completely solid."

Shaking my head, I walk over to the big window, jerk open the curtain, and open the window. I wave my hand and say, "Just toss him over the side."

He laughs.

"I'm serious."

"You can't do that. Stu—"

"I don't care what Stu wrote, what he asked, what he wanted! He's not here anymore!" I stop myself, release my suddenly clenched hands, and draw in a deep, steadying breath. The smell of fried grease from some nearby fast-food establishment makes me cough. Feeling foolish for my outburst, I meet Ben's stare, know he's waiting for my decision. But I have none. I turn on my heel. "I'm going to bed."

But sleep doesn't come. I lay in the dark for what seems like hours, questioning myself, questioning Stu. "Why would you send me on this journey?" I whisper in the night's quiet. "Why?"

Silence is his answer. Much like God's answers to my prayers.

I remember a time when Stu was sick, his head propped in my lap. I tried to soothe his brow, easing out the tiny lines with my fingertips. Chemo gobbled up his hair like a ravenous tiger. "Why is this happening?" I asked, not expecting an answer yet needing one. He didn't respond. In a moment or two, I realized he'd fallen asleep.

I slam the cabinet on that memory. I want to remember happier times, healthier times. But I can't get past remembering Stu ill, weak, waiting to die.

A college memory surfaces of two young men—one wiry, the other bulky—cutting up and laughing. Ben and Stu shared a friendship few men ever experience. They didn't just grab a basketball and hoop it up through the afternoon. They didn't just go fishing together. They also had long serious discussions about their faith, about God. And they'd prayed together.

"God isn't some distant being out there in space," Stu had explained to me.

"That's right," Ben said. "He's more than that. He wants more than that from you."

"He wants to live right here," Stu clapped a hand on his chest.

A chill seeps into my bones as I sit on the hotel bed. The beige sheets have been worn smooth by many washings. Had I believed because Stu wanted me to? Had I believed to be closer to Stu? Had I believed what they'd said at all? They seemed to understand so much more. They seemed to have an actual relationship with God.

Unable to dwell on those questions, I rifle through my thoughts, deliberately going back to an argument Stu and I had several months after I'd come home from the hospital and found he'd taken down the baby bed and repainted the pink room a plain-Jane builder's beige. We hadn't spoken of our loss.

"I want a baby," I said, tossing the topic we'd been avoiding out like a stone. It hit the water with a splash, and the waves undulated outward.

Stu looked at me over the toes of his sports socks. His green eyes narrowed. Slowly he sat up, put his drink on the coffee table.

I clicked off the television. "I want a baby."

"I know," he said quietly—too quietly.

Maybe that was the end of the discussion. Maybe it was going to be easier than I'd anticipated.

"But I don't anymore," he said, his tone gentle, as if it could soften the blow.

I felt the air yanked out of my body. "But you did. Once."

"That was before. But now I don't. I'm happy with just you and me. Let's not mess with it."

"But we always planned to have a baby, maybe two. What about those plans?"

He wouldn't meet my gaze. "I can't watch you go through that again."

I sat on the edge of the couch. Hot tears seared my eyes. I blinked, tried to think of a response, some argument that would sway him, blinked again. "But I want a baby."

"Why?"

"I don't know. Because I do."

"Because it's the thing to do?" He took a swig of his soda. "None of the guys at the office are happy parents. Look at the heartache. You give yourself to these kids, and they grow up and bad-mouth you, back talk, and you get to foot the bill. You pay for all their activities. All their mistakes. Do you know how much hockey costs?"

"Hockey?" I asked, bewildered.

"Hockey. Or horses. Or dance or whatever the kid is interested in."

No more than that stupid Cadillac he'd bought and was renovating.

"What if the kid gets sick . . . even dies? It happens. The cost is greater. And I don't mean monetary expenses."

I knew then I'd lost. Our baby had turned into "the kid."

"Then there's college. Do you know how much a good college costs? And then there's a wedding to pay for."

When he stopped ranting and raving about money and the price of textbooks, I said, "But I want a baby."

"I don't."

"We could adopt," I suggested.

"No."

"But that's not fair! Why do you get to decide?"

"*We're* deciding."

"How? I want one, you say no, that's a decision? You're deciding for both of us! That's not fair."

"Life isn't fair, Claudia. Or have you forgotten how devastating losing . . ."

He couldn't say her name. He couldn't say the name we'd decided on while staring down at her little cold body. "Emily."

"Why can't we just be happy with us?" He challenged my desire with a sharp glare, then left the room.

I stared at the blank television, knowing the decision had been made. I thought about leaving. I could have filed for divorce on the grounds we had different dreams, different hopes, different goals. But I knew instantly that I wouldn't. I would stay. And I would try to make us happy. Just us.

I realize now, sitting in the hotel bed all alone, that I've tamped down my anger into a black hole in my heart.

IN THE MORNING, bleary-eyed from lack of sleep, I pad out into the main living area. Ben is snoring on the couch where he fell asleep. Pale rose light slants through the parted curtains and spotlights Elvis. I stare at the American icon, the King. Did I put Stu on a pedestal? Worship him rather than God? I'd glorified him, certainly in college and even more so when he was sick and beaten by cancer. Purposefully I'd blocked out pages of our history in my own form of selective censorship. But it hadn't been our whole story. The Stu I kept in my memory most of the time wasn't the real Stu. Just like this bust wasn't the real Elvis. He'd been just a man, no better or worse than any other. Just a man.

Ben said Stu identified with Elvis. Stu had had good points and bad. He'd done good deeds and made mistakes.

So had I.

Suddenly I could relate to Stu in a way I never had before. I was beginning to understand why Stu had sent me on this wild ghost chase with a bulky Elvis bust in tow.

Chapter Twenty-One

It Is No Secret

"Help me, will you?" I ask, bending over Elvis. He's more awkward than heavy, much as Stu was in his last days.

Without questioning me, Ben leans into the car from the opposite side and picks up the bust all on his own. I remember him helping the hospice nurse move Stu into a wheelchair, Stu's legs limp and almost useless. Ben had knelt in front of his friend, his shoulders seeming wider than normal, his skin healthier and tanned, his muscles working the way they should. Gently he'd placed Stu's socked feet onto the metal slabs, his motions tender, not the way the two men had bruised and roughhoused with each other through the years. His love was pronounced in gentle kindness.

"You sure about this?" Ben asks me, his voice compressed, pulling me back to the task at hand.

"Let me help," I say as he pulls the bust out of the car. Behind me I hear the jangle of Rae's bracelets as she waits on the curb.

"Just tell me where you want him." Ben grunts, shifting Elvis in his arms, jabbing himself in the gut with one corner of the base.

"Myrtle is not gonna like this." Ivy taps her flip-flopped toe on the pavement. The granite sign glitters in the morning light. Faithland. Do I have enough faith to let Stu go now? Am I ready to say good-bye?

I nod encouragement for Ben to continue, meeting his gaze over the top of Elvis's pompadour. I hope he doesn't wrench his back as he wrestles with the King. He motions with a dip of his head, indicating I should lead. I pull open the heavy door to the chapel and hold it for Ben to walk past me, then Rae enters, followed by Ivy.

Ben stops in the middle of the main aisle. The lights have been dimmed, giving the chapel a soft, golden glow. It's empty except for us. Out of the hidden speakers comes Elvis's rendition of "It Is No Secret (What God Can Do)," his voice reverent and deep.

"Put him here." I pat a back-row pew. The scarlet velvet cushion makes a soft throne for the King. I don't want to be presumptuous in placing him on the pedestal up front.

I stand there a moment, not knowing what to say, what to do, looking down at Elvis. I try to imagine him at the front of the chapel, hoping to get some flash of insight that this is where he belongs. But to me, the bust just looks stupid sitting there in the pew. Deflated, I sink into a seat behind Elvis. Slowly the others settle around him like groupies. I glance toward the private entrance door that leads to the office and home of Myrtle and Guy, where they housed Ivy overnight.

"What now?" I ask, my voice sounding too loud in the stillness of the chapel.

"Wait," Rae says. "They'll come."

"I've heard that before," Ben jokes.

"Who do you mean by 'they'? Guy and Myrtle? Or Elvis and Stu?" I laugh but no one else does.

"Want me to go knock?" Ivy asks.

"No," I say too abruptly and not sure why. "Let's see if they come out."

"We could be waiting here all night," Ben says. He's been on his cell phone with vendors for the nonprofit on the way over to the chapel. I can't believe I haven't thought of work in days. I know he's anxious to head back to Dallas. I promised we'd go this afternoon. Or so I hope. If all goes well with Myrtle and Guy.

"Okay," I say, rising from the pew, "I'll knock—"

But at that moment, the private door opens a crack. I hear Myrtle saying something about the toilet needed unclogging, then she steps through the doorway. "Well, hello!" She moves toward us, her smile tightening into concern. "Is everything okay? Ivy, how are—"

She stops between the third and fourth pew, her facial muscles going lax, making her look even older. Myrtle's tanned skin suddenly pales. "Oh, my," she whispers and grabs onto the nearest pew. She's wearing a tight-fitting orange tank top that clashes with her red hair and shows her well-rounded bosom heaving with each breath. "Wh-wh-what is . . . I mean, how on earth . . . ?"

"Myrtle," Ivy says, going to her, "are you okay?"

"Seems you do know Elvis," I say.

Myrtle stumbles, then sits in the nearest pew, across the aisle from Elvis. She looks as if she's seen a ghost.

"I told them not to bring it, Myrtle," Ivy cries. "I told them!"

"Are you okay?" I ask, suddenly worried.

Myrtle ages in front of us. Her whole body sags, the loose skin of her arms and neck drooping. She gives a slow nod, but she keeps nodding, as if she's forgotten what she's doing. "But how . . . how did this happen? Was *he* here again?"

"He?" Ivy hugs her friend. "We brought it."

"It wasn't a ghost," I say, "who took the bust. It was my husband."

"You don't know who or what was involved, Claudia," Rae cautions, but I ignore her.

"Your husband?" Myrtle looks confused.

I tell her about Stu, his penchant for practical jokes, his weekend in Memphis (minus the grizzled man on the side of the road), and Stu's last note to me. Feeling the weight of my husband's responsibility, I whisper, "I'm so sorry."

"That can't be what happened," Myrtle says. "I saw . . . I know I saw . . . *him*. Elvis. Right here at the chapel." She looks around with crazed eyes, as if she's reliving the moment. "I saw him myself!"

"It's okay." Ivy pets her arm, trying to soothe her friend.

"You probably just saw my husband and mistook him for—"

"No! It was—"

"What's going on?" Guy asks as he walks through the private entrance and into the chapel. "Myrtie?" He rushes forward. "You okay, baby?" He puts a hand on her shoulder, kneels beside her. Pure concern darkens his eyes. "What's happened? Ivy, are you back? You doin' okay? What's happened?"

"It wasn't my fault, Guy," Ivy says. "I told them not to bring it. But they wouldn't listen to me. What does a teenager know, right?"

"Bring what?"

"This," I place my hand on Elvis's head and repeat my story.

Guy looks equally shaken.

"It's not possible," Myrtle repeats. "I saw Elvis that night. And there was no man . . . no human being with *him*."

"You only saw part," Guy says gently. "I've always wondered how a ghost could have lifted the bust. Now we know he recruited somebody to help him."

"Recruited?" I keep the rest of my dissident thoughts silent. I can't believe they still think a ghost is responsible rather than a more practical explanation of a thief. But I'm relieved to see their genuine shock at the sight of Elvis without twinges of guilt, which I hope means they had no part in its disappearance. Only in the legend. And from Myrtle's shocked expression, she's either an Oscar-worthy actress or has come to believe her own propaganda about a restless, wandering Elvis.

"Well, it's yours," I say. "You can have it."

"No harm done, right?" Ben stands. "Okay, now that—"

"No, you keep it." Myrtle clasps her husband's hand. "Or else Elvis will be back."

"I ain't scared of no ghost," Guy says, crossing his arms over his chest. "But the bust still can't stay."

My heart thunders. We came all this way only to be thwarted because they don't want the bust? "But why? It's yours."

"It's the principle of the thing." He pats his wife's shoulder. "We learned a valuable lesson back then. We was putting Elvis on a pedestal, looking to him, worshipping him instead of who we was supposed to.

"Remember that story of Elvis, Myrtie? The one where some girls were sitting on the front row of a concert. And they waved a sign declaring Elvis as the King. Elvis stopped right there and looked at those girls all serious like and said—"

"'I'm not the king,'" Rae interrupts.

Guy nods. "'Jesus Christ is.' That's what he said."

Elvis's tender voice floats out from the hidden speakers as he sings "In the Garden." Stunned, I don't know what to do, where to turn, what to say.

"And those girls," Guy continues, "put that sign down. Just like we can't put Elvis back up on that pedestal. So," he looks at me then, "I'm sorry, miss. But Elvis can't stay."

"But you've still got the pedestal, the shrine. Right there."

"Sure, it's a good reminder how wrong we were."

"But my husband . . . it was his last request." I look at Elvis. In that moment I hate the bust as I never have before. "I can't take it home again." Tears come, and I can't push them back. "I'll never have my own life if I don't get rid of Elvis."

Suddenly Ben's beside me, his arm around my shoulders. "It's okay," he soothes. "We'll figure something out."

"Guy," Myrtle says, "do something."

Her husband hands me a tissue.

"Maybe there's a back room," Rae says, "someplace you could store him. Elvis would find no fault with that. Neither would the Almighty."

"Don't matter about Elvis, what he'd think." Guy says.

"This isn't about a bust or Elvis," Ben says. "It's about you, Claudia. Stu knew that. And it was his greatest wish before he died. Do you know why he sent you on this—"

"Wild ghost chase?" I'm shaking my head as I wipe my nose with the tissue.

"Because he knew you'd lost your faith. He wanted you to get it back."

"But—"

Ben drops to his knee beside me, cups my hands in his. "Stu knew you'd lost your way. He felt guilty for that."

"It wasn't his fault. Maybe I never believed enough."

"No." Ben squeezes my hand. "He knew the loss of your baby, your mom, even Stu had worn away your hope. He knew it all started when your dad died."

I can't look at Ben. The truth of his words slices clean through me.

"He wanted you to believe."

"What if I can't?"

"Because God didn't answer your prayers?"

I shrug, my throat tight.

"I bet Jesus felt the same as you," Guy says, "that night in Gethsemane."

I look up. My tears make Guy seem blurry and distorted, like the reflection in a fun-house mirror.

"Think about it," he says. "Jesus was praying he wouldn't have to die. Didn't want to do it. But God said no.

Jesus Christ, the son of God, was told no. Imagine that! So he knows exactly what you're feeling."

Glancing at Myrtle, then Rae, Ivy, and Ben, they're all watching me, nodding in agreement with Guy. My mind wrestles, twisting and turning over his words, but my heart maintains a slow, steady beat.

"Faith," Rae says, "isn't some miracle. It's not magic. It's not some elusive thing, unattainable by most. It's simply a choice, Claudia."

"Faith is being sure of what we hope for . . ." Guy says.

"Certain of what we don't see," Myrtle finishes.

"That's it," Ben adds. "Pretty simple. We hope for more. But we can't see it. Can't see God. But we can see God's hand in things."

"So how do you believe through all you've suffered, through all that's happened to you?" My voice wavers.

"One step at a time. One day at a time." He sits back on his heels. "I know that sounds trite, but it's true. There've been days when I don't think I believe anything. There've been days when I railed at God. But it all comes back to what I hope for and what I can't see. And so I keep walking forward."

♪♩♪♩.♩♪♩

FIRST IVY EXCUSES herself to go to the restroom. Then Myrtle and Rae leave to fix the teen a sandwich. Slowly Guy and Ben follow. Until I am left alone. In the chapel. With Elvis.

I stare at the black pompadour and stand-up collar for a few minutes. Ben's words roll around my head. Somewhere high above me, Elvis's soulful voice drifts out of a speaker singing "Without Him." I toy with the idea.

I remember back before I'd taken the first tentative step toward God. We did a dance of sorts for a while, one step forward, two steps back. I was scared. Uncertain. Bewildered by what it all meant. But soon it became scarier thinking God wasn't there, watching over me, guiding me. I wonder now if I want to return to a place where I didn't believe or if I want to take a tentative step toward God again. I believe it is a choice. And I'm standing on the brink.

I push up from the pew, walk past Elvis and on up to the front. There are two steps up to the altar. The red carpet is plush and inviting. I sit and fold my arms around my knees.

I close my eyes, squeeze them tight. I don't expect to feel anything, to hear anything other than Elvis singing an old spiritual. But as I begin to voice my objections, my doubts, my prayer that doesn't exactly sound like a psalm or the Lord's Prayer, a peace sweeps over me.

Finally, spent of words and tears, I press my cheek to the altar. There's no Elvis on it, no Stu, nothing of this world.

Across the chapel Elvis stares at me from his seat on a back pew. Suddenly I think I grasp Stu's connection with Elvis, the tug of war between hedonism and spirituality. I have felt it in my dance with disbelief and belief.

It's a first step, and I know it won't be the last. The rhythm of Elvis's jaunty "If the Lord Wasn't Walking by My Side" makes me think of this awkward dance of mine. I'm no longer dancing with a memory. It feels as if God has reached his hand out toward me. He's chosen me.

I'm simply a wallflower, blending in with the others. I've got a list of excuses for why I shouldn't tango. But here we go. There'll be steps forward and backward, side steps, twirls, and dips. I'm not leading but following. At least I'm dancing again.

♪♩♪♩. ♩♪♩

"ARE YOU OKAY?" Ben touches my shoulder.

"I think so." I do feel better, just stiff now as I push myself to my feet. "Is everyone ready to go?"

He nods. "Myrtle and Guy have agreed to keep Elvis till we get all packed. Then we can come pick him up. No sense in carrying him back to the hotel."

I look at the bust sitting on a pew as if he's an orphan, waiting for someone to want him. I don't hate him anymore. In fact, I think I'm beginning to like him. "I still don't understand why Stu wanted us to come here. Seems like an awful lot of trouble for nothing."

"Getting your faith back is not nothing," he says as if he's read my thoughts, my heart.

I rub the tension out of my forehead. "I feel like I've been so stupid, so blind."

"Grief does strange things. Your tears blinded you. But I think you're starting to see more clearly."

"I think you're right." I watch as Ivy and Rae emerge from Myrtle and Guy's private quarters.

"Everything okay?" Rae asks.

"Of course." We move to leave.

"Elvis will be safe here," Myrtle says, following behind us.

I pass Elvis still sitting in the pew. I feel a need to reach out and touch him. My finger brushes a stud in his upright collar. This should be good-bye. Instead it's "see you later."

We'll pick up Elvis on our way out of town. Then we'll take him back to Dallas. Or dump him along the highway. Or sell him to the highest bidder. I guess it doesn't matter anymore. Ben is right. It's not about Elvis. It's not even about Stu anymore.

Ben touches my arm, leads me to the car. I remember he was there, leading me away from Stu's grave. There's comfort in his touch, in his presence.

"Do you want me to drive?" he asks.

I shake my head. "No, I'm okay."

Then I know the truth. I am okay. I don't have the answers. I can't see God. But I know what I hope for. And that's enough in this moment. Even if I have to keep Elvis in the attic forever.

When Ben and Ivy settle in the back, I start the engine, give a quick wave to Myrtle and Guy standing on the top step, then pull away from the curb. My plan when we reach the hotel is to pack and leave. It's time to say good-bye, just as Baldy said.

With a glance at Rae, I say, "You were pregnant with Elvis's baby, weren't you?" I imagine the headline: *Elvis's Love Child Discovered!* "That's why you left Memphis, right?"

"I was pregnant," she says.

"Was it Elvis's?"

"The father was . . ." She shrugs. "This wasn't an environment I wanted for a baby. My baby." She says the words slowly, as if savoring the fact that it was her baby.

Slowly, like a small child connecting the dots on a mimeograph page in school, I connect the things I know about Rae. "So then you gave the baby up for adoption? To an agency?"

She looks at me, her eyes dark. She touches my hand.

"I gave the baby to my sister."

Braking at a red light, I feel her words grip me like brakes clamping down on a wheel. For a moment it feels as if my heart doesn't beat, as if everything stops. I can't hear the road sounds, a siren wailing in the distance, the drone of a song on the radio. Silence. My chest feels compressed, like a heavy weight is pushing against it, restricting my breathing.

As if in the distance, I hear a faint *thumping.* It grows louder, and I recognize my own heartbeat pounding in my ears.

Slowly I look at Rae. She meets my gaze, steady, sure. Regret and fear cloud her eyes. I recognize the emotions, know them personally.

A car horn blares behind me, makes my skin contract.

"Light's green," Ben says.

But I can't move. Can't speak. Can't breathe.

Chapter Twenty-Two

It's Now or Never

The silence in the car feels like the pregnant moment when a balloon has been inflated beyond its capacity to stretch and an explosion is imminent. As I hastily park the car, I step on the brakes too hard, jarring my passengers and myself. Without a word to anyone, I slam the car door and walk toward the hotel and our room. My one thought is to pack, leave, and go home. It's safe there. I want to crawl into my own bed, pull the covers over my head, and forget this weekend.

A small part of me collapsed when we left Elvis at the chapel. But now my lungs compress, my mind reels from Rae's confession. Is she telling the truth? Maybe she made it all up . . . about Elvis . . . about my mother.

I've returned to Topsy-Turvyville.

I pause at the elevator. Before the doors open, Rae reaches my side. When we step onto the elevator, she stands across the small space, looking at me, her eyes wide and watchful. I stare down at the floor and realize we are alone.

"Where'd Ben and Ivy go?" I ask, my voice sounding strange to my own ears, as if my mouth is disconnected from my body.

"Ivy was hungry," she says. "They went to get a bite to eat."

I wonder when that conversation took place. Had they told me? Had I not heard? Or had they whispered it behind my back? I know how that happens. After Stu's funeral I heard the whispers—

"How is she doing?"

"Has she eaten?"

"Think someone should stay the night with her?"

Then I'd simply walked on, not caring. But for some reason today, their whispering seems subversive and makes me angry. "Well," I say, stepping off the elevator, "they could have asked if anyone else was hungry. I hope they won't be long." I stick the plastic key in the slot and push open the door. "I want to pack and hit the road."

"They wanted to give us a few moments alone," Rae says, her voice soft.

"Why would they do that?" I want to lash out at her, but it doesn't make me feel better.

"Do you not want to discuss it?"

"No, I really don't." But I do. She knows it, and so do I. But I can't stop my waspish words any more than I can calm the anger pulsing through me. There's an iciness inside me, penetrating my bones, frosting over my words.

She watches me for a long moment and blinks her eyes, assessing me. "As you wish."

She walks toward her room. I've acted foolishly, like a child. I just don't want to agree with her. Which sounds a lot like Ivy. "So," I say and she stops, "why'd you lie to me about something like that?"

She turns slowly. Instantly, hot regret presses against my eyes.

"It wasn't a lie, Claudia. I wouldn't lie to you."

She walks back toward me. She doesn't seem rattled by my accusation or ruffled by my brusqueness. It's as if she expects it, knows exactly what I will say in response to what she's told me. Maybe she's even said it to herself. I'm at a distinct disadvantage. I'm the one shaken to my very core.

"I spoke the truth," she continues. "I gave you to my sister to raise. She was your mother. She raised you. I am not usurping her, trying to get you to call me Mom. I'm telling you this, not for selfish reasons."

I open my mouth to ask her why, but the words can't push past the lump gathering in my throat.

"Nor should it change the love you have for your mother. She wanted you. Very much. She made you who you are."

My world tilts. Slowly, shakily, I sit on the edge of the couch, grasping its arm for support.

"She needed you, your mother did. She couldn't have children anymore . . . after her miscarriage. It was, you might say, providence."

The bald-face truth glares at me. I want to turn away from it, to hide, but it also draws me closer, like a child with a magnifying glass. I wonder if that's why Mother never told me about her miscarriage, even after I suffered one myself, because it might have led to my discovering my real birth mother. Birth mother . . . Mother. My thoughts and memories fracture.

"Then why? Why tell me this at all?"

"Because Stuart asked me to."

"Stu? He knew?" Another blow slams into my stomach. "When?"

"Toward the end, when he told me about Elvis."

"Cozy. Any other little secrets you want to tell me now?"

"No."

"Why didn't Stu tell me?"

"I swore him to secrecy. As he did me with Elvis."

"Why should I believe either of you. I mean, you believe in ghosts." It was an irrational statement, but I couldn't seem to think clearly or rationally.

"It's your choice to believe or not. You must make that step yourself."

"But why? Why not tell me six months ago? Or when Stu was alive? Or when you first came back from Oregon?"

"It wasn't the time. In the end his will prevailed. That's the other reason he wanted me on this trip."

"But I don't understand. Why would he want so desperately to tell me that you . . . ?" I can't force the words out. "And about Elvis?"

"I don't know about Elvis. But he believed you had a right to know who your birth mother was. That's debatable. Mostly he knew you'd feel alone after he was gone. He wanted you to know you aren't alone."

Questions crowd my head, clog my heart with emotion. I don't know where to begin, where to stop.

"So you want me suddenly to call you Mother?" I hear the contempt in my own voice.

"No," she says simply. "That's not my wish. Beverly was your mother. Always will be. She rocked you, held you, took you to the doctor, cared for you every day that I could not be there with you. I told you because I want you to see the possibilities. There are other relationships than those you've known, those you cling to. I expect nothing from you, Claudia. Maybe you'll reject me. I'm fine if that's what happens. I've lived estranged from those I loved most. I can continue . . ." Her shoulder lifts in a slight shrug, making her charm bracelet jangle.

"You asked me once what these charms were for." She fingers a pointed ballet shoe. "I added one for all the things I didn't get to experience with you, for the milestones in your life. It was my way of staying connected to you."

Tears are usually salty, but these are bitter and tighten my throat. I think back to the times I thought Aunt Rae didn't care about us, didn't think about us. And all the time she was wishing she could be a part of my life.

It feels as if I've been told the last answer to a crossword puzzle. The answer is a word I'd never heard of, one I can't comprehend, could never have considered. Yet it fits the spaces perfectly.

"I tell you all of this because it's the truth, the truth I've always lived with. It's why I had to go away. Why I lived so long far away from you."

"How could you . . . how could you . . . give away your baby?" I hear the pause in my own voice, the inability to say "give *me* away." But that's the real question. And yet there are more, many more.

"It wasn't easy, and yet I'm sorry to say it was. I was afraid—afraid of you, afraid I would fail you. It broke my heart to be near you and to hear you call another 'Mother.'"

She faces the window. Her long silvery gray hair flows

down her back. It's naturally curly, like my own. Where she lets hers loose to be wild and free, enjoying its wantonness, I keep mine short, tamed, which, as Mother always pointed out, is more practical. Am I really more like the eccentric, extravagant aunt whom I never knew, than I am the woman who raised me? Or was I some hybrid combination that would take me a lifetime to sort out?

Rae turns her head to meet my curious, hurting gaze. "I tell you, Claudia, because it is time. I tell you because you cling to the past, to your memories. Memories are fine. But they are not all of life. You must reach out. There's more out in the world for you. I hope, with this news, you realize that.

"I know what I've done. I know why I gave you to my sister to raise. Painful as it was, I don't regret it. It was the right thing to do. It gave you a good, healthy, stable life. It helped heal my sister.

"But I hope you'll see the possibilities in others now, reach out to others in friendship and love. Your mother's dead. Stu is, too. You, Claudia, are not. You must go on with your life and enjoy it to its fullest."

I turn away from her then. The tears start to flow. But I swat them away with the back of my hand. Anger swells and explodes inside me. "Did Mother ask you not to tell me?"

"No." No bitterness coats her voice. "It was her right, though. Your father, however, did ask. He asked to protect Beverly, to keep her from being hurt, to protect your family. And I respected that wish. But now they're gone. The truth needs to be told, if only for you to understand, for you to see the possibilities of your life. I'll go if that's your wish."

I want to tell her to get out of my life. She hasn't helped me. She's confused me. Angered me. Destroyed my memories. But I can't. The constraints my mother taught me now benefit Rae. "I don't know what I want anymore."

"One day you will." She reaches out and touches my hair, running her fingers over the curls. "So much alike," she whispers, "yet so different."

"Who is my father?" I ask, looking at her again, this time not hiding the tears. My voice cracks, revealing the gaping hole in my heart.

My own father—my beloved father—died of a massive heart attack when I was in college. "The widow maker," the doctor pronounced sagely with a sad shake of his head. I mourned him as a daughter should. But he wasn't even my father. Yet he raised me as if he were, as if I was his own. In this moment I love him more. And the love I've always known for my mother swells inside. She never hinted, never indicated I was anything but her daughter. They loved me. I know that without a single doubt.

When Rae doesn't readily answer, cold fear slides down my spine. I think of Graceland, the house, the gaudiness, the Elvis bust sitting in the pew at Faithland Chapel. "Oh, no. Is Elvis my father?"

"I don't know, Claudia. The name of your biological father is one thing I can't give you. But I don't think it was Elvis. There are tests these days . . ." Shame pinches the corners of Rae's eyes. She says she doesn't regret, but I wonder if that's true.

Sure, medical tests can determine the truth easily enough—and create headlines and nightmares. I could never pursue that.

"It was a crazy time, the sixties. We were coming into our own as women. We were learning everything our mothers hadn't taught us, maybe because they hadn't known themselves about sex, joy, power, freedom. And so it was wild and irresponsible."

Then a thought strikes me. "Could Howie . . ." I can't finish the question.

"No. I'm no prude, but no. Not with Howie. Even *I* had standards."

I breathe a sigh of relief, but it still doesn't relieve the pressure in my chest. "Do you remember that story you told me as a child, the one about Topsy-Turvyville?"

"Yes."

"I think I've just moved in."

"I knew, one day, you might." Sorrow fills her eyes and deepens the lines around her mouth. "I'm sorry."

I believe her. I'm not sure why, but I do. "When you said I needed faith . . . what did you mean?"

"Faith is being sure of what we hope for—"

"—and certain of what we do not see."

"It doesn't matter if I'm your mother," Rae says, "or if Beverly birthed you herself. I don't care if you came from Mars. What matters is that you're loved."

My throat closes as tears course down my face. Rae wraps her arms around me, and I hold on tight.

"I gave you up because I loved you and wanted what was best. Beverly mothered you for the same reasons. But God loves you, too. Even when you can't seem to muster the faith to believe in him, he never gives up on you. He still believes in you."

She holds me while the bitterness and anger flow out of me.

Chapter Twenty-Three

Way Down

I sit beside the window looking out at the late afternoon shadows falling over Graceland, though it's a stretch to think I can see even the gates from here. Rae has gone to lie down, but I know she's giving me space to take in and absorb all she's told me. I don't know where Ben and Ivy are, but I'm grateful for the silence, the time alone.

Rest seems impossible. My brain feels like an engine trying to catch and not fully able to engage. Images and snippets of conversations zip around so fast in my mind that I can't lock onto anything for any length of time. I feel the empty place in my heart pulse and throb. I wonder if it's like a tomb locking away memories, sealing me from any more hurt, or if it's a doorway welcoming something new into my life.

For minutes or hours, I'm not sure which, I remain seated on the couch. I stare at nothing but the blank spot Elvis occupied. I miss him, which seems absurd. Maybe it's only Stu I miss. I don't sense any answers. There's only silence still. Yet something has changed. Maybe it's me. Most certainly it's my heart.

I don't hear God's voice. I don't hear trumpets or angels wings. There's no miraculous sign flashing in front of me. Yet I feel peace. It's not something I can explain. It's just there like a warm blanket tucked about my feet.

I've questioned and berated myself for not having enough faith, not believing enough to save Stu. Yet maybe I was wrong. I am certain of what I don't see. And for the first time in a long, long while, I'm hopeful.

♪ ♩ ♪ ♩. ♩ ♪ ♩

TIPTOEING INTO THE room, Ivy belches, which gives her away. I turn from the window.

"How ya doin'?" she asks.

I shrug, then nod. "Okay."

"You had kind of a shock today." She walks the rest of the way into the darkening room and touches her stomach. "I know how that feels."

"I'm sure you do." Honesty has always been solid footing between us. "How are you feeling?"

"Not as pukey as I was."

I offer a sympathetic smile. I know those days will come and go. "How far along are you?"

"Three months, I think. Myrtle helped me figure it out with dates and stuff. Dad wants me to go to the doctor when we get back to Dallas."

"That's a good idea."

"It'll make it seem more real. But there's not a doctor for you to go to, is there?"

I laugh. "Maybe a psychiatrist. Think I'm going crazy?"

"You'll be okay. You're strong."

"Stronger with good friends."

A blush creeps up Ivy's features, and a dozen emotions dance across her face.

"You're wise for such a young woman."

Ivy laughs this time. "Dumb enough to get myself in this situation."

"But for the grace of God, go I." That's what Stu must have felt when he looked at Elvis. It wasn't pride. It was gratitude and humility. And a big helping of grace on top of it all.

"Do you believe in God?" Ivy asks.

I consider the question for a long moment. A week ago, even a year ago, I would have probably answered differently. Is it easier to believe in good times than in bad? I don't know the answer. Maybe for the first time I am reaching toward God where before I would have reached for a human security blanket like my mother or Stu.

Finally, I answer, "Yes, I do."

"Dad does, but I don't know how—what with all he went through with my mom."

"Maybe it was the rope he clung to that got him through. I think my husband Stu believed when I had doubts."

Ivy sits on the arm of the couch. "I don't understand how all this could have happened to me. Myrtle and Guy say God loves me. But if he does, then why would he let my life get like this?"

"I don't know the answers. But I do know it's okay to ask them. Keep asking."

"Well, I know it's my fault I'm pregnant."

"Yours and some boy's. Remember it takes two to tango."

"I know." She blushes. "But why did my mom . . . ?" Her mouth twists. "How come you get two moms and I don't get any?"

I go to her and wrap my arms around her. "I don't know." I soothe my hand over her soft hair. "I think it all comes down to choices. Your mom made a choice. So did mine. And you and I had to live with the consequences."

She presses against me. For a long moment we simply hug. Then she looks up at me, tears streaking her face. "But what about Stu?" As a toddler Ivy use to call him Tutu, which we all thought funny. I forget that others mourn him, too, when I'm caught in the grip of grief myself. "Why'd he have to die?"

I shake my head. I don't have the answers. Maybe I never will. Life doesn't come in neat little packages with ribbons and bows. Answers can't always be found in song lyrics. Life is messy and incomplete and awkward and difficult. "I don't know. I just know we have to keep believing."

The questions lie between us. Unanswerable. Yet there is a fragrance of hope like a soft, alluring scent drifting through the room.

Slowly Ivy pulls away from me, stands, and straightens her clothes. There's a damp spot on my blouse from her tears. "My dad wants to talk to you. That okay?"

"Sure." I turn back toward the window.

THE SKYLINE IS turning orange as Ben enters the room.

"Some weekend, huh?" he says.

I laugh, not expecting that. "I guess we've both had a few shocks."

"Enough to last a lifetime." He sits on the couch. "We've both been through a lot. You've seen me face my wife leaving. I've watched you deal with Stu's death. Both shocks. But we handled it. And we'll deal with the new ones."

Tears once more clog my throat. He's right. He makes sense.

"We've always controlled things, you and I," he says. "We've controlled our emotions. We've controlled our environments. I tried to keep everything as calm as possible for Ivy, as stable as it could be with only one parent. And you kept things sane for Stu in the end. But I guess life isn't controllable."

"No. You're right. So what are we going to do about all this?"

"It's not so horrible, you know," he says, his voice craggy. "Hey, I'm going to be a grandpa. Can you believe that?"

I laugh again. With him sitting there in his shorts and baseball cap, I can't quite imagine it. I see him more as he looked in college when he roomed with Stu. Now with tiny gray threads sneaking into his hair, he's only a couple of years older than me. If he's old enough to be a grandparent, then so am I. It's a sobering thought. "No, I can't believe it. But you'll be a great one."

"I don't know. I hope so. I wanted to be a good dad but—"

"You are a good dad." I cut him off. "The best. But I know how you feel. You think you let Ivy down in some way, but you didn't. Your wife made her own choices. Bad ones. Or maybe not. What if she'd stayed? She was depressed, confused, disturbed." I wipe the leftover tears off my face.

"What if she'd stayed and hurt Ivy? Killed herself, right there?"

He nods, unable to speak for a moment. "You're right. It could have been worse. I tried to minimize the hurt, the pain. It's not always possible though." He meets my gaze. "Do you think you let Stu down?"

It feels as if he's sliced right through my defenses. My eyes instantly fill with tears. I put a hand out to stop him from speaking, but he clasps my hand and simply holds it. A surprising warmth sweeps through me. "I do feel like I let Stu down. For his death. For this weekend. For living when he couldn't. Everything. I know, I know, I'm not at fault for Stu's illness, his death. I couldn't have prevented it. Maybe it's survivor's guilt."

"I've felt that, too," Ben's voice deepens, resonating pain. "Guilt. For enjoying Ivy's birthdays when Gwen should have been there watching her daughter grow. For things I thought I should have done or said in our marriage. But guilt's a funny thing. It clouds your mind and heart. It also implies blame, and there isn't any. You are not to blame for Stu, for his death, for living longer than he did."

I nod, unable to speak. We sit there for a long time, just holding hands. Our friendship was born of Stu, yet it has grown deeper over the years, stronger through adversity.

"You know . . . if I can be a grandpa, then you can be a daughter again."

I pull my hand back, turn away. A fresh wave of tears rushes over me. My defenses have been destroyed, my emotions depleted. I'm not sure why I'm crying anymore.

He moves toward me, curses under his breath. "I shouldn't have said anything. Don't cry, Claudia. I'm sorry."

I shake my head, try to stop the tears. I feel his closeness as if it's a part of me. It's different from when I held Ivy. This makes my insides squirm. I can't think and move away. "It's not you. It's not Rae. Not really." I face him, laugh at his dubious expression. "Really. It's . . . it's . . ."

He keeps his distance and just watches and waits for me to sort through my thoughts and feelings.

"I don't want to lose someone again." I look at him, aching for him to understand, to agree.

"What do you mean?"

"I've already lost my mother, my father, my husband. If . . . if . . . Rae will die one day. And I'll have to go through that all over again."

Something in his expression shifts, and he pulls me against his chest. His arms embrace me, comfort me. "You can't push yourself away from everyone just so you never have to let go again."

I give in to the need to hold and be held. I wrap my arms around his body, and we stand that way for a long while. Finally, I look up at him. "You think I'm crazy, right?"

He touches my face, smooths away my tears with his thumb. "No, I don't. I've felt those same feelings, too. When Gwen left, I was angry, resentful. When she died, all those emotions turned to blame. I never wanted to care about anyone, never wanted to risk loving someone . . . never wanted to be left like that again. But a funny thing about having a kid . . . that kid needs love and opens the heart."

"But," I venture, "you've never dated much since Gwen. Aren't you open to those possibilities? I mean, a child doesn't fulfill . . ."

"I know."

His eyes darken with understanding and sympathy. Then his gaze drops to my mouth. My insides plunge to dark, unknown territory. Then he dips his head lower, breathes once, twice. My pulse pounds in my throat, my temples. I swallow hard.

Part of me wants to say, "Don't." But I'm transfixed, not knowing what to do, how to respond, experiencing familiar feelings that transcend time and age and new ones I've never imagined. My mistake comes when my gaze drops to his mouth, out of curiosity and trepidation. But he takes it as an invitation.

His lips touch mine, testing at first. Automatically, I close my eyes. To block him out? Or to absorb his strength? I'm not sure. His mouth is warm, his lips surprisingly soft. I think of kissing Stu the last time, his cracked lips cool to the touch.

I lean into Ben, suddenly needing him, his aliveness. He eases away from me slightly, repositions us, then slants his mouth more fully over mine. His tongue touches the seam of my lips, teases and tempts me. Startled by the need welling up inside me, I push against his shoulders, step back.

He releases me. "I'm not going to apologize." His voice sounds tight. "So sue me."

Uneasy, I laugh. "I won't. But . . ." Uncertain, I don't know what to say. "Ben, I, um . . ."

"We should head back to Dallas tomorrow." His tone remains flat.

I nod, at a loss for words. My emotions jumble and tumble inside me. "Okay."

He turns away, stops and looks me in the eye again. "What if I accepted this grandbaby, loved it, cradled it, and then Ivy decided a few months down the road to give it up for adoption? I'd be crushed. Devastated. Hey, I'm already wondering if I should get it a baseball cap or one of those pink frilly dresses."

My heart goes out to him. I know how helpless he must feel, the same way I felt when I looked at Stu, wanting to help, knowing I couldn't heal him.

"I'd have to let it go, right? Should I push away the joy of holding a newborn baby? Should I reject the baby before I can feel any loss?"

I want to say it isn't the same. But in many ways I know he's right.

"Look, Claudia, it comes down to this: Are you going to reject Rae because one day she's going to die? Are you going to refuse to ever love someone—maybe me—because one day I'll die? Sure, you'll keep from being hurt. You won't feel any pain. But you won't feel anything else either. No joy. No love. That, to me, is a wasted life."

"But you . . ." I accuse. "Don't point fingers at me. You haven't dated. You haven't loved anyone else . . . not since Gwen left. And that's been—"

"You're wrong. I've loved *you*, Claudia." His voice wraps my name in thick emotion. His words are as big and bold as the Elvis bust, undeniable, unavoidable, unmistakable. With that he turns and walks out of the hotel room.

♪ ♩ ♪ ♩. ♩ ♪ ♩

"WHERE'S MY DAD?" Ivy asks sometime later when it's getting close to dinnertime.

Since Ben's so-called declaration, I've been sitting in

the darkening room, getting my bearings on life. When Ivy came out of her room, her door banged back against the wall, startling me.

The noise unearthed Rae from her room. "Everything all right?"

Unsure whom to address, and still in shock over the weekend's many *24*-like revelations, I say, "I don't know."

Rae comes fully out of her room and flips on a table lamp. "What's happened? What's wrong?"

"My dad! Where'd he go? He never goes anywhere without telling me."

"I'm sure he's okay." I shrug, unable and unwilling to explain. "Everything is f—" I stop myself from saying *fine.* It doesn't fit. "Everything's okay," I correct. "And your dad . . . well, I don't know where he is. He's around, I'm sure. Couldn't go far without keys." I glance at the Cadillac's keys on the glass coffee table. "Did you call his cell phone?"

"No."

I laugh. How could a teenager *not* think of using her cell? It seems a bit ironic for a teen to be checking up on her dad using the same tool he's often used to keep tabs on her. "Well, why don't you try?"

She walks back into her room, and I hear the familiar beeping of her cell phone as she punches in the numbers.

Rae looks intently at me. I feel a slight bobble in my equilibrium. "You sure you're all right?"

"We should think of dinner," I suggest.

"Did something happen between you and Ben?" Rae asks.

Her question makes my skin contract, my face burn. "Aren't you hungry?"

Rae narrows her eyes at me, then says, "Why, of course. Our last night in Memphis should be grand."

I don't think it should be a big celebration but more perfunctory—something we have to do, especially with Ivy in her condition. It feels awkward, considering all the things I suddenly know about my companions. I find myself staring back at Rae, watching her move, studying her nose and chin, wondering if she's simply an older version of myself and if I carry any of her traits that I've never noticed before.

"Are we alike?" I ask, putting voice to my questions. I've often caught a glimpse of myself in the mirror, triggering memories of my mother. I don't want to lose that.

"What?" she looks up from the magazine.

I fling my hand outward. "Are we alike? You and me?"

"In appearance or behavior?"

"I don't know. Both maybe."

"Sometimes I see myself when you turn or walk, when you speak or use your hands a certain way. Other times I see Beverly. A good case study for genetics, right?"

I nod, not trusting my voice.

"Mostly Beverly comes through in your speech, the way you respond to others, always watching and waiting. I'm not one for waiting."

And yet I realize she waited a long while before telling me the truth. "Why . . . why did you wait so long to tell me?"

"There were many factors. I've told you of your father's request. But also . . . I was afraid."

"Afraid?" I ask, having a hard time imagining Rae afraid of anything.

"Yes, afraid. You could have kicked me out of the car. Never wanted to see me again. I feared losing the relationship we shared . . . not knowing what would be on the other side. I still don't know."

"Neither do I."

"It's enough that we're talking."

"It's going to take me a while—"

"Of course."

"—to get used to all of this."

She touches my arm. Her hand is warm, soft, undemanding. "Everything has changed, yet nothing has. You'll see. Only your eyes have been opened to the truth."

Nothing has changed, yet everything has. Forever.

My gaze turns to Ivy's doorway where she has appeared. "Dad said for us to meet him downstairs when we're ready for dinner."

A lump lodges in my throat. I wonder if I'll feel awkward around him, if we'll act like kids in junior high, knowing one has a crush on the other. But he's a man, not a boy. Could his love be called a simple crush?

Will he try to date me? Court me? I cringe. Will he be standoffish? Act irritated. Angry even? Make me wonder and worry about our friendship, maybe even my job? Will he pretend he never spoke those words? The words that confounded, confused, irritated, aggravated, and amazed me.

And how will all of this affect our working relationship? I don't want to think about that now. He joked that I could sue him. Even though I know it wasn't sexual harassment. I'd never seek litigation against Ben. I know his heart. Still, it's awkward. I will have to take one step at a time and see how tonight goes.

Chapter Twenty-Four

You Don't Have to Say You Love Me

I walk into the lobby, dragging my feet behind Rae and Ivy. My gaze searches the odd assortment of colorful and oddly shaped chairs and couches. A cardboard cutout of Elvis driving a red sports car, a girl by his side, stands beside a small, old-fashioned television. I'm hoping to see Ben first. Maybe I can get an early reading on how he's going to respond to our kiss.

Suddenly I feel a hand at the back of my waist. Although the touch is soft, gentle even, I startle. But it's Ben. Maybe all the ghost talk has me skittish. Or maybe it's that around every corner a secret seems to jump out at me.

He whispers in my ear, "Are you okay?"

I nod, turning only enough to see his face. "Are you?"

"Of course." Now he sounds like Rae. "Ready, ladies?"

Nothing in his words can be construed as anything. I'm not sure what I want to find. Hidden meanings? Suggestive remarks? I don't want to read things that aren't there either. But at the same time I'm fully aware of a tingle that ripples down my spine at the touch of his breath on my neck. As quickly as he touched me, he moves away and greets the others with a casual smile and quick hug for Ivy. I'm left standing alone, watching him as he moves with ease. Is he too festive? Too animated? No, he seems normal. Just Ben.

But what does that mean?

He leads us out the doorway and into the sticky-warm heat of the night. He drives the Cadillac, and fifteen minutes later we arrive at a yellow, rectangular building. Bars cover all the windows.

"What's this?" Ivy asks.

"Neely's is supposed to be the best barbecue in Memphis."

Ivy, Rae, and I glance at one another. "Okay," I say, "I'm game."

Is there something to read behind his smile? His eyes contain the same spark, nothing more, nothing less. It makes me wonder if the spark has always been there and I have only been ignorant of the facts.

Nothing has changed. Except me. I have become aware. Aware of him. Aware of my own reaction to him. It makes me edgy. Even those stupid glasses I bought him look good as he studies the menu. Although Ivy complains about them. Still, I question everything I think, say, and do around Ben. I don't want to lead him on, not when I have nothing to offer. Not when I don't know my own feelings.

The words he spoke earlier encircle my heart, tighten with the truth. I know he's right—I can't just push people away. I have to open my heart to possibilities. But how? Is faith the key? Have I already taken the first step?

I try not to look at Rae during dinner, or Ben either, which leaves few options except Ivy, who finally says, "What?"

"Nothing." I dab the napkin to my mouth, trying to cover my confusion.

"You're staring at me. Do I look funny? Fat?"

"No, no, you're fine." I glance from Rae to Ben, then back to Ivy. "It's just been a long day. My mind's drifting, and I didn't realize I was staring. I'm sorry."

She grabs another roll out of the basket in the middle of the table. "It's been a long weekend. I'll be glad to get home."

"You will?" Ben asks.

"I miss my friends."

I almost laugh but catch myself. I'm not sure how she can miss them when she's been on the cell phone to them half the time. But I understand, too. After all, I was young once. Her need to see her friends is actually a good sign; it means she still wants to be a part of that crowd.

I remember making friends during college. I didn't meet Stu until I became a sophomore. Once we'd started dating, he'd taken me to his apartment off campus, and there I saw Ben again. I hadn't seen him since that one date we shared. I don't remember much about him then, just a sweaty guy coming in from football practice and downing a whole container of Gatorade in several gulps.

After that first visit to Stu's—when I also met the Elvis bust for the first time—I got to know Ben in bits and pieces, mostly when Stu had to run out to the 7-11 to get snacks and other essentials. I'd sit on the couch waiting for Stu.

"How ya doin'?" Ben asked, flipping the channel to a *M*A*S*H* episode. He'd broken up with his girlfriend, . . . or she'd broken up with him. My memory is blurry on the details.

I crossed my legs, then stood and moved to a brown chair. Elvis made me nervous. So had Ben. "Okay. And you?"

"Ready for football season to be over."

I noticed then he had scabs on his knees and elbows.

"Y'all are doing well, aren't you?"

He laughed. "Been to any of the games?"

Embarrassed, I ducked my head. "Two."

"I bet you watched Stu taking pictures of the game."

A shy smile tugged at the corner of my mouth. "Of course."

Rae's laughter pulls me back to the present, to the restaurant table. I'm not sure what she finds humorous, but Ben and Ivy join her, so I give a lifeless chuckle that seems out of place. Rae's laugh is full and robust, as if she knows how to enjoy herself. I remember it from way back in my childhood, as if it's always been there, a part of my life. My mother's laugh was more reserved, more self-conscious, more like my own.

My life spins around inside my head, making me question every memory. What all have I missed, been oblivious to? If I'd been paying closer attention, would I have known I was missing a mother before today? Would I have sensed Ben's interest? Suspected Ivy's pregnancy?

My head begins to throb, and my vision blurs from unshed tears. I realize I've been focused on my own pain rather than others'. I've turned inward, locking up my heart. It's not that I can't feel empathy for others, but I've been so overwhelmed by my own grief that I gave no time to anyone else's. I stopped looking outward, searching, seeking God. I tried to control events, tried to handle Stu's death, my grief, myself. And I failed. Maybe that's the key: Faith is simply reaching out to others, to God. No guarantees. Nothing promised in return. It just starts with hope.

"You don't like?" the waitress's nasal voice penetrates my fog.

"Huh?"

"Your chicken? Didn't like it, honey?"

"Oh, no." Rae and Ben stare at me with concern. "Uh, it's fine." Each bite tasted like cardboard, but I don't think it has anything to do with the food, the seasonings, or the way it's been roasted.

"You can order something else," Ben suggests.

"Oh, no. I'm, uh . . . full."

"But you've hardly eaten!" Ivy seems genuinely shocked since she's all but licked her plate and has scarfed down all the rolls.

"Let her be," Rae says. "She's tired. Overwrought. She must figure out what to do with Elvis."

"Elvis," I whisper. I almost forgot about him. "There's nothing wrong with keeping him. In fact, I think he'd look pretty good on the coffee table. At Christmas I could stick a red ball on his nose, like Rudolph."

A frown creases Rae's brow. Ben narrows his eyes. Ivy tilts her head to the side, her mouth open.

"I'm kidding. That's a joke."

Obviously relieved, they all laugh, but it isn't full throttle, and I realize how concerned they all are about my mental stability.

"I'm okay, really. Just not hungry."

"I should have chosen a different restaurant."

"No, no. Really. This is fine. Very nice. It wouldn't have mattered where we went tonight . . ." I can't explain my feelings, which seem to bounce from sorrow to panic. I twist my paper napkin in my lap.

"Those were the best baked beans I've ever had." Ben leans back in his seat. "Dessert?"

Everyone groans.

The waitress has already cleared most of the dishes off the table when she asks me, "Want a to-go box?"

"No, thanks." Guilty, I glance at my full plate. "We're traveling."

She nods and removes my plate. With her other hand she leaves the bill, which Ben accepts. Both Rae and I protest, but he insists, saying, "It's the least I can do for all the help you've given Ivy."

Yeah, I thought, *we let her run away!* But I keep my guilt to myself. Maybe faith is letting go of that, too, releasing my failures and mistakes. Letting go of my relationship with Stu, the pain and the joy.

When Ben pays, we leave the restaurant, gathering together on the sidewalk outside, feeling the warm night air drift over us.

"Rae," Ivy says, walking toward the car. Rae pairs up with her as Ivy continues, "I wanted to ask you . . ."

I decide it's a private conversation and hold back.

Ben waits with me. "Ivy likes her."

"Doesn't everyone?" I ask.

"I don't know. But I think she's good for Ivy right now. They've been through similar things. Different times maybe, but still . . ."

"Yes, I know." But I don't want to think about Rae as a young woman facing an uncertain future, her belly ripening with me. She had a tough decision to make. I wonder if she considered telling one of the men she'd been seeing or if she hadn't wanted to be tied down.

Ben's presence beside me makes me tense. I twist my watch around my wrist. "Rae will give her solid advice."

He nods, still quiet though. I cross my arms over my chest.

"She's wise," I say, feeling awkward. "She is."

I glance at Ben beside me. His hands are stuffed in his pockets, his shoulders hunched. He stares at the uneven sidewalk, lost in his own thoughts.

"She'll be okay. She can go to school. No one will—"

"I know all that."

"Oh."

"It's you I'm worried about."

"Me?"

He meets my gaze. "You."

"Oh."

"I know you're not ready. I'm not asking for anything. I just want you to know that."

"Okay." I didn't expect he'd be so blunt, so straightforward about all of this. Feeling awkward, I glance over at the car, wish we were inside it and headed back to the hotel. I don't want to have this conversation. "What if I'm never ready?"

"Then you'll be giving up a lot in life." He laughs suddenly, startling me. "That sounded conceited, didn't it? I didn't mean *me* specifically. I meant, if you don't open yourself to love, to whomever it might be, then you'll be missing out." Looking down, he shakes his head. "I'm bungling this, aren't I?"

"No." I smile sympathetically, wanting to help and yet unsure of myself. "I think you're handling this better than me. I keep thinking back on things . . . things you've said or done . . . and it makes me wonder—"

"If I'm just a big jerk?"

"No, I didn't mean—"

"Believe me, I've questioned myself. I didn't want to do anything for the wrong, sleazy reason."

"When did you, uh, know?"

"College. Finals before I graduated. Just hit me one day."

"Really?" Stunned, I feel flattered and unnerved at the same time.

"Yeah."

"So what did you do?"

"I studied harder than I'd ever studied to get you off my mind. You were my best friend's girl." He shrugs, looking as if his well-starched shirt suddenly doesn't fit. "I knew that wouldn't change. You only had eyes for Stu."

"Is that why you married—"

"No. I loved Gwen. We met the year after I graduated. I'd accepted my feelings for you by then, pushed them away as much as possible. When Gwen left, it took me a long time to get over her."

He glances over his shoulder at Ivy and Rae talking beside the Cadillac. "When you came to me, applying for the position in my company . . . I thought long and hard about it. Probably gave you a harder study than others I hired. I didn't want to hire you with a secret agenda. I didn't want to love you and have to look at you every day. So I examined my heart. And really, back then, I didn't feel anything. I couldn't feel anything. My heart had been shattered by Gwen. It had no feeling. Like when I got hit in football and cracked my cheekbone and I couldn't feel half my face for a year."

"Oh, Ben." I remember those years after Gwen left, the silence of his grief.

"Over the years, working closely with you . . . I don't know. I just knew. I knew it wasn't time. Might never be. Knew you weren't ready. You were married to my best friend. You might never want me the way I wanted you. So I tried to forget, focused on other things." He pauses. "But I won't fight a ghost. I won't fight Stu over you. That's a battle I can't win."

"He wasn't perfect," I say, touching his arm, feeling his muscles tighten beneath the fabric of his shirt, solid and warm. I know I idealized Stu in my mind during the last year, martyred him. But he wouldn't have wanted that.

"I'm not either."

Touching his arm was a simple, friendly gesture I've done for years. Now I question if I should have. Reluctantly, I let go.

"It's okay," he says. "I won't read anything into what you say or do."

I laugh as we begin walking toward the car. "Good. Because I am."

He laughs, too. "I know. You'll get used to it."

I'm not so sure about that.

"And," he says, his tone deeper, more serious, "I won't believe anything, think anything . . . until you tell me your feelings have changed. Until you kiss me."

I stumble. Literally, over a crack in the sidewalk. He catches my arm, steadies me, then releases me. I know he'll always be there for me, ready to catch me before I fall. I give a terse nod, understanding. His terms are clear, precise. I can't help thinking about the warmth of his kiss, the curling need inside me. My gaze shifts to his mouth, then away.

"Okay." I doubt I'll ever be ready or able to take that kind of a step.

Chapter Twenty-Five

Seeing Is Believing

The moment I step into the hotel room, I need to leave. I can't breathe. Too many emotions wrestle inside me. I need time alone, away from everyone, and I won't get that kind of privacy in the hotel suite.

"I think I'll go swimming," I announce. Not that I brought a swimsuit. But I can fake it, I suppose, and dip my toes in the heart-shaped pool.

From the couch Ben looks over at me. "Okay. Want company?"

No. "Well, I—"

"I'll go," Ivy interrupts. "I brought a swimsuit."

"Okay." I'm both relieved not to be alone with Ben and disappointed I can't find space to myself. But at the same time I'm surprised and delighted that Ivy would choose to go somewhere with me.

"I'll change." Ivy heads to her room.

"If you don't mind," Rae says, settling on the couch beside Ben, "I'll stay here."

"That's fine. I don't think we'll be long."

"Just don't let Ivy get in the hot tub," Ben says. "Not good for the baby."

"I don't think there is one. Just a pool."

"Heart shaped," Rae adds.

Ten minutes later Ivy and I flip-flop our way down the hall toward the bank of elevators. Wearing a pair of shorts and a top, I carry two hotel towels over my arm. Ivy wears a pair of cut-off shorts and a bikini top. There's a slight swell to her belly, but she doesn't look pregnant. Not yet anyway.

Empty lawn chairs surround the vacant swimming pool. Chlorine taints the air. We plop our towels down on two lounge chairs. Ivy slides her shorts off her narrow hips and dives right into the pool. Her black hair floats out behind her, her long legs kicking up foam and waves. I sit on the dry decking and put my feet in the cool water. Little waves swell around my calves. I notice a line has been painted along the bottom, giving the impression of a broken heart.

Ivy turns at the end of the pool and swims sideways, making long sweeping motions with her arms and legs. She stops in the middle of the pool and treads water. "How come you're not getting in?"

"I didn't bring a suit. I just came out here to . . ."

"Get away from everybody?" she asks.

"Something like that."

"Me, too. Are you mad I tagged along?"

"Not at all. You're easy to be around."

"So are you." A warmth spreads through me.

She swims closer, props her arms on the tiled edge. "Did Dad tell you to babysit me?"

"Not exactly." I wink at her. "I'm supposed to watch you."

She huffs out a breath. "Dad thinks I'm still a child."

"Well, he is your dad. It's hard for dads to realize their little girls are growing up." I decide not to reiterate that she did run away and give us all the scare of our lives.

"Was your dad that way?" she asks.

My heart lurches. Not only did my father, the man I will always consider my father, not live to see me to adulthood, but he wasn't really my father. Grief overwhelms me momentarily. He's been gone for more than twenty years, yet I still miss him, wish I could crawl into his lap and he could tell knock-knock jokes until my troubles are left far behind in the wake of laughter.

"I had a great father," I say. Then I realize my father was much like Ben. "Like yours."

She looks down at her belly. "I think Dad's handling it better than I expected."

"He'll be okay. And so will you. What about the baby's father?"

She shrugs a slim shoulder. "Heath wasn't interested in being my boyfriend anymore, much less a dad."

I wonder if my biological father would have reacted the same way as Ivy's boyfriend if he'd known Rae carried his child. Or if he would have wanted to be a part of my life. "Probably a shock to him," I say in defense of young fathers. "Maybe—"

"He accused me of screwing around on him. Said it

wasn't his. You know, all that stuff. Told me he didn't love me. But I don't think he ever did."

Some lessons come hard. I watch her face change, petulant one minute, angry, shamed, and sad the next. Why did it seem a rite of passage for young women to be treated poorly by men? I'd had my own experiences of heartache in my teens. I'd just come out of a bad relationship with a guy named Bob, who'd two-timed me, when I met Stu.

There are so many good guys in the world—my father who stood by my mother when she became pregnant, Stu, Ben. Each fallible, but each had a good heart, honor, and a strong sense of right and wrong.

"Men aren't all like Heath, you know," I say.

"Maybe. My dad's okay. He's a good guy. But it's hard to tell the good guys from the not so good."

"I know. Lots of frogs out there. But you'll start to recognize them."

"You think you'll marry again?" Ivy asks.

Her question shocks me as if I had fallen into the cold pool. I want to shut down the conversation immediately. I've done it a million times over the last year with overly concerned friends. But Ivy's different. I force myself to open up to her, think of what Ben said about how kids make you open your heart to new possibilities. "I don't know. I loved my husband. It's hard to think of being with someone else."

"But you could live to be like sixty or something. All alone."

Like sixty or something. I almost laugh. How old that seems to Ivy, how young it's starting to look to me. Yet it's twenty years away. Will I be all alone? What if I live to be eighty or older? I realize it's the first time since Stu's diagnosis that I've even thought about my life and what might become of me.

"Rae's sixty or something," I say, "and she seems content." Maybe I can be, too. Yet Rae seems more independent than me. More of a loner. Was I made to be part of a couple?

"They say if you love once, you can love again," Ivy says.

I smile at her. "Sounds like something Mother Theresa would say."

"Who?"

I laugh. "Where'd you hear that?"

"*Sleepless in Seattle.*"

"The movie?"

Her eyes sparkle. "Have you seen it?"

"A long time ago."

"It's really good. And it makes a good point. His wife died . . . can't remember his name. But he's Jonah's father. And he found love again."

"At the top of the Empire State Building." I remember Tom Hanks pining for his wife in the movie and Meg Ryan going in search of the passion missing in her own life. "I live far from New York."

"Didn't the terrorists burn it down?"

I sigh. "That was the Twin Towers."

"Oh, yeah. Anyway, so you can find love again, too."

"We'll see."

"Do you think I will?" Ivy asks, her voice suddenly reticent. Then I understand her purpose in finding love for me. "I mean, after some guy finds out I've got a kid . . . or had a kid . . . or whatever . . ."

"I'm sure there's a really special guy out there just for you." But I also know that many guys might shy away from her. Stu would have.

He hadn't been interested in kids. We got pregnant only because I wanted it. Then when we lost the baby, our baby, he didn't want to try again. He hadn't really wanted a baby in the first place. It wasn't that he was a bad guy, a "frog"; he simply wasn't interested in fatherhood. He tried, for my sake, with the baby. Or maybe he wanted a baby more than he admitted. Maybe the loss of our own was more painful than he conceded. Maybe then he closed himself off from the possibilities. Maybe he lost faith in what could be. Maybe it was his way of closing himself from hurt.

The whys and wherefores don't matter now. I suppose it's for the best. If we'd had a child, then I'd be raising him or her alone. Our child would have to grow up without a father. Which makes my thoughts return to Ivy.

"I hope there's someone out there for my dad," she says, her legs kicking under the water and making a ripple along the surface.

The nerves in my body tighten. Would Ivy be pleased or defensive if she knew we'd kissed, if she knew Ben loved me? She's never shared her father's affections or attention.

"He's been alone a long time," she says.

I wait, unsure what to say.

"Why do you think my mom killed herself?" Ivy asks.

"I don't know, Ivy." Tears burn my eyes.

"She was sick. Depressed," Ivy says as I nod agreement. "I always imagined she'd come back for me someday. But I was wrong. I blamed myself when I was little. Then

I started to blame Dad, thinking he'd made her go away. But now . . ."

Words fail me. I hurt for Ivy who aches for a mother she'll never know. I hurt for Gwen who will never know the joy of watching her beautiful girl become a woman. "It's hard to understand why someone would do something like that. I know it wasn't you, Ivy. And I doubt it was your father. There was probably something in your mother . . . something that overwhelmed her, made her feel hopeless. She just didn't know there's always hope. If only she'd opened her heart, shared her fears, her struggles. But I think she closed herself off, from me, your dad."

My own words surprise me. For so long I've felt hopeless. But maybe . . . maybe this trip has helped me find the hope that was missing in my life and see possibilities rather than despair.

"Last year," Ivy says, "a boy in my grade shot himself in the chest. He died. It was weird. He was a loner, always by himself." She shrugs. "I don't want to be like my mother."

"You won't be." I reach out for her across the cold water, grab her hand. Her fingers are cool, slender, and slippery wet. "You have to have faith."

"I'm trying. I listened to what Myrtle and Guy said. They talked about God like they really knew him. I've kinda started to pray."

"Me, too." It's been a long time for me. But I'm realizing I can't do this life all alone.

"I ran away. Just like my mom." She squeezes my hand, then lets go. "I'm sorry, Claudia. I shouldn't have scared you like that."

"It's okay. We all do crazy things sometimes."

"Have you?" Her pointed questions jab at tender parts of my heart.

"I'm here in Memphis with a butt-ugly Elvis bust, aren't I?" I laugh and she joins me. "Just know this, Ivy: You ran away to get *help*. You're different from your mom. We have to keep reaching out. You've helped me do that. I've learned a lot because of you."

"Really?"

Her fingers trace the lines in the tile along the edge of the pool. Finally, she nods. "I want to keep my baby." She blinks away tears. Her nose turns red. "But I don't know if it's possible."

"You don't have to decide now. You'll know when the time comes. Maybe you should just keep your options open."

She nods. Her face pinches as she fights back tears. "I don't want to abandon my baby like my mom did me. But also . . . I know how hard it is to grow up without a mom. Is it fair to make my baby grow up without a father?"

"You know what, Ivy? You're far wiser than I was at your age. I know whatever you decide, it will be the right decision for your baby . . . and you."

"What about God?"

"He has a plan."

"I just don't know what it is."

"AT LEAST I don't have to fly back to Dallas," Ben says, loading his suitcase along with the rest of our luggage in the trunk.

"No, you get to ride in a vintage Cadillac," Rae says.

"Stylin'," Ivy says, dumping her backpack in the front seat. "With Elvis!"

Ben glances toward me. "You sure you want to take him back?"

"I can't leave him at Faithland, where he's not wanted. Maybe this was all a big joke by Stu to get me to appreciate Elvis more." I'm feeling weepy for some reason and jiggle the keys against my palm. "Let's get gas for the car, then we'll pick up the King."

"I saw a place not far from the chapel with the best gas prices in town," Ben advises.

I pass about ten gas stations on our way to Beale Street. With Elvis belting out "Mean Woman Blues," I feel like the woman he's singing about.

"It's just down this street," Ben points to the left.

But I pull into a parking space along the street. I grab a couple of coins out of the ashtray, where Stu liked to keep change, and stick them in the meter. "I'll be right back."

Before anybody can ask a question, I grab my purse and head across the street to a record store. It boasts original Sun Records, Elvis, Johnny Cash and the like.

"Can I help you?" an older woman asks.

"Do you have any CDs?"

"Of course." She dog-ears a page and closes the paperback novel she's reading. With a slight grunt, she walks around the counter. "Are you looking for anything in particular?"

"Anything but Elvis."

"Too much of a good thing, huh?" She points me toward a side wall. I grab a variety of CDs from Josh Groban to U2 to Michael Bublé and hand her my credit card.

A few minutes later, back in the Cadillac, Ivy, being the youngest with the most know-how and most nimble fingers, pulls the shrink wrap and tape from the new CDs.

We pull into a gas station that has seen better days. But, as Ben said, the price is lower. He volunteers to pump the gas. He also refuses to accept my credit card. I busy myself punching out all the Elvis CDs from the player and inserting our new play list.

"Holy guacamole!"

"What is it?" I turn, afraid that Ivy is feeling sick or going into labor or something equally horrible.

She points out the side window of the Cadillac. Rae and I both look past the pumps. A red pickup truck, swarming with college-age boys, parks at the next pump. Their sound system throbs and pulses. Is Ivy salivating over some potential frog? Or maybe her boyfriend has shown up.

"Elvis," Rae whispers.

"What?" I ask, searching over the frat-house-on-the-move. Then I see it. Tied down with bungee cords in the bed of the truck is Elvis. The head. The butt-ugly bust.

Before I formulate a complete thought, I jump out of the car. "Hey!" I yell and walk around the front of the Cadillac toward the group of young men. "Hey!"

"What are you doing?" Ben asks.

As if from a long distance away, I hear Rae and Ivy alight from the car and follow me. But my focus is on the pickup truck carrying the bust of Elvis.

"Hey!" I call again.

This time one of the college boys who sits next to Elvis turns. "Hey," he calls back. "An Elvis fan? He don't give autographs."

"What are you doing with him?" I ask.

The loud, beating bass suddenly stops. All of the college boys look at me. "What's the problem, lady?"

"What are you doing with Elvis?" I ask. "He doesn't belong to you."

"Uh, well, he does now."

"Since when?" I challenge.

"Since last night."

"I'm going to call the police. You can't get away with stealing—"

"Claudia," Ben warns.

"Let them have it," Rae says.

"Do you want my cell phone?" Ivy asks.

I put my hand out, and Ivy pushes her cell phone into it. "You better start explaining, mister, while I figure out how to dial 911."

"We didn't steal it," a guy with black hair gelled into a shape like he'd just slept on it says. "Honest."

"That's like a bank robber holding a bank bag full of cash and saying he won the lottery," Ben says.

"No, really," one of the guys who wears a University of Tennessee shirt says. "This guy gave it to us."

"Gave it to you?" I ask. "What guy?"

If he gives a description of Guy, I'm going to drive back to Faithland Chapel and crack the Elvis bust on his head.

"Come on," I say, anger swelling inside me. I punch in the numbers and put my thumb over the send button. "What guy?"

"It wasn't Guy or Myrtle," Ivy says. "They wouldn't—"

"You don't know that." I look back at the young man. "Tell me. Now."

"We were out drinking last night on some back road," the driver says.

"We didn't even know where we were," another adds.

"We were lost," somebody else says.

"And this old guy was trying to hitch a ride. So we pulled over."

"What did he look like?" Ben asks.

"Look like?" the driver looks down at his topsiders. "He, uh . . ."

Another kid shrugs.

"Like Elvis," the blond says, his ears reddening. "Or that's what I thought."

"Like an old Elvis impersonator," another says.

"What were you boys drinking?" Ben jokes.

They laugh, but the driver scuffs his shoe on the pavement. "It was kind of eerie actually."

"It was." The guy wearing the Tennessee shirt jumps down from the bed of the truck. "I rode in the back with him. And he didn't talk much, other than telling us where to drive."

"How gullible do you think I am?" I ask.

"No! I swear."

"It's true, lady."

"We swear . . . on whatever Bible you want."

I cross my arms over my chest. The only thing keeping my finger off *send* is that their story sounds way too familiar. "Go on . . . tell me the rest."

"Well," the driver says, "we ended up at this chapel. The dude asked us to wait. He went inside, then came out, asked us to help him. He said it was okay. The bust was his."

"It was dark. Nobody was there. But in the corner was this Elvis bust. The guy asked us to carry it out to the truck."

"I told him we couldn't steal it," the orange-shirted guy says.

I glance from him back to the driver. "Go on."

"He said it was his. So we carried it for him. We put it in the truck and hauled a—" he cuts his eyes toward Rae, then Ivy, and says, "out of there.

The kid glances at the other guys, who nod back at him.

"Tell her," the orange-shirted guy says.

"Otherwise she'll call the cops."

"She might call the psych ward."

"Okay. All right. The dude disappeared. One minute he was in the truck, and the next . . . he was gone. I swear. I know it sounds made up but—"

"It's the truth," another adds.

I swallow hard, clicking shut the phone and handing it back to Ivy.

"What are you going to do with him?" Ben asks.

"Take him back to our frat house," the driver says.

"Back in Knoxville?" Ben asks.

The kid nods.

"Seems appropriate," Rae says, low enough for me to hear. She and Ben are watching me, waiting for my reaction.

I give a nod and back away toward the Cadillac. "Take care of him."

"Sure thing, ma'am."

Tears spring to my eyes as I watch Elvis drive away and

disappear from sight. I remember what Baldy said, "Some answers can't be known. It takes faith."

Was that the faith Stu had known, that there was something bigger than himself? That there were answers he couldn't know in this life that only came in the next? My heart feels full, and I can't speak. Stu had that faith all along. But telling me wouldn't have convinced me; I had to see it to believe it.

Suddenly I feel an arm around my waist and I look to see Ivy standing beside me. Then Rae encircles me with her arm on the other side. At the beginning of our journey, I thought we three were as different as the seasons. But now I realize even the seasons are connected and dependent on one another.

I wrap my arms around their waists, and we stand there together. It's then I realize why I'm here, what my own unique purpose is: I was made to care for others. It's one reason my life has been so empty during the past year. I closed myself off to everyone. But now I feel my heart opening, expanding, and for the first time in a long time hope fills me.

Letting go, I realize, is not forgetting or sending Stu off to heaven with a full lunch box and a kiss. Letting go of Stu means remembering him—the good, the bad, the ludicrous . . . all of him, while stepping out into my own life . . . whatever that may mean.

We climb into the car and head in the opposite direction of the truck. I punch the button for the CD player, and a song floats out of the speakers. It's a song about home. I realize that's exactly where I want to be. Not as a place to hide but as a place to live again.

Epilogue

Can't Help Falling In Love

I awaken with a smile on my lips, realizing I actually dreamed. And Stu was there. He'd been in an Elvis-style jumpsuit, swiveling his hips. Elvis rock 'n' rolled into my dream, too, showing Stu his best moves. Part of me wants to close my eyes to the coming day and drift back to sleep to find that dream again. But a quick glance at the bedside clock reminds me what I have to do.

In the garage Rae has already started stacking and displaying Stu's sports equipment and Mother's linens, the things I couldn't let go of before. "Are you ready?"

"Here goes everything," I say and punch the garage-door button, which slides open easily. A cool fall breeze brings crusty leaves and rustles Stu's ties on the table.

Ben's the first customer to arrive. "You're selling your George Foreman?"

"You want it?"

"No thanks. I like my chicken juicy."

I laugh. "Where's Ivy?"

"She'll be by later. She wants to show off her new driver's license." He glances up at the garage-door mechanism attached to the ceiling. "How's it working?"

"Perfect." I raise up on tiptoes and kiss his cheek, surprising him, thanking him for fixing the garage door. And yet I know it's just an excuse.

He gives me his usual smile, then narrows his eyes at me.

I nod slowly, feeling a warmth sweep over me.

"Doesn't count."

"I don't get points for trying?"

"Not like that." He grins, his eyes crinkling, his features relaxing. "Try again."

"But . . ."

He raises his eyebrow, asking what I'm so afraid of. I'm not sure anymore. My stomach twists into knots.

Bracing my hands on his shoulders, I turn him to face me fully, raise up on my toes and plant a kiss right on his lips. At first I feel awkward, aware of the chilly morning, but the touch of his hands on my waist warms me. I begin to melt into him.

"The lawn mower for sale there?" a customer asks walking into the garage.

I pull away from Ben, feel my face burning. But his hands remain on my waist. He's grinning.

"Not the mower," I manage.

"Everything," Rae says. She brushes past me carrying an armful of old records, Elvis included. "It's about time. Don't you think?"

I smile at her, feeling her encouragement as I make tentative steps toward a new life.

By midafternoon we've sold most of the big items, like Stu's desk. Someone's looking at the crib, and I'm hopeful it will sell, too.

Ivy arrives, her belly looking very full. She shows me her driver's license and the used car Ben purchased for her. Over the summer she's visited me often, invited me to go to movies, and our friendship has grown along with her belly. She glances at the crib.

One thing we haven't discussed much is the baby. She's kept her options open. When she's mentioned keeping the baby, juggling school, or talked about adoption agencies, I've listened. But she hasn't solicited any advice from me.

"If you want the crib," I say, running my hand along the wood railing, "I won't sell it."

"No, I'm not looking for that." Her hair has grown even longer during her pregnancy. She now has blond roots showing above the black.

I try to read into her answer. Maybe she still hasn't decided what to do. But the baby's birth is approaching, and time's running out.

Ben's shared his concerns with me after hours at the office. I've been proud of his ability to continue loving Ivy and supporting her without being overly domineering. Sometimes he's ranted and raved about the situation to me in private. Other times he's almost wept, grieving for his daughter's lost childhood.

"I'm looking for—" Ivy moves closer to me "—a mother."

I stare at her, not comprehending.

"A mother for my baby," she clarifies.

"So you're going to . . . your decision is adoption?" I ask. Ben hadn't told me. But then maybe he didn't know yet.

She nods. "I don't think I'm ready to be a mother. You know, old enough. But I want to pick the mother."

"And father, right?"

She nods, her gaze sliding over to Ben, who's helping a customer load Stu's desk and chair in a truck.

"Are you going to sign with an agency?" I ask.

She mouths the word *no.* Tears spring into her eyes.

I reach out to her, grasp her hand. She clasps my hand in return. "It's going to be okay. Whatever you decide. It's going to be okay. Your dad and I . . . even Rae will help you."

She swallows hard, then licks her lips. "I want you . . ."

I tilt my head to the side. "I'm here for you, Ivy. Whatever you need."

"I want you to raise my baby."

"Oh, Ivy," I breathe, her name barely audible.

"I know you wanted a baby. Once. You have a crib."

"Don't you have to have more requirements than a crib?" I try to joke, but tears choke me.

"You have the heart of a mother."

I hug her close, unable to imagine how difficult it's been for her to ask me, to honor me with her choice.

"Will you?" Her hard, round belly bumps into mine.

"I don't know." Then I feel the baby move between us. And I know. Right then. I don't have to think about it, contemplate the consequences of my decision. It's the closest thing to having felt my own baby inside me. "Yes. Okay."

Through tears, Ivy smiles at me, her face relaxed, her eyes shining. My heart feels full and wide open, accepting of this new possibility. Holding Ivy close, I whisper, "Thank you." God has answered the cry of my heart before I ever voiced my prayer.

Acknowledgments

Gary, thank you for always being supportive of my writing. Thank you for saying, "Yes," and "Go" to conferences or classes. Thank you for reading through synopses and chapters. Thank you for encouraging me to pursue my dream. I am blessed to be married to you.

Thank you, Graham and Caroline, for always being supportive as Mommy works at the computer. Thank you for being patient when Mommy holds up a finger and asks you to wait to tell me something important before a piece of dialogue gets away from me. Thank you for praying for Mommy's writing and for this book. Always go for your dreams, for God places them in your heart for a reason.

D. Anne Love, thank you for your friendship but also for setting me on the path for Memphis. I will forever be grateful for your encouragement and support through the ups and downs of writing.

Thank you, Jane and Hock. You guys rock! Hock, you are the one who said get Elvis into the title, and look what happened!

Dee, Jenny, and Mary, thanks for the encouragement along the way, for reading bits and pieces and whole chunks of manuscript. I appreciate your generosity.

A special thanks to my sweet prayer partners, Leslie and Maria. You guys are the best. Thank you for praying for me, for my writing, and for this book. May God's blessings shower down upon you. I am so blessed to have you in my life.

I would be remiss if I didn't thank Fellowship Church and my pastor, Ed Young. For three years I prayed about whether God wanted me to write. During that time each service spoke to me in unique, creative ways and allowed God to speak to my heart. I not only get wonderful messages that are personal and meaningful for what I am going through in my life, but I get wonderful insights into characters at the same time!

Natasha, thank you for your honesty and compassion. Thanks for believing in this project and in me.

Finally, thanks to David and Karen for reading this book, seeing its potential, and putting your wholehearted support behind it. The entire staff at B&H Publishing Group has been incredible! I am so blessed to work with such a talented, enthusiastic team.